"It's time you learn about how to perform a B&E."
I strode out of the d_____ _____ hallway to my bedr_____ to me.

"What's a B&E?"

"Break and enter."

I reached my room and grabbed my sword. Spelled by my former best friend, Milly, it would cut deeper than any other blade and was nearly impossible to break.

The handle was a comforting presence—a perfect fit—in my hand.

With my sword, I felt better. Like I could face anything down. I didn't bother to shut the door behind me, just strode back into the hallway. The library was at the far end of the house. Our steps were muffled by the thick rug, which hadn't seen a proper cleaning in what looked like a decade. Pamela struggled to keep up with me without jogging every few steps.

"Jack will be angry. Doesn't that bother you?"

"Jack is going to be angry at me no matter what I do. There comes a time when you can't dick around anymore. And I'm at that moment." I paused in front of the doorway. "This might give me a clue at least as to what the hell is going on, and if he will ever teach me."

"You think it's something bad?" She whispered, her eyes going wide, a glimmer of the child she still was showing through.

Damn, that was exactly what I thought.

PRAISE FOR SHANNON MAYER AND THE RYLEE ADAMSON SERIES

"If you love the early Anita Blake novels by Laurel K. Hamilton, you will fall head over heels for The Rylee Adamson Series. Rylee is a complex character with a tough, kick-ass exterior, a sassy temperament, and morals which she never deviates from. She's the ultimate heroine. Mayer's books rank right up there with Kim Harrison's, Patricia Brigg's, and Ilona Andrew's. Get ready for a whole new take on Urban Fantasy and Paranormal Romance and be ready to be glued to the pages!"

—*Just My Opinion Book Blog*

"Rylee is the perfect combination of loyal, intelligent, compassionate, and kick-ass. Many times, the heroines in urban fantasy novels tend to be so tough or snarky that they come off as unlikable. Rylee is a smart-ass for sure, but she isn't insulting. Well, I guess the she gets a little sassy with the bad guys, but then it's just hilarious."

—*Diary of a Bibliophile*

"I could not put it down. Not only that, but I immediately started the next book in the series, *Immune*."

—*Just Talking Books*

"*Priceless* was one of those reads that just starts off running and doesn't give too much time to breathe. . . . I'll just go ahead and add the rest of the books to my TBR list now."

—*Vampire Book Club*

"This book is so great and it blindsided me. I'm always looking for something to tide me over until the next Ilona Andrews or Patricia Briggs book comes out, but no matter how many recommendations I get nothing ever measures up. This was as close as I've gotten and I'm so freakin happy!"

—*Dynamite Review*

"Highly recommended for all fans of urban fantasy and paranormal."

—*Chimera Reviews*

"I absolutely love these books; they are one of the few Paranormal/urban fantasy series that I still follow religiously. . . . Shannon's writing is wonderful and her characters worm their way into your heart. I cannot recommend these books enough."

—*Maryse Book Review*

"It has the perfect blend of humor, mystery, and a slow-burning forbidden-type romance. Recommended x 1000."

—Sarah Morse Adams

"These books are, ultimately, fun, exciting, romantic, and satisfying. . . .Trust me on this. You are going to love this series."

—*Read Love Share Blog*

"This was a wonderful debut in the Rylee Adamson series, and a creative twist on a genre that's packed full of hard-as-nails heroines. . . . I will definitely stay-tuned to see what Rylee and her new partner get up to."

—Red Welly Boots

"*Priceless* did not disappoint with its colourful secondary characters, unique slant on the typical P.I. spiel, and a heroine with boatloads of untapped gifts."

—*Rabid Reads*

SHADOWED
THREADS

Books by Shannon Mayer

The Rylee Adamson Series
Priceless
Immune
Raising Innocence
Shadowed Threads
Blind Salvage
Tracker
Veiled Threat
Wounded
Rising Darkness
Blood of the Lost

Rylee Adamson Novellas
Elementally Priceless
Tracking Magic
Alex
Guardian
Stitched

The Venom Series
Venom and Vanilla
Fangs and Fennel
Hisses and Honey

The Elemental Series
Recurve
Breakwater
Firestorm
Windburn
Rootbound

Contemporary Romance
High Risk Love
Ninety-Eight

Paranormal Romantic Suspense
The Nevermore Trilogy:
Sundered
Bound
Dauntless

Urban Fantasy
A Celtic Legacy Trilogy:
Dark Waters
Dark Isle
Dark Fae

SHADOWED THREADS

A RYLEE ADAMSON NOVEL
BOOK 4

SHANNON MAYER

TALOS

New York

First Talos Press edition published 2017

Talos Press books may be purchased in bulk at special discounts for sales promotion, corporate gifts, fund-raising, or educational purposes. Special editions can also be created to specifications. For details, contact the Special Sales Department, Talos Press, 307 West 36th Street, 11th Floor, New York, NY 10018 or info@skyhorsepublishing. com.

Talos Press® is a registered trademark of Skyhorse Publishing, Inc.®, a Delaware corporation.

Visit our website at www.talospress.com.

10 9 8 7 6 5 4 3 2 1

Names: Mayer, Shannon, 1979- author.
Title: Shadowed threads / Shannon Mayer.
Description: First Talos Press edition. | New York : Talos Press, 2017. | Series: A Rylee Adamson novel ; book 4
Identifiers: LCCN 2016038955 | ISBN 9781940456980 (softcover : acid-free
    paper)
Subjects: LCSH: Missing children--Investigation--Fiction. | Paranormal
    romance stories. | BISAC: FICTION / Fantasy / Urban Life. |
    FICTION /
    Fantasy / Paranormal. | GSAFD: Fantasy fiction.
Classification: LCC PR9199.4.M3773 S53 2016 | DDC 813/.6--dc23
LC record available at https://lccn.loc.gov/2016038955

Original illustrations by Damon Za: www.damonza.com

Printed in Canada

ACKNOWLEDGEMENTS

With each book I write, the list of people who've stepped up to the bar and helped me present a book of high quality keeps getting longer, and I can't thank them enough! Editors Melissa Breau, and N.L. "Jinxie" Gervasio, who help me smooth out (sometimes with a steam roller) the rough edges until the pages are presentable to the public. Thank you to my proofreader Jean Faganello a.k.a. "Mom" who despite all the bad words still finds it in her heart to read my books, and point out anything I've missed. (And still crosses out every bad word she comes across with a red pen.)

A brilliant thank you to Damon Za; the cover art he produces knocks my socks off every time. My assistant, and now close friend, Lysa Lessieur, for your unwavering support, encouragement, and for the ridiculous amounts of wicked awesome that you are in my life. Thank you!

Now to my husband. Without you at my side, I never would have begun to chase this dream of writing. You are the guy my readers should all be thanking, not me. You saw in me more than I ever could, and you believed in me more than I even do now. You are my "Liam," my heart, and my life. I love you.

CAST OF CHARACTERS

Rylee Adamson: Tracker and Immune
Liam O'Shea: FBI agent
Giselle: Mentored Rylee and Milly
Millicent: AKA Milly; Witch who is best friend to Rylee
John: Motel owner; friend of Rylee
Mary: Wife of John
India: A spirit seeker
Martins: O'Shea's FBI partner
Kyle Jacobs: Rylee's personal hacker
Doran: Daywalker and Shaman
Alex: A werewolf and friend of Rylee's
Berget: Rylee's little sister
Dox: Large pale blue-skinned ogre. Friend of Rylee
Maria: Mother of missing child
Don: Father of missing child
Louisa: Shaman
Eve: Harpy
Agent Valley: Senior in command in the Arcane Division of the FBI

1

Long white teeth bared to the icy cold, running with his belly low to the ground, the wolf breathed in the scent of his quarry. Fear and magic filled his nose, the distant tang of witch made him hunger for the screams that would precede the man's dying breath. Never again would the wolf be held against his will; never again would he be collared and commanded to obey.

Sunlight sliced through the trees, illuminating the man as he spun to see behind him. The wolf dropped to his belly. The man—the witch—stood still, his chest heaving for breath. His eyes were wide, dilated, and the wolf could see the rivulets of sweat sliding down his face even with the crisp dawn air here in the north. Birds sung as though the drama below them wasn't happening, which the wolf preferred. Let the man believe he was safe; let the bird's songs soothe him. Let him hope for rescue.

The witch lifted his hand and a light bloomed over his head, shooting into the sky. The wolf *knew* what would happen. More witches would come. They would see the light and they would come to the aid of this one. Perfect.

Creeping forward, the wolf advanced on the witch, one that would collar him if given the chance. Each step closer made his lips curl higher over his teeth until they rippled with his fury.

Sinking to his knees, the man clasped his hands in front of him, his lips moving in a low rumble of words in a language the wolf didn't understand. Ten feet away now, the wolf hesitated, pausing in mid step.

Cocking his head, the wolf listened to the rise and fall of the man's voice, almost remembering, almost wanting to.

No. We aren't going back. Ever.

In an explosion of powerful muscles, the wolf catapulted toward the man on his knees. Black fur slammed into white flesh, blood flew as powerful jaws clamped down on the fragile skin, bursting through to the pumping lifeblood inside.

The wolf bore down, felt the miniscule thump of magic against his side, the last ditch effort of a dying man trying to save his life. It would do him no good. The wolf's teeth dug deep into the man's neck, and he ground his jaws around the spine until the satisfying snap of vertebrae rang in the morning air; a symbolic clash against the birds' raised songs amongst the trees.

The man twitched once, limbs falling like dead branches to his side. Lifting his nose to the sky, the wolf let out a long, shattering howl. Around him the world went silent, birds stilling their songs, wind stilling its breath, bowing to him, as it should, in recognition for who he was. Here he was King; here he ruled.

Let the witches come.

He would show them the meaning of fear as he hunted them one by one, and tasted their dying screams on his tongue.

The black panther slammed into my chest, dropping me to the ground. I rolled, and struggled to reach my whip, the only weapon I had on me. Heart pounding, I fought with all I had, but the cat was big and solid, nothing but muscle and predatory reflexes. I jammed my legs between our bodies and kicked hard with both feet, prying the big cat off, giving me some space. At least for a second.

"Rylee wins!" Alex cheered me on, but didn't make a move toward us. Not that I was complaining, I'd specifically told him to stay put, and stay out of this. For once he'd listened to me.

From the corner of my eye I caught a glimpse of the werewolf giving me his—quickly becoming trademarked—two claws up, with a goofy grin on his muzzle.

"She did not win," Pamela said, and though I couldn't see her, I had no doubt her hands were on her slender hips. "Will was knocked off, not pinned. Those are the rules, Alex."

"Rylee always wins. Will stinks," Alex grumbled, his tipped claws drooping.

With Will's weight off me, I yanked my whip free and rocked back on my shoulders, then flipped to my feet. Will paced ten feet away, tail lashing. Waiting for me.

Too much of a gentleman, this training was as much for him as it was for me. He had to learn to fight, and fight dirty, if necessary. There was too much cop in him, despite the fact that he was big-ass shapeshifter.

I adjusted my grip on the whip's handle, and shifted my weight, finding the balance I looked for. The makeshift training room was in what had once been Jack's carriage house. Bare walls and floor, we'd painted a circle on the concrete floor. The rules being what they were, you either had to toss your opponent out of the circle, or pin them in such a way that you could, if circumstances were such, kill them.

Something of our own fight club.

I beckoned to Will with my free hand. "Come on then, let's see what you've got . . . Pussy."

His lips curled back over teeth that made Alex's look like stubbed off Tic Tacs. Will didn't sprint toward me. Nope, he made a move that took me by surprise.

He leapt; one powerful spring and he was in the air. A single heartbeat was all I had to react. The whip let out a crack as I slung it forward, the braided leather coiling around his neck, a perfect catch on the cat. A pretty new collar for the big boy.

His eyes bugged out as I yanked the whip, putting my entire body into the pull. The coiled leather tightened on his neck and dragged him to the ground at my feet, his kitty cat green eyes bugging out.

I didn't loosen the whip, but stepped forward as he scrabbled to get the leather off, and put my foot on his shoulder. I made a slashing movement with my free hand, as if I had my sword in it.

"You're dead."

Alex let out a howl of triumph. I bent and loosened the whip from around Will's neck. Gacking and choking, he backed away from me, a low growl of irritation escaping him. Third time in a row I'd bested him and, by his hunched back and narrowed eyes, he wasn't pleased about that. Apparently, he wasn't the only one.

Pamela stepped in front of me, blue eyes glaring. "Why do you have to be so mean? This is supposed to be training, I thought. Not just you beating him up."

Ah, here we went again. She struggled with the harshness of my techniques, particularly when it came to her crush, Will. This was not the first time she'd tried to get me to ease up in the last few weeks.

"You want him to survive?" I coiled the whip and re-attached it to my hip, not even needing to see the clasp anymore. "You want me to survive? Alex? You? Because this kind of training is the only thing that can do that."

Her lips tightened and the air tensed around us. Witches, what the hell was with them anyway? Moody and hormone driven to the extreme. Most days Pamela was fine, but the minute Will showed up, she was a different girl.

She lifted her hands and the air around her stirred. "Then maybe you and I should train together more, instead of me and Deanna."

My eyebrows shot upward of their own volition. "And you think that if you best me, that will make Will feel better about me besting him? All it will do is show him that both of us can take him. Not the way to make him feel like a strong, tough man."

Her hands lowered, and her thin shoulders quivered, but no tears fell. No, not Pamela, she was turning out to be tough as nails, if still somewhat ruled by teenager angst and hormones.

"Come on then, you want to fight? Let's do it." I beckoned her forward with a single finger. No, not that finger.

She tipped her chin up and lifted her tiny fists in front of her face, stepping into the circle as Will stepped out from behind the screen we'd set up for him to shift behind.

His eyes darted between the two of us. "What are you doing?"

"Pamela wants to train with me." I didn't look at him, just waited for her. Stilling my body, my muscles relaxed, stance balanced to move quickly.

Her first swing was true, aimed at my chin, but easily seen coming. I took a step back and slapped her hand away from me. "Again."

Lips tight, she punched, missing me as I sidestepped and batted her hand down with ease. Over and over we repeated the motions, as if we had planned it, a dance that involved me slapping her fists, and her fists, and then feet, coming at me as fast and as hard as she could.

"You getting angry yet, witch?"

No, I didn't need to ask her. I knew she was pissed. Maybe I should have had her training with me like this sooner, but I'd thought she needed more time to get over some of the trauma she'd experienced in her young life.

Again, apparently I was wrong.

Her swings started to get wild, the strain on her under-developed muscles showing in the tremor along her arms, the beads of sweat on her forehead.

But she didn't back down, didn't pull away. Just kept swinging. Damn—I batted her fist away, reached in and shoved her shoulder, making her stumble backward—she was so much like me; it was more than a little scary.

Finally she broke, going to her knees, chugging her air back as if it were water and she was dying of thirst.

"Done?" I asked, crouching beside her.

A shuddering breath rippled through her body. "Yes."

"Every morning from now on you and me will work on this." I stood and turned to see Will frowning at me as he slipped a shirt over his head—tawny hair getting mussed in the process—then sliding it down on over his rock-hard abs. Yeah, I could see why Pamela had a crush on him. I could.

Only thing was, I had a wolf waiting on me. And if Jack didn't start training me soon, I would go after O'Shea without the extra knowledge the old Tracker could give me. Screw the consequences.

Will stepped back into the circle and tossed Pamela a bottle of water, but addressed me. "You don't have it in you to go easy on people, do you?"

"No. Going easy gets people killed in the long run. And I'm tired of the people I care about getting killed and hurt."

He reached over, touched my elbow and tipped his head to one side. I followed his lead, calling back to Pamela as we left the carriage house. "Cool off and then go to the dining hall. I'll meet you there."

Will closed the door behind us and headed across the lawn toward the pond out back. He stopped at the edge of the marshy water, and folded his arms across his chest.

"Deanna and Daniels are going to have it out soon, but they won't tell me when. If Deanna doesn't win, Daniels has already said that she plans on purging the land of all those who oppose her." His eyes flicked over to me, the concern in them apparent.

I shrugged and mimicked him, folding my arms. "If she comes after me, I'll kill her."

He nodded. "I know. But I wanted you to have a heads up."

"Thanks."

Will stared over the pond, and I watched the emotions dance across his face. Uncertainty first and foremost.

"If you've got something to say, spit it out; otherwise, I've got to go finish Pamela's lessons for the day and try to figure out why the hell Jack is stalling on me."

"Still won't teach you?"

An unease settled over my shoulders as I shook my head. "No, he won't. And I can't figure out why." That was a problem. If I was going to learn all I could about being a Tracker, I needed Jack to teach me. Stubborn old coot that he was, he'd been avoiding me one way or another for the last three weeks, locking himself in his library where he wouldn't let anyone in.

The rain pattered down on us, more of a heavy mist than a rain, but it was still getting me wet, which only worsened my mood and irritation at Will's inability to wrap this up.

"Say what you've got to say, Will."

He closed his eyes and shook his head. "No. I've nothing more to say. Just be careful. Daniels has tricks up her sleeve, and she's power hungry beyond anything we all realized before. She won't stop. Not ever."

I raised an eyebrow. "Then why don't you just kill her, and be done with it?"

"Because I have no cause, just suspicions. Not everyone has your latitude when it comes to taking a life, Rylee." He snapped, his eyes flashing.

My jaw tightened, and I flipped him off. Yes, that finger now.

"You know what, Will? Go fuck yourself."

I turned and strode back toward the house. What did he know about life and death? Nothing. He'd never fought for either, never been placed between a rock and a gods-be-damned hard place. Never seen the light in the eyes of someone he loved get snuffed out while he begged them to stay.

There was no way he could understand me, or the choices I had to make.

There was only one person who did.

And I had no idea where the fuck he was.

2

The next morning Pamela sat across from me, her blue eyes narrowed, lips pinched together, bangs hanging down past her chin. I reclined in the Easy Boy that I'd dragged in from the sitting room, the springs creaking under me as I shifted in an attempt to get comfortable. My eyebrow twitched upward with her intensity. "You done yet trying to lift me up?"

"No." She stared harder, finger twitching.

As an Immune, I wasn't affected by her magic, but Pamela was just stubborn enough to try and find a way around it. Sure, I could have peeled my Immunity back, but where was the fun in that? There had been instances in the past where a spell would slip through the Immunity, but it seemed that the older I got, the less that was the case. Which was just fine by me.

Thinking back to when my abilities had come on-line, I could see that over the years my Immunity had been strengthening. It had been a long time since a spell had slipped through it.

I closed my eyes, my throat tightening. O'Shea had been with me then. I missed his constant presence in my life. I'd spent so long wanting him gone; then as soon as I changed my mind, he'd been ripped away from me.

I glanced up at Pamela and smiled as she threw her hands into the air. Now that Will had gone back to work, she'd gone back to being her normal self. Or at least as normal as a witch got.

"I don't understand, how you cannot be affected? It's magic, it affects everything." She let out a gust of air that blew her bangs off her face.

Pushing with one foot, I rocked in the chair. "Magic does affect everything; you're right. But there is a balance in the world. There has to be. I guess as an Immune, I'm here to balance out all of you crazy witches throwing magic shit around."

She stood, stretched, and wandered over to the pictures hanging on the wall of Jack's dining room. Alex, Pamela, Eve, and I had been staying with him since he'd been released from the hospital. His cancer seemed to have gone into remission and Jack had been allowed to go home. At least for now.

Home to Jack was a two-story sprawling mansion that covered close to ten thousand square feet. When he did venture from his damn library, he grumbled and cursed the fact that we were here, taking up space.

As I'd pointed out to him the night before, if he'd just teach me what I needed to know, we would get the hell out of his way. The only thing he'd helped me with so far was calming me down when I'd Tracked Berget and felt nothing once more. He'd pointed out that she'd probably been taken, or had gone, across the channel to the mainland. That had been his one contribution to my life in these last few weeks.

"Do you think these paintings were here before Jack, or do you think he had them put up?" Pamela reached, standing on her tiptoes, and touched the ornate edge of a painting five feet across, her fingers skimming along it lightly.

"They were probably here. I don't think he cares much for paintings."

She tipped her head to one side, staring up at the monstrosity of an oil painting. Nothing like the one O'Shea had in his home. Again, a pang of longing shot through me. I had to go after him soon.

The door opened on silent hinges and Jack stepped into the room, using a cane but nothing else.

I got up out of the recliner—it was his after all—and he glowered at me.

"Fucking houseguests warming up my goddamn fucking chairs everywhere I go." His tri-colored blue eyes sparkled up at me, but not in good humor. Not that I was bothered by his potty mouth, mine was almost as bad. Almost.

Pamela spun and glared at him. Funny how she defended Will from me, and me from Jack.

Her chin tipped up slightly, a sure sign she was setting her heels in. Oh, this was going to be good. Wouldn't be the first time the two of them had a go round since we'd been here.

"Don't you talk to her like that; if you'd teach her, we'd leave and be out of your way."

He thumped over to her and poked at her stomach with his cane. "Smart-mouthed little witch. Mind your own fucking business."

She flicked a hand at him and lifted him into the air. "I'm on Rylee's team, and you promised to teach her. So teach her."

He squirmed and huffed, and I let out a sigh. Yeah, playing referee wasn't my idea of a good time, but I seemed to be doing it more and more with this motley group.

"Put him down, you might break him."

The bastard had the nerve to spit at me, the gob hitting the floor at my feet. "Break me, my ass."

I glared up at him. "Don't you have an appointment to be at?" I knew damn well he had another session with Deanna.

He glared right back, eyes flashing with anger. "What is it about women and the need to run every gods-be-damned piece of my ever-fucking life?" He squirmed, but Pamela held him just above the floor, teasing him.

"Pam, put him down."

"But—"

"Just do it!" I pointed to the floor and she lowered him the last foot.

With a snarl, he hobbled away from us, muttering all the way out to the front door.

We watched him go, in silence. Jack was hiding something from me, on top of not teaching me. Well, I was damn well tired of waiting on him to teach me, and his fucking secrets could stay that way for all I cared. Except for the somewhat large possibility that his secrets, and his inability to find the time to teach me, were likely intertwined, knowing my luck. Damn.

With all the time he'd been spending in the library, that was probably the best place to start. I made my decision and didn't question it.

"It's time you learn about how to perform a B&E." I strode out of the dining room and down the long hallway to my bedroom. Pamela trotted to catch up to me.

"What's a B&E?"

"Break and enter."

I reached my room and grabbed my sword. Spelled by my former best friend, Milly, it would cut deeper than any other blade and was nearly impossible to break.

The handle was a comforting presence—a perfect fit—in my hand.

With my sword, I felt better. Like I could face anything down. I didn't bother to shut the door behind me, just strode back into the hallway. The library was at the far end of the house. Our steps were muffled by the thick rug, which hadn't seen a proper cleaning in what looked like a decade. Pamela struggled to keep up with me without jogging every few steps.

"Jack will be angry. Doesn't that bother you?"

"Jack is going to be angry at me no matter what I do. There comes a time when you can't dick around anymore. And I'm at that moment." I paused in front of the doorway. "This might give me a clue at least as to what the hell is going on, and if he will ever teach me."

"You think it's something bad?" She whispered, her eyes going wide, a glimmer of the child she still was showing through.

Damn, that was exactly what I thought. When he'd promised to teach me, I thought it would take a day or two. Not three weeks of him dodging me.

Which could only mean one thing.

That whatever the hell was going on was no good. Son of a bitch, what was it with the men around me lately that they couldn't just spit things out? Nothing like O'Shea, who always spoke what was on his mind.

Again, a sharp stab of longing gutted me. I breathed in slowly through my nose, working around the pain. Focusing on my task, I lifted my sword and slid it between the two massive doors. Whoever had built the house had done a sloppy job on them. While they did lock, there was a half-inch gap between them. Though it was a tight fit, I could still draw the blade down, slicing through the old lock with very little effort.

"The trick is to make it look like you were never here." I pushed the door open. "Unlike this B&E, where Jack will know that I was here the second he goes to open his door."

She bobbed her head, taking my words in like a sponge. Scary. "You did it that way on purpose then? You want him to know you were in his library?"

I glanced around the library, took it in with a single sweep of my eyes. Two sets of floor-to-ceiling windows that were bordered by long red curtains, also floor to ceiling. Rows and rows of books, again, floor to ceiling. A huge oak table with a few wooden chairs, a couple of overstuffed recliners, and not much else.

"Yes. I want him to know I've had enough of his games." So I would play my own and do my best to force his hand. Either he would teach me, or we would leave. But no more of this shit he was pulling.

Rolling my sword in my hand, it caught the light from a lamp on the big table. I strode to the open book under the light. Open wide, the book was easily three feet across, the words within it written by hand in a scrawling black ink.

I jammed the tip of my sword into the floor at my feet. It would leave a gouge mark on the old wooden slats, but at least it was within easy reach if I needed it. Not that I should, but one can never be too damn careful.

I wrinkled my nose, the musty smell of the pages strong now that I was this close. I grabbed the edge of the book and partially closed it so I could see the front cover. Black leather, a texture that felt familiar to me, but that I couldn't quite place, engraved with a single word.

Demons.

Oh shit, that was just fucking awesome. I grit my teeth and opened the book again, reading the page that Jack had been studying. Had he been trying to find a way to conjure a demon? Maybe to cure him of his cancer? I didn't know if that was even possible, but then again, I didn't really know that much about demons.

"What does it say?" Pamela leaned closer and I pushed her back, not wanting her too close to a book about demons. The one thing I'd learned from Deanna since I'd been here was that witches were susceptible to demons, more than any other supernatural creature. The last thing I wanted was Pamela getting mixed into that shit.

And what about Milly? Yeah, there was a growing suspicion in me that whatever she was up to had to do with more than just a simple vampire . . .

Leaning over the black book, I read it out loud for Pamela.

"And when the Veils shall fall to Orion, there will be no hope for mankind. For with his Rise, the Tracker will die and our glory shall be forever as we bathe in blood and crush those who defy us." I swallowed hard. Shit, that did not sound good. And that name, Orion, it sent fear tracing along my synapses, like my brain wanted me to remember something . . . I couldn't place it though, no matter how many times I read the name. The rest of the page was similar. Orion, whoever the hell he was, would rise, and with him humanity was doomed. We were all doomed by the nasty fucker of a demon. This was not good. . . but why was Jack studying it? Did he think he was the Tracker meant to die?

That would make sense, would explain how freaking cranky he was being.

Pamela moved around the table. "There are more books, made kind of like that one."

She was right, though they were closed and spread out; they were all made with the same kind of leather as the book under my fingers.

I stared at the one furthest from me. The book at the far end was a shade of blue I'd only ever seen on one other supernatural creature.

Dox.

"Shit, these are ogre-skinned books." I stared at them, shocked by the variety of colors.

I knew about Black, Blue, Gray, and Green. But Red, Brown, and—I walked over to the book next closest to me brushed my hand against it—Violet were new to me.

Pamela hefted the gray book. "This one says 'magic' on it."

I moved around the table, taking in each book, memorizing the color that was attached to it.

Winged: Blue
Fanged: Red
Furred: Brown
Magicked: Gray
Blooded: Violet
Psychic: Green
Demons: Black

Pamela flipped each book open to pages that were marked with scraps of paper.

"Do you think the colors have anything to do with the groups?"

"I don't know. Probably. There is very little coincidence in this world, things happen for a reason, not just for shits and giggles."

She gave a shaky laugh, and I really looked at her. "What is it?"

With a shaky finger, she pointed at the open page in front of her. "The words, I can feel them under my skin, like ants, moving." She scrubbed her hands over her arms.

Gods be damned, what the hell had Jack opened up here?

"Go over to the door; just stay there and keep an eye out for Jack."

She didn't argue with me, just backed away from the table and the books, kinda like how I wanted to.

I didn't really want to read what these books said. Not really. But that was the only way to find out what the hell was going on, because I seriously doubted Jack was going to come clean. Even once he saw the less-than-subtle B&E.

I moved to the book that Pamela had said made her skin crawl, the Green one, and read the page Jack had marked. Reading was slow going with the hand-written script, and I found myself reading the words aloud.

"Thus shall one Tracker stand between Orion and the darkness he brings. She shall be either our destruction or our salvation. No matter the outcome, her blood will be taken, drained to the last drop." What the fuck? Chills raced along my spine, my skin rising in gooseflesh I couldn't control. This was not sounding good. But, again, why wouldn't Jack want me to read this, unless he thought that the 'she' was . . . shit, he didn't think this was about me, did he? Yeah, it looked like I'd more than stumbled on Jack's deep dark secret he'd been keeping.

The Gray book came next and my heart leapt higher into my throat with each word.

"Orion shall twist the magic of the Great One, and shall bring her to her knees with his lies. For when he possesses the heart of her soul, salvation shall fall to one bound by oaths to stay his hand of death over the world. The Tracker must break her oaths to save the world, or we will all be doomed."

"I don't like the sound of that. It sounds like the Tracker could be you." Pamela's voice softened with each word, echoing what I was thinking.

This was too close to sounding like it was about me. Like these were prophecies for each of the different groups of the supernaturals, and maybe they all were about me. No, that couldn't be. I was Immune, there is no way they could Read me. So this was just stupid.

My fingers traced the words, and with each touch, my gut clenched and I fought to keep myself standing there. Stupid or not, I knew that I was staring at pages that would change my life.

"Yeah. Let's not jump to conclusions." I kept my tone smooth, but inside I was doing my best not to freak out.

Fuck, fuck, fuck! Each word from the books resonated with me and I couldn't deny that they *felt* as if they were directed at me. I made myself go slowly, so I wouldn't trip over my feet scrambling to get to the next book.

Blue, the Winged supernaturals.

"And our wings shall carry the Tracker into the final storm, and together, bound by blood, they will battle Orion."

Brown book, the Furred.

"The Great Wolf shall howl the Tracker's name, and claim her as his own, and shall spill his blood for her. And the Tracker will teach the submissive to stand; to shift and fight alongside her as Orion's darkness rises."

I gripped the edge of the table, struggled to keep my breathing even. No need to have Pamela wigging out. I skimmed the words again. These couldn't be true, couldn't be. I was Immune; they couldn't have read me. This was about someone else. They had to be about someone else. Teeth clenched, I shook my head. Maybe other people could lie to themselves, but it wasn't one of my talents.

"Rylee, I think Jack is home." Pamela whispered, peeking around the edge of the door.

I barely registered her words, so stuck on what I was reading. Fuck, how could this be about me? But what other reason would Jack have in hiding them from me? Moving sideways, I stepped in front of the Red book. The one attached to the Fanged.

"The Tracker will bring the Teeth together, making the mouth whole that it may bear down on the black rising horde with all its venom. For together, our bite will destroy all in our path." Not much better, maybe a little if only because I had no idea what Teeth were, or why they'd be brought together.

One more book.

Violet, the Blooded group. That made no sense to me; I would have thought Blooded and Fanged would be the same thing. I flipped the pages until I found a heading that actually made my heart stutter, the words wavering in front of my eyes, echoes of Giselle's voice whispering through me.

In my hands, I held the Blood of the Lost.

3

Shaking, I closed the book before I could read the words. I just needed a second to take it in—

"What the fuck are you doing?" Jack roared, pushing Pamela out of his way. Face almost as bright red as his hair, he stomped over to me. He swung his cane, catching me on my upper arm. The sting of the blow was nothing compared to the anger that built in my gut.

"What the fuck are *you* doing hiding this kind of shit from me?" It took everything I had not to scream at him.

He glanced over his shoulder, straight at Pamela. "Get her the hell out of here, this isn't for her ears."

Her eyes narrowed and she opened her mouth as she lifted her hand, no doubt to wrap him up in a spell to remind him she wasn't to be pushed around.

I cut her off, giving her a look. "Pam, go bake some cookies." That was her cue to leave, one we had decided on just a few days after moving in with Jack. Every time Jack and I needed to have it out, I would tell her to go bake cookies.

In the last three weeks she could have easily supplied a bakery.

From down the hallway came a scrabbling of claws and the thunk of a body falling. Most likely Alex had spun out on one of the rugs that lined the wooden floors in a mad dash to get to us.

Three seconds after the word 'cookie' had been spoken, Alex burst into the library, the doors flinging open around his two-hundred-pound frame. Stuck forever between man and wolf, he was covered in black, silver-tipped fur and had the ability to cause mayhem and destruction. But he didn't, that wasn't Alex. He was loyal to the core, had the mental capabilities of a two-year-old, and was submissive to the point of it being deadly to his health. Which made for some interesting days and a hell of a lot of laughter. He was the reason I could still smile despite all the shit that went on in my life.

Sliding to a stop on his butt, he turned huge golden eyes to us and rippled his lips up over his teeth into his version of a smile.

"Alex gets cookies too?"

Pamela put a hand on his collar as she glared at Jack. "Let's go then, they aren't going to bake themselves."

The two of them left the library without Jack saying a word. No, he waited until after they'd gone to start in on me. But that's what I was supposedly here for, whatever training he could give me before I went after O'Shea. Because there was no guarantee Jack would be here when I got back. Now, I wasn't so sure why I was here, or if Jack even had anything else to teach me.

Not after reading through those books.

"You care about them too bloody much, you know that, don't you?" He tapped the floor with his cane. He wasn't an old man, but the cancer had stolen much of his vitality, had eaten away at a life that should have been far longer than it would end up being. Even supernaturals couldn't cure cancer. He scrubbed a hand through his bright red hair, and then pointed at the chair across from him.

"Sit."

"No. You tell me what the hell is going on. Now." I widened my stance, as if preparing for a fight.

He huffed and cursed, but I waited. I wasn't going anywhere now.

I looked up at the ceiling, counted the branches of the chandelier hanging over our heads. "What are you going to teach me, Jack? Anything? Because I have some gods-be-damned serious deadlines I've got to keep."

He snorted. "Anything?"

I lowered my eyes, and met his in a glare I didn't hold back on. "Yeah, Jack. I know you don't want to die alone, but you're being a shit if that's the only reason you'd keep us here. The only reason I stayed is so you could teach me. I've been here three weeks and no teaching yet. Not to mention this shit, this prophecy crap you are obviously buying into." I swept my hands to encompass the table, fought the sudden nausea that clawed at my throat. I refused to let it slow me down, as I tried to find the words that would spur him into action. Because it looked like even mine and Pamela's B&E wasn't going to be enough to provoke him.

Jack's lips curled into a sneer. "You think I'm lonely?"

"I know you are."

We glared at one another, two stubborn Trackers, neither willing to back down without at least a small fight. With a slam of his cane on the floor, Jack broke first. I always had prided myself on my bitchy eyes.

He picked up the silver letter opener on the table beside him, flipped it along his knuckles. "Goddamn it. Fine, you're right. I don't want to die alone, my body shriveling up into a husk while the world goes on and no one even knows I'm gone. Is that so fucking wrong?" He tapped the floor with his cane, three beats in quick succession. "There isn't a lot left to teach you. Probably could do it in an afternoon."

For once, understanding took the lead over my anger.

"Jack, we'll come back. You know that, right? Even if you kick the bucket while we're gone, we'll come back. I'll come back. You won't be forgotten."

He shook his head and put the letter opener back on the table, spinning it in place. "This is one of the problems you've got to learn to deal with, kid. The downtrodden, the miserable, and lonely, they will be drawn to you. Those that are lost, whether in the physical sense or in their souls, they are drawn to you, and they will fucking use you up if you let them."

I clenched my hands tight. I thought about Eve, Alex, and Pamela. Even O'Shea to a degree—Jack was right, they had been all lost in one way or another. "So, I try not to take on too much, that's what you're saying?"

"Not just that, even me, I want you to stay, I want you to not leave. I've been fucking stalling." He took a breath, and in the split second I could see the fear on him, heavy like a gargoyle sitting on his shoulders, gripping him tight. "We're both Trackers but, as a woman, you have some characteristics that I don't carry. Almost like a maternal instinct to protect, to care for those who can't care for themselves."

"Not news to me, Jack." I rocked on my heels. That had been my whole life really, why should this be seen as something new?

He held up his cane, poked me in the chest with it, right where the demon mark was etched into my skin. "Maybe not, but you aren't grasping what it *means* to you. They will bleed you dry, surround you with their needs, and you will *never* be free of it. You will end up no longer able to Track because you are too busy taking care of those around you. Stop taking on the goddamn fucking charity cases. Or be ready to stop Tracking."

His words jammed my brain, and in a burst of understanding, I realized he could be right. Taking on Eve, Pamela, and even Alex, though it had been nearly a year ago, they had all taken some of my focus. Before Alex had come into my life, there had been nothing other than bringing children home to their families. Though I hadn't stopped Tracking, maybe I hadn't been as dedicated? No, I had still gone after missing kids, that hadn't changed.

Had it? Doubt nagged at me. Maybe he was right.

I shrugged, but lowered my eyes so he wouldn't see any of the indecision I knew would be there. "Fine. No more charity cases. What else you got?" I itched to go after O'Shea and Milly. Though I knew Track-

ing Milly might not get me anywhere, I could Track
O'Shea. Free him from her.

Have him back in your arms and your bed.

Yeah, that too.

Jack grunted. "You master the group Tracking?"

"I Tracked some Druids, I think in some ways it
was—"

"Easier, yes." He nodded tapping his cane in rhythm
with the bobbing of his head. "Easier, but also harder.
You don't know if the group you Track are the exact
ones you seek. Try Tracking a human, for example.
Not a person, just humans in general."

I frowned and thought about the traits of humans
that I could use to Track them as a group. Contradic-
tions: love and hate, fear and bravery, oblivious to the
supernatural. Using those simplistic traits, I sent out
a thread of Tracking to the closest human.

What happened was not what I expected. Like feeling my head expand, curiously filled with millions of
sparkling lights that hurt my eyes, frantic and pan-
icked, the sparks danced around the inside of my skull,
each one desperate to be seen, to be heard, demanding
my attention. Painful? No, more overwhelming than
anything, in their calls for attention, their desperation
and fears, all crashing around inside my head. Each
spark was a life, a human within my proximity, which
apparently was the whole of Britain. Fuck me.

I let go of the thread, unable to take the sheer vol-
ume of humanity. Somewhere in that brief moment
I'd fallen to the ground, and had ended up curled on
the floor, hands over my ears as if that would stop
what I'd been feeling.

"That's why you bloody well never Track humans as a whole. When it comes to them, make sure it's only one at a time." Jack held out his hand and helped me stand up. My legs wobbled as if I'd been running flat out for miles.

"Holy shit." I put a hand to my head. I wouldn't be doing that again anytime soon.

Jack let out a grunt and settled himself back into his rocking chair. "Your blood will be favored by anyone who works magic. For some fucking unknown gods-blasted reason Tracker blood is a catalyst."

I nodded, my thoughts whirling to the piece of paper I had tucked between my mattress and the box spring at home. A recipe of how to turn a Daywalker into a true vampire. My blood was in that recipe or, more accurately, the blood of a Tracker.

"You don't seem surprised by that," Jack said, lifting his cane to poke at me again.

I batted it away. "No, it makes sense with what I've run into before." Perfect, ridiculous sense.

Jack gave me a tired smile, one that drooped on the edges and didn't reach his eyes.

"It gets worse. Much, much worse."

Oh fuck, how could it get worse than having half the magical world after my blood? I rubbed my hands across my face, feeling the distant tang of a headache at the back of my skull. "Just spill it, Jack. The theatrics are getting tiresome and I have to get my ass in gear and go after O'Shea. I've dicked around long enough waiting for you to find your balls and tell me what I need to know."

Jack didn't frown, didn't lash out at me for once. He laughed. Barking until he heaved for breath, he ended up bent over his knees, pounding his cane into the floor. It took him a full two minutes to get himself under control, and by that point I was really starting to get pissed off.

"Oh gods, Rylee, I needed that." He swiped at his eyes with the back of his hand. I realized he was stalling, trying to divert my attention away from not only the supposed training, which I realized now was just superficial, but more importantly, he was avoiding the issue with the prophecies.

Well, there was one way to fix that. "What's with the books?"

Leaning heavily on his cane, Jack made his way to the far side of the library and stood in front of the big oak table. I moved to stand beside him, though he didn't answer me. I tried another question, tried to find a way to get him talk.

"Is this ogre skin?"

"Yes, it holds the old books together better than anything else, but it has to be taken from their bodies while they're still alive. Good eye; you run into many ogres?"

Diversion, diversion. Like a magician, he just kept trying to keep me occupied.

I thought about Dox, "Just one. He's a good guy."

"Must be a blue." Jack stared down at the books, his hand hovering over the black-skinned tome, and then he surprised me. "You read them all?"

"Except the violet-skinned one." I pointed to it, a web of fear tangling along my spine.

Whatever good humor he'd had running through him was gone. His tri-colored blue eyes were angry again, and maybe even a little afraid. "You had no right to this. None of these were for your eyes."

"Are they about me?"

"Get out of my library."

I stepped up, put my nose to his. "Are. They. About. Me?"

He slammed his cane onto the center of table in a small depression, and the air shifted, a spell he'd obviously planted there. With a crack, the books disappeared.

"You're an asshole, Jack." I grabbed my sword and strode from the room, equal parts anger and fear biting at my insides. I clung to the anger.

Much easier than admitting that the words I'd read scared the shit out of me.

4

The November rain hammered down on the conservatory where I'd chosen to hide, though if anyone asked, I'd tell them I needed a place to think things over. Jack never went to the conservatory, and Pamela didn't like the way the shriveled up plants looked. She said it reminded her too much of Anna's rooftop and what had happened there.

Me, I was just happy for the peace and quiet as I let my head try to sort things out.

So there were some supposed prophecies that *looked* like they could be about me. But none of that really applied to me now. Not really.

Really?

I shook off my doubts, had to if I was going to move forward. Fear was a paralyzer, that much I knew. Right now I had to find O'Shea; that was the first and foremost issue I had sitting in my lap. And if I was going to find him, I couldn't be scared out of my mind because of things that might, or might not, be about me.

Not much of what Jack had told me was going to be helpful; in fact, there wasn't much at all I hadn't already learned. A few quirks of Tracking, like not being able to feel people's life threads across large bodies of water, the ability to Track groups of supernaturals. All good information to have. But not worth waiting three weeks for.

And sitting here was getting me no closer to going after O'Shea. There was nothing in my way now, I just had to get my gear, my weapons, and I'd be off after the FBI agent turned werewolf, kidnapped by a witch and held captive against his will.

Yup, no problem at all.

I stood, already planning the things I would need, as Jack hobbled into the conservatory, much to my surprise.

"What do you want?"

He leaned on his cane, his face even more haggard than just an hour before.

I opened my mouth to ask if there was anything else he had for me, anything he could teach me, when Alex came bounding into the room.

"Cookies, cookies, coookkkkiiiieeeessss!" He howled and then took off running around the conservatory at top speed, tucking his tail between his legs and grabbing at plants with his mouth and paws as he ran. Twice he stopped to spin in place, not chasing his tail, just spinning as fast as he could. Tongue hanging out, spit flew and I put myself between him and Jack. Just in case.

Jack grumbled and took a swing with his cane at the werewolf as he raced by for the third time. "Let's go get some damn cookies." Again, a diversion. Even though I understood some of his reasoning, his diversionary tactics pissed me off. As in royally fucking pissed. It took everything I had to not lash out at him.

Walking beside him, Jack acted as though we'd never had a fight.

Classic male pattern avoidance. Fine, I'd pretend like I didn't remember the previous hour either, then.

"The last thing you need to know, you already know part of it. You can Track people who are dead already."

I nodded, and he gave a double tap of his cane. "Then you need to know that you can also Track the spirits of some people. Not all. But those who have work left, or who are in limbo. They float between the first level of the Veil and the human world."

"Ghosts you mean."

"Ghosts. You can Track them. They move around a helluva lot more than most people realize, going wherever the fuck they want."

"Do I have to know them? Or can I Track them like I would a group?"

"Both. But be careful because Tracking ghosts has its downfalls too. They can yank you through the Veils. Heard about Brin getting dropped into the third level once. When he came out, his hair was white as snow and the prick was only twenty-one at the time." He paused and then gave me a tired smile and a wink. "The ladies loved it though."

We made our way into the oversized kitchen. Copper pots hung above the granite-topped island, wooden barstools lined up along the edges. The kitchen was equipped with two of everything. Handy

I suppose, but—I glanced at Jack—I wondered how many people it had served since Jack became the owner of this place.

The kitchen was warm; both stoves were running full tilt. Pamela had flour all over her face, the floor, the counter, and even on a few of the hanging pots. But she was smiling and pointing at a cooling rack covered in irregularly shaped cookies. The smell of chocolate and peanut butter wafted through the air, and my stomach growled loudly, demanding some the warm, calorie-packed treats.

"I made chocolate chip peanut butter." Pamela dropped a dirty mixing bowl into a sink full of sudsy water, earning a glare from Jack.

"Don't break my shit, witch."

She opened her mouth and I shook my head, stalling her. Her lips turned down in a hard frown, but she kept her mouth shut.

Alex side-stepped closer, and then sat on his haunches, drool slipping from his lips in great gobs that splashed onto the white tile floor as he stared without blinking at the cookies. Subtle he was not.

"Give him a cookie quick before we get flooded the fuck out," Jack said, taking a cookie for himself. Pamela handed Alex a cookie, which he took without hesitation and popped into his mouth.

I grabbed one, and tossed it back and forth between my hands to help it cool off. Alex downed at least three in the space of ten seconds, Jack had his eyes closed as he savored the cookie. Pamela puttered about, cleaning up the mess. All so fucking domestic it made my head hurt.

And me? I bit into the cookie, the perfect blend of sweet chocolate and nutty flavors doing nothing to still the roll of my gut. Between the prophecies I'd read, the desire to go after Milly and O'Shea, the knowledge that Berget was alive and, whether she knew it or not, waiting for me to Track her, not to mention attempting to train Pamela, and keep Alex and Eve out of trouble . . . I wasn't sure what I was feeling was true gut instinct and what was just stress. Fuck, I hated stress. I wanted things to go back to the way they were. Simple and easy. Get called out on a salvage and go after the kid. In that, at least, Jack was right. With everything else going on, I was being pulled away from what I should be doing—Tracking kids. How many back home were waiting on me? Just the thought of how many kids would die, how many were going missing as I stood there eating a cookie, made me sick to my stomach.

The phone in the kitchen rang, actually jumping in its cradle, startling me. Jack walked to the wall where it hung and lifted the receiver, a sour look twisting across his face.

"What the fuck do you want, witch?"

I choked on the cookie in my mouth. Jack was a Reader, like Giselle. Which meant he would know who was on the phone the minute he picked it up.

Pamela's blue eyes went wide and she mouthed the name I had come to hate.

Milly.

I strode to Jack's side and he handed me the phone, but didn't let go right away.

"Don't let her manipulate you. Remember what I said about people using you."

I pulled the phone out of his hand and put it to my ear, the crackle of static hissing ever so lightly. "You need to let O'Shea go, Milly."

"He's already gone. There is no way to bring him back, Rylee, so don't bother trying. The wolf in him has taken over completely."

The phone creaked under my grip. "You calling to gloat, you piece of shit?"

"No, I'm not. You should know, though, that he will be taken care of. You won't have to worry about him anymore."

"What the fuck is that supposed to mean?" I didn't care that my voice rose in intensity, didn't care anymore that Pamela was hearing me swear.

"He is hunting witches, actively hunting them. The local Coven has sent a team to deal with him."

"You mean kill him."

She drew in a breath and I could almost see her bite her lip before answering me. "Yes."

I had to find O'Shea. As in now.

"Why are you telling me this?"

She was silent for a heartbeat, maybe two before answering. "You're like my sister, I don't want you to be hurt—"

Anger, sweet and hot, made it hard to speak evenly. "The next time we meet, witch, be ready to pay your penance to the gatekeeper, because I *will* be taking your head. You don't give a shit about anyone, just yourself."

"Don't hang up!" She called out, like I hadn't just threatened her life. "Please, Rylee."

The phone was already away from my ear when she screeched out words that stopped me.

"I'm calling to ask if you would be the godmother of my child."

Not much could have thrown me for a loop. But that did. I stared at the wall. Milly was pregnant?

She kept on talking, quickly, as if to stall me.

"It's Ethan's baby. I thought he was going to come to Europe to be with me, but *Terese won't let him.* I need to know my baby will be safe if something happens to me. I don't expect you to help me or anything— I know better than that. I get it, we are on opposite sides; you've made that very clear.

"But if anything happens to me, I need to know that you will take care of my child, that you'll raise him and protect him. Please."

This was not happening. It couldn't be. The 'Milly is pregnant' scene wasn't what was throwing me for a loop. Shit, that had been coming for years. But for her to think that after she tried to kill Alex and Eve, compelled O'Shea, and now O'Shea was being hunted by other witches as a result of what she'd done, not to mention she'd essentially killed Giselle, that I would for one instant do what she wanted—

"You took an oath to protect and save children at all costs, even to the loss of your own life," she said softly, her voice dropping into a whisper. "Please, Rylee. For whatever love we had as sister-friends, promise me this."

I struggled to find the words. "How far along are you?"

"I'm due in April, right around Easter."

Jack's admonition still rung in my head. "I'm not promising you anything." I slammed the phone back into the cradle before she could beg anymore. Before I could buckle under the weight of my oaths.

The kitchen was still; no one moved. Jack, Pamela, and even Alex stared at me, waiting for me to say something. Saved by the bell, a buzzer sounded through the house announcing someone at the front door. Jack glared at us, and then glared at the general direction of the door. The buzzer went off again. And again. And again.

"Company, who fucking needs it? You three, you need to get the hell out of here so I can bloody well die in peace." Jack thumped his cane into the floor with each step he took as he left the kitchen, presumably to greet whoever was buzzing us with such glee.

Pamela walked to my side and slipped her arm around my waist. "I can feel it in the air, things are changing, aren't they?"

I draped an arm across her shoulders, as my mind once more saw the prophecies as if stamped inside my brain. "Yeah . . . yeah, I think they are."

5

If you'd asked me to guess who was at the door and had given me ten tries, I still would have gotten it wrong. I assumed it would be Agent Valley (who still hadn't given up on me joining his agency), maybe Deanna, or even Will.

Nope. None of those.

I think my jaw might have actually unhinged as the punk rocker-esque Daywalker strode into the kitchen. Jack muttered under his breath as he trailed behind his newest houseguest.

Doran strode right up to me and kissed me on the cheek, dark-green eyes all lit up with happiness, as if seeing me had just made his fucking day. His white-blond hair was still tipped in black, the silver piercings above his eyebrow and in the side of his lip still glinted at me, teasing little winks. All of it was the same. Except that he was here, in London, instead of in New Mexico where he should have been.

"What the fuck are you doing here?" I blurted out, shoving him away from me, wanting space between us. If he was here, something was wrong. And the last thing I needed was more wrong in my life.

With a smooth fluid grace he lifted himself to sit on the counter, right next to the cookies. He took one, broke it in half, and then took a bite.

"Oh my gods, these are fantastic. Surely you didn't make them, did you, Rylee? If you tell me you can bake as well as kick ass with the best of them, I may have to make an exception to my 'no marrying' rule." He smiled around the bite of cookie in his mouth.

"I made them," Pamela said, her voice coming from the other side of the kitchen where she stood pressed against the industrial fridge. Her blue eyes were narrowed to slits. Her past experience with a fanged supernatural hadn't gone too well. No, not too well at all. Her hands twitched, no doubt prepping a spell.

Alex climbed up onto the counter to sit awkwardly next to Doran. "Alex sits too."

"Get off the counter, Alex." I pointed to the floor. He slid off like a boneless Gumby doll, until he was splayed out on the floor flat on his belly.

"No fairs."

I had only my bowie knife and my whip on me, stupidly having put my sword back in my bedroom. Not enough if I had to fight Doran. Shit. Of course, that was assuming he was here to cause problems. Again, I had to think he was. To come all this way for tea and cookies? Nope, that just didn't fit.

"I will ask you only one more time and then things are going to get nasty." I fingered the whip's handle. "What are you doing here?"

Doran leaned back, popped the last of the cookie into his mouth and dusted his fingers on his black leather pants. His eyes had an odd glint in them and they flicked quickly around the room. A single bead of sweat budded on the left side of his face. Yeah, something was wrong. Shit, I hated being right.

"May I speak with you in private, Rylee? Somewhere your new witch and the old Tracker won't hear us?"

I tipped my head toward the door and he slid off the counter, following me. Jack lifted an eyebrow and I pointed at Alex and Pamela. "Keep them with you."

I would deal with Doran on my own, it was better that way. My skin twitched as I walked; I could feel the Daywalker's eyes on me, feel the desire he had to pierce my skin with his fangs. Fuck, and I still owed him a kiss. I fought the urge to groan. Had he come all this way for a kiss? Shit, I was good, but I wasn't *that* good. No, it had to be something else. Something I wouldn't want to hear. Or something he wanted from me.

I led him to the library. Seeing as the door was busted, there was no hiding behind it now.

Doran took a step in, turned and shut the doors. "No lock?" He fingered the clean slice of the dead bolt, and then grabbed a chair and slid it under the doorknobs for extra security. Or an extra precaution to keep me in the room with him? What the fuck was going on with him?

"No need for us to be interrupted." His voice was soft, but carried across the room easily. Shit, something was seriously off with the Daywalker. For all his quirks, and the few times we'd spent together, this was not like him.

Without any hesitation, I pulled the bowie knife out and un-looped the whip from my belt. When Doran turned, his mouth opened and his step toward me stopped in mid-air.

"I'm not here for that kind of a visit, as much as I wouldn't mind sparring with you. Though I'd prefer we did it naked." He gave me a wink, but I didn't lower my weapons. I was learning that supernaturals with fangs just couldn't seem to help themselves, no matter what they said, they would always want what they couldn't have. Blood, sex, power, one or all three of those options, whatever they could get.

"I think I'm good as I stand now."

"Have I not been helpful to you, Rylee?" He stepped toward the big table, ran his fingers along the top of it.

"Yes, sort of."

"Have I not sent you gifts that have aided you?"

I thought about the pendant he'd sent for Giselle, how it had helped on the last salvage. "Perhaps."

He smiled, maybe hearing the hesitation in my voice.

His eyes flicked up to mine. "Have I not drawn a demon's poison from you? And in doing so, saved your life?"

"You all did that, you and the other Shamans."

Laughing, he shook his head, the piercings catching the light and flickering against his skin. "I didn't need them, I could have done it myself."

"Then why didn't you?"

"Ah, well, I was under orders. Sorry about that." Again, he winked, but his eyes were strained, like his mask was finally cracking. I had a feeling that whether I liked it or not, I was about to see another side of Doran.

"Orders?"

He ran a finger along his lips, a second bead of sweat joining the first. "Can't tell you anything else."

Fuck, this was getting irritating. "Why the hell are you here, Doran?"

With a hop, he sat on the edge of the table and leaned back, spreading his arms out, fingertips stretched. He let out a heavy sigh.

This was weird behavior, even for him, and my gut told me I needed to move, get out of there. The thing was, if O'Shea was lost to the wolf he carried now, I would need help to bring him back. And Doran was a powerful Shaman.

"I am here because . . . ." His hands waved loosely in the air above him.

I waited, but never lowered my weapons. He remained silent, so I asked him the question that burned the back of my throat with its intensity.

"O'Shea is lost to the wolf in him. Can you bring him back?"

Doran tipped his head up so he could see me and blinked, as if seeing me for the first time. "Bring him back? Maybe. Perhaps. But it won't be easy, even if it would work. Worse than what you went through with the Hoarfrost demon, I think. Perhaps. Maybe not. Possibly."

The knot that had tied itself around my gut when Milly had told me O'Shea was lost loosened. A chance, that was all I asked for, a chance to save him.

Before I could ask another question, Doran sat up and scrubbed a hand through his short hair, grabbing at it as if he would try to yank it out. "Rylee, I'll tell you why I'm here, but you're not going to like it. I've been compelled to come. However, I thought that once I was here I could keep myself in check, but it's proving harder than I expected. Perhaps I should have tried harder to stay away." He was rambling, which was totally unlike him. "I told her I would help you; so I helped in the beginning, because it's what she wanted. But—"

I cut him off. "Spit it out, Doran."

He swallowed hard. "I don't want to hurt you." He took a big gulping breath, his pain-filled green eyes flicking up to mine. "She wants me to kill your little witch."

I licked my lips, heart thumping hard with adrenaline. Fuck, I did *not* want to fight Doran. "Who wants you to hurt me? Who wants to kill Pamela?"

"The Child Empress, the one that would rule the vampire nation. She is a power in her own right and she isn't even fully fanged yet. Because she carries the memories of her parents, she has all their strengths as well as her own."

Oh fuck, wasn't it bad enough that I was already dealing with Faris? Did I really have to deal with this Child Empress too? And what the hell did she have against Pamela?

The thing was, I didn't know what to do. Killing, or trying to kill, Doran would lose me a powerful ally. And while I might not always trust him, the same could be said for many of my allies. Not to mention that Doran hadn't gone after Pamela when he had the chance. He could have attacked her there in the kitchen, but he hadn't, he'd held himself back somehow. Add in the fact that he'd just told me he could possibly help me bring back O'Shea if he was lost to the wolf as Milly said.

"Why would she send you to me, why not one of her vampires who could have cleaned my clock and be-spelled Pamela in a heartbeat?"

I wanted to move, to pace or prep for a fight, but at the same time, I needed him to keep talking. If I *was* forced to kill him, then I needed all the information I could get out of him ahead of time. Brutal, cold, but no less than the truth for all that.

"You let me right in, didn't you?" His dark-green eyes were full of sorrow, but he couldn't seem to sit still. His hands jumped and twitched as he talked. "I walked right up, kissed you on the cheek and you didn't even lift a weapon. The Child Empress knew that. I can get close to you; it's what she's wanted all along. But I can't stop her from commanding me, the binding goes too deep."

"Fine." I rolled my shoulders, loosening my muscles. "Then how the fuck do we unbind you from her, stop her from compelling you?"

"We don't." He lunged at me, and I barely got the bowie knife up between us. He stopped, his eyes wild, mouth open as he panted for air. His muscles twitched, as he lowered himself to the ground, face down, neck exposed to me.

"Kill me swiftly, that's all I ask." His body jerked and jumped as if tied to strings I couldn't see. Like the puppet he was. Fuck it all to hell and back.

"There has to be a way to unbind you from her." I held the knife above him, poised on the edge of slicing it into his neck, holding off the inevitable.

"I would have to bind myself to another, someone else. There is not time; I can barely think straight with her in my head—"

His hands snaked out and grabbed me by the ankles, jerking me to the floor. I hit hard, but stayed on my back so I could see him. He crawled up my body, fangs bared, his eyes wide with fear.

"Kill me. You must."

"I never did like doing things the easy way," I said, as I flipped us over so I was on top and his back was to the floor. Even though he tried not to fight me, his body struggled to obey his mistress.

"Rylee, you have no ability to bind me. And she is pushing me hard. If you don't kill me, I *will* go after Pamela." He groaned, his body bucking underneath mine.

I balanced my knees on his arms, but I knew that he could throw me off if he wanted to. What the hell was I going to do with him? I couldn't kill him, not if I was going to bring O'Shea back, but how did I let him live with Pamela's life on the line?

A tentative knock came on the door, then the sound of a cane rapping against the wood.

"Go away!" I yelled, glancing over my shoulder. Doran threw me off him, pushing me straight up into the air. My head brushed the fifteen-foot ceiling before gravity took over, yanking me back to the floor. I landed in a crouch, eyeing up the Daywalker who had plastered himself against the far wall of books.

"Rylee, I can't hold on much longer. Send her away, I can smell her on the other side of the door." He said, sliding to the floor, books falling around him as he went.

From outside the door came a resounding curse and then the wooden panels were blasted open. Jack strode in, a snarl on his lips, eyes flashing with anger.

"This is my fucking house, and I don't give a shit." He came to a stop as he rounded the table and Doran came into view for him.

I put myself between Doran and Jack. "Fuck, Jack, this is why I didn't want you in here, I knew something was wrong."

Pamela stepped into the room and lifted her hand. With an ease that belied her experience, she pinned Doran down, and his face relaxed. "Should have asked the witch along. Always ask the witch along. That's advice you need to start taking."

"Shut up, Doran," I snapped, knowing he was right. The struggle was using Pamela to help me, but not getting her killed. A fine line in our world. One I didn't like walking.

Jack made his way to his recliner and slumped into it. "Who has you bound?"

Doran rolled his head toward the old Tracker. "The Child Empress. I know of no way to break the binding; Rylee must kill me or I will attack her, kill Pamela, and make a general mess of things for all of you."

Jack snorted and leaned back in the chair, putting his feet up. "All these things you know, and yet so bloody fucking much you don't, Daywalker. And you've been around for what, three hundred years?"

Doran gave a grunt. "Close enough."

I felt my eyes widen, couldn't stop them. Three hundred years? Seriously?

Jack pointed at me with his cane. "She *can* break the binding, but are you ready to be free of the Child Empress, to stand with Rylee instead?"

Okay, now I was confused. "I can't break any binding, Jack. I have no magic."

"The magic is in your blood. In mine too, but I don't have any extra to spare."

Doran and I were talking over each other, but I shushed him with my hand. "Doran has drunk my blood before. So your theory falls short."

"Straight from the vein, or out of a cup?" Jack tipped his head back, and closed his eyes.

Doran's eyes met mine and I saw the confusion in him—and the fear.

"From a cup," I said.

"From any major artery, or from the last of your life, the magic in your blood will act like the catalyst it is. It is a driving force in the most powerful of spells, and will break the bond between him and the Child Empress." Jack let out a jaw-cracking yawn, as if all this were just the every day for him, as if he didn't really care about the outcome.

Doran shook his head. "I don't think this is a good idea. If I bite you, she could have a connection to you through me. I'm not sure I won't rip you open if she commands it of me."

"I need your help, which means we are doing this." I walked toward him, rubbed my wrist. This was going to hurt like a son of a bitch.

"Think big artery, Rylee. I'd say neck or inner thigh if you want to be sure it will work," Jack said, stopping me in my tracks.

Fuck, this was just getting better and better, wasn't it? Neck it was.

Doran couldn't move, held as he was by Pamela's spell. I turned to face her. "You let him go when I tell you to, okay?"

"Are you sure?" Her fingers clutched Alex's collar, the werewolf having crept in without me noticing. Both of them had eyes the size of silver dollars. Children, I had children for allies. Fuck, I needed Doran to snap out of this binding he was under so I had at least one able-bodied adult backing me up.

I was in front of Doran, our bodies maybe an inch apart. He was still shaking his head. "Rylee, this is a bad, bad idea."

"So is killing you, so is killing Pamela. There are no good choices here. If this will break the tie, we are doing it. So stop your fucking whining." I closed the distance between us and did my best to ignore the thundering race of my heart. I closed my eyes and pressed my neck against his closed mouth. "Do it."

He groaned, his lips brushing against my skin, tongue darting out to taste. I shivered and my heart sped up even more, sweat beading up along my spine. He whispered my name, kissed my neck, and I pulled back to glare at him.

"None of that shit. Just bite me, damn it."

Doran gave me a smile. "Can't blame me for trying."

I leaned back in, pressed my neck hard against his mouth, and this time he wasted no breath. His fangs popped through my skin, and I stiffened at the sharp piercing. He groaned and I lifted a hand. "Let him go, Pamela."

The second her spell left him, his arms snaked around me, holding me against him as he drew my blood into his mouth. For most people, it would have been a sensual, sexual moment, and by the way Doran's lower half felt, he was definitely in the mood. But he hadn't be-spelled me, so his bite wasn't doing a thing for me. The bite hurt, and his hard-on dug into me with the unpleasantness of a drunken come on. Overall, not an experience I'd want to write home about.

I felt a distant twang on my senses and the Child Empress's attention focused on me. I could feel her gaze through Doran. Shit, this *was* a bad idea.

"Jack, how long?" I tried to look to the old Tracker, but one of Doran's hands snaked up to cup the back of my head.

Jack had the nerve to laugh. "The first drop of blood would have done it, he's just getting off now."

I slid two fingers between Doran's mouth and my neck and popped him off like I would a leech; the connection that had started up between me and the Child Empress cut off. Thank the gods.

The Daywalker reeled back, stumbled across the floor, and ended up flat on his back, a trickle of my blood leaking down the edge of his mouth.

"Sweet mother of the dark goddess, Rylee. That is the most amazing blood I've ever tasted." He giggled, sounding drunk. "And the binding is gone. I can't feel her in my head. You are a goddess, a queen, a sweet aphrodisiac that I will never grow tired of."

I put a hand to my neck, the bite tender, though I could tell he'd not dug in as he could have. I had a bite on my lower back from a pissed off Daywalker— I knew how bad it could have been if Doran hadn't been holding back.

"Great. The binding is gone. You can behave now. Pamela" —I strode across to her— "come with me."

I left Jack and Doran in the library and headed to the nearest bathroom. Digging through the cupboards, it took me several searches to find what I was looking for. The towel was too big, so using my bowie knife I cut it into strips.

"Pamela, run this under the hot water, will you?" I handed her the smallest strip.

She did as I asked, her eyes watching me in the mirror. "Do you think he's safe now?"

"Safe as he's going to be."

"Then why did you take me with you?"

I sat on the edge of the tub and she handed me the strip. Pressing it against the bite I let out a sigh. "Because he's never going to be *safe*. Not really. There are very few supernaturals that I would leave you with. Will and Deanna, Jack, Eve. Not Doran."

Alex slunk into the bathroom. "Leave Pamie with Alex."

"Yes." I patted him on the head. "I'd leave Pamie with Alex. You would keep her safe."

He grinned up at me, and then leaned into the sink to play in the water, drawing designs in it with his oversized claws.

Pamela eyes were shadowed, like she was still worried. Fuck, this was what I'd been worried about when taking her on as my ward. Not only how the hell I was going to keep her safe, but how was I going to allow her to still be a kid when she needed to be?

Unfortunately, I already knew the answer. Her days as a child were done, and even though she was only fourteen, I had to depend on her as the powerful witch she was.

It took everything I had to say the words that came out of my mouth next. "You want to go and check on Doran, make sure he and Jack are all right while I clean up?"

A flare of excitement lifted the shadows from her face. "Are you sure?"

"Yes. Just be careful. If he so much as steps toward you, wrap him up again and holler for me." She was running back the way we'd come before I'd even finished speaking. Eager to take part, eager to be of help. Eager to be a grown up.

The gods help me, I was going to need her when I went after O'Shea.

Gods help us both.

6

Doran was passed out when I went back into the library. Still flat on his back, he was snoring, which to me just seemed weird. Where was the grace and the mystery, the fear-inducing reputation that was supposed to go along with the blood drinkers?

He snorted and rolled onto his side. Maybe not so much after all.

Jack didn't look up when he spoke to me. "Between the binding being broken and the high of your blood coursing through him, he'll be passed out for days."

"I don't have days. Milly said there is a team of witches going after O'Shea now. I have to leave."

"I'll keep an eye on him. He's got some interesting parts to play in the future." Jack's eyes narrowed as though squinting to see something—maybe that was exactly it. As a Reader, he could pick out what people were going to do, and even what they needed to do, just like Giselle had been able to.

Maybe when I got back with O'Shea, I'd ask Jack how he'd avoided the madness that had stolen Giselle from me long before she died.

I scrubbed my hands over my face. "Listen, Alex has to stay here."

The werewolf let out a high-pitched whine.

I glared at him, something I didn't often do, but I needed him to obey me. "You can't come. O'Shea is dangerous and he might go after you again. I don't know that his last orders from Milly aren't still in play. You stay here with Jack and Doran. Got it?"

His lower lip trembled, drooping a good inch. "Gots it."

Next I turned to Pamela. "Go get your trench coat, the black one, and your tall boots. Dress warm for flying."

Her lips crept into a smile. "You're taking me with you?"

"I need you to hold O'Shea for me. Once we find him, you need to hang onto his furry ass until we get back here to Doran."

She bobbed her head, blonde hair dancing as she ran from the room.

"You going to be okay here, Jack?"

"I've been fine alone for a long fucking time before you bloody well showed up." He grumbled, and then poked Doran with his cane. "Besides, somebody's got to keep an eye on the fanged asshole here."

"Thanks." I touched Jack's shoulder and he reached up and put his hand over mine in an unusual show of affection.

"Be careful. I may not be able to read you, but everyone around you has a lot of shit coming down the pipeline. Very little of it good."

I swallowed hard, pushed the spurt of fear that curled around my chest. "Got it. Anything else?" Here it was, he could come clean, tell me what he knew about the prophecies. Nope, no such thing.

He waved his cane at me. "Nah. Now fuck off, go find your wolf."

Walking down the hallway to my room, I mulled over the best course of action. Experimentally, I Tracked O'Shea, something I hadn't done for some time, not since I'd been home in North Dakota. I'd been too busy dealing with a rogue Necromancer, Milly, and Faris. No, that wasn't entirely fair. O'Shea had gone off on his own and that had hurt. He hadn't trusted me enough to let me help him. So in turn, I'd ignored him.

I let my abilities work, opened them up to trace O'Shea's threads. There was nothing, not even a glimmer. The only way I wouldn't be able to feel him is if there was a large amount of water between us. Shit, had he gone back to America? Son of a bitch—that would not make my life easy. I slipped into my bedroom and shut the door behind me.

"Come on, O'Shea, where the hell did you go?"

While my mind worked over what to do, I dressed for flying with Eve. Leather pants were not my favorite, but they were lined with fleece and were damn warm, which was what I needed. Tank top and long-sleeved shirt were next. November in England was a bitch of cold and wet. I much preferred the dry, cold, windy snow of North Dakota. Holding the straps that would keep my two swords attached to my back, I paused. Milly had spelled all my weapons so they would cut deeper, hardening the metal so it wouldn't break under pressure. She had made so much of what I did possible with her magic. Even now, knowing everything she'd done to hurt those I loved, I struggled in those quiet moments to understand where my friend had gone. Why she had turned against everything we had fought for in our years together with Giselle.

I let those thoughts go, slipping my two swords on. Next was my belt where I hung my bowie knife, whip, and a hip holster for arrows. Though I was still gaining proficiency at long distances, the crossbow was a sweet addition to my arsenal. So far it hadn't jammed up or given me grief in the middle of a fight.

Over top of everything I slid on my leather jacket, fingering the tears and ragged stitch jobs that criscrossed over it. The thing was almost as patched up as me.

A soft knock on the door that I was sure would be Pamela turned me around. "Come in."

"Gladly."

I spun, not recognizing the voice, pulling a sword from my back as I faced the man in the doorway. Average height, average build, brown hair, brown eyes. Nothing that screamed danger. If it hadn't been for the crescent moon axe he held in his hand, I would have thought he was there for tea and biscuits.

Right.

He swung at me, still smiling, which was more disturbing than if he'd snarled or grimaced. I ducked and rolled while he dealt with the backswing of the larger weapon.

"That's the bitch with axes." I swung my sword up, the tip opening a shallow cut from his hip up to his armpit. "Always dealing with the backswing."

The man stumbled back from me and then threw a spell my way, straight at the floor in front of me.

Minor, one I'd seen a thousand times via Milly and even Pamela, but had never had used on me before. A sticky spell, one that would plant my feet to the ground and force me to stay where I was standing.

"Hah, good luck with . . . ."

Shit. I tried to lift my foot and nothing happened. This was the first time in a long time my Immunity had buckled, damn it all to hell and back. The timing was a bitch.

His grin widened. "Shoes and floor aren't you, little girl. Immunity doesn't spread to those bits, do they?"

Fuck, this was bad. He swung at me again and I did a limbo backward, stared at the shimmering blade as it skimmed along the front of my body, caught a glimpse of my wide, green, gold, and deep brown eyes in the reflection of the polished steel. There was no time for me to play around, I had to end this fast or I was dead. Using the leverage of my feet glued to the floor, I lunged my body toward him, sword aimed at his throat while he dealt again with the backswing and miss of the heavier weapon.

My blade slid through his neck with ease, the spelled edge beyond razor sharp. His eyes bugged out then closed, the smile forever etched onto his face as the axe slid from his hands. The weapon hit the floor with a thud and my feet unglued, the spell dying with him. Blood poured out of the wound in his neck, spreading across the floor as it first spurted and then just gushed from his body, until there was nothing but a steady trickle of blood coursing out of him.

"What the fuck was that?" I kicked his body as I walked past him to check the hallway. Cocking my head,

I listened for the sounds of fighting. The axe man was no ordinary robber, he had magic, and he'd known about my Immunity. He hadn't been here for the silverware and fine china. Keeping my back to the wall, I made my way to Pamela's door. I knocked softly.

"Pam, you ready to go?"

A voice that wasn't hers called out. "Yes, come in, Rylee, you can help me pick out my weapons."

How stupid did they think I was? I slid out of my leather jacket and pulled the crossbow from my back, loading it as fast as I could, talking to keep the intruder, whoever it was, lulled. "Okay, but I thought we could discuss your use of magic first—"

I kicked the door open, saw the intruder and fired without a second thought. The bolt took her between the eyes, her mouth a perfect 'o' of surprise. I barely spared her a glance after that; her death was nothing to me.

Pamela was laid out on the bed, her eyes closed, her body still.

I rushed to her side, a spurt of panic driving me. She couldn't be dead. I wouldn't believe it.

"Pam, wake up, come on kid." I put my fingers to her neck. Her pulse was steady, easing the panic that had gripped me for that split second. Fuck, what the hell was going on here?

I scooped her up in my arms and jogged back to the library. As I drew close, raised voices greeted me. Son of a bitch. The door to my left was a closet. I slid Pamela into it and shut the door; that was the best I could do for now. Loading my crossbow again, I peeked around the edge of the library door.

Other than Jack, Alex,—who sat trembling by his side—and Doran—who I could still hear snoring—there were two new visitors. One I recognized, one I didn't. The one I didn't recognize was tall, hulking even. He would give Dox a run for his money in both height and width. Black hair curled around his ears, and he wore only a pair of threadbare pants, his upper body naked. A Celtic knot was tattooed over his heart and his muscles actually rippled with each breath he took, as he stood still in the center of the library. What the hell was he? Because he didn't feel like someone who carried magic, he was much more primal than that.

Actually, he reminded me of the tribal Guardians I'd met the last time I'd been in New Mexico. His eyes flickered around the room and I caught a glimpse of silver. Shit, he *was* a Guardian of some sort, which meant I couldn't kill him. Fuck me, this was turning out to be a bad day.

The one I recognized, I could kill her and not lose a moment of sleep over it. Dr. Daniels, my own personal nemesis from my first day in London, stood with her back to me, facing out the window.

"You see, Mr. Feen, Rylee is standing in the way of progress. The world of the supernaturals is on the brink of coming into our own, of taking our rightful place as leaders, as gods amongst the humans. Rylee has sided with Faris, and so she is against this progress."

My mouth curled up in a sneer. What a bitch, I wanted to just shoot her and be done with it, but I also needed to hear where this was going. Not to mention

I knew from experience that the Guardian with her would be impossible for me to kill. I really didn't want to get on his bad side if I could avoid it.

Jack gave a grunt and his hand tightened on Alex. "She hasn't sided with anyone. Whatever information you've got, it's fucking wrong, you dumb bitch."

I silently cheered Jack on. Alex lifted his nose, his head turning my way. Fuck, not now, Alex!

Big, gold eyes blinked at me, then one gave me a slow wink and he turned his face back to Dr. Daniels and the Guardian with her. For once, Alex seemed to get the severity of the situation and rolled with it. Thank the gods he was learning.

"No, no. My information is very clear. Killing Rylee will be best for all involved. If my people don't manage it, then my Beast here will. But fear not, you have my oath—you and the others in your home will not be harmed. That is not the Druid way." She turned to face Jack, giving me a full view of her gloating smile.

The Beast, as she'd named him, nodded his head. "I am yours to command, Mistress."

Not good, not good at all.

Dr. Daniel's advanced on Jack. "You are pitiful, dying, and even Deanna's little bag of herbs won't save you. You know that, don't you?"

He flipped her off. "Fuck yourself. Seriously, you think I care . . . ." He was lifted into the air, his face going red as he struggled for air.

"I may not kill you, I may not harm you, but I will not take that kind of language in my presence." She spoke to him as if she were a Queen and he her misbehaving servant.

That was enough. Time for me to make my entrance.

I stepped around the corner and fired, as she stepped sideways and my bolt missed her heart, instead slamming into her arm. She screamed, and Jack fell to the floor with a gasp as he yelled at me.

"Run, Rylee. They aren't after us, just you. Run!"

"Not really my style, Jack," I said as I dropped the crossbow and slid the two swords from my back. The Beast cricked his head sideways, silver eyes taking me in with a single sweeping glance, and then shifted into his animal form. His shift was like watching liquid bend and slosh in a cup as his body slid from human to cat in the space of half a heartbeat. It didn't look real, nor did I think it was how regular shifters made the change. The faint shadows of rosettes under his black coat and the shape of his body were all panther. The shape of his head, the thickness of his body spoke of dark jungles and thick foliage where the cats of his ancestors still lurked. But the size of the Guardian was most definitely not panther. He was easily a thousand pounds, the size of a freaking horse, not a goddamned cat.

Daniels smiled at me, though smiled would imply mirth, and she was all but baring her teeth. "Beast, take her."

The Beast roared, the scent of fresh meat on his breath spreading through the room. The sound reverberated through the house. My skin went cold; this was going to be bad.

He lunged at me, paws that were at least five times the size of Alex's slashed through the air above my head as I dove deeper into the library. Dr. Daniel's screeched at the top of her lungs. Maybe she had a right to it, after all, it wasn't the first time I'd hurt her without her being able to defend herself.

I ran to her, slid an arm around her neck, and pulled her tight to me, my other hand holding my sword so the tip pressed under her chin.

"Call your kitty cat off," I growled, squeezing her body tight to the point where I knew she would struggle to take a breath.

"You will pay for this," she choked out.

I snorted. "Jack, do the bad guys ever come up with new lines, or is it always the same old shit?"

"Same old shit, doesn't matter how many idiots you face," he coughed out, rubbing his throat. Alex trembled where he stood, peeing on the floor. Fuck, I wasn't far behind him. The Beast crouched in the library doorway, tail lashing through the air.

"Call your pet off." I pushed on my sword, popping through the first layers of skin.

"No."

I had to give her credit, she had balls.

But I had no time to make a move. Something hard, a book from the feel of it, hit me from behind. I gripped Dr. Daniels harder, but she used that momentary distraction to escape my grasp.

Spinning to face me, a sneer curled her lips. "Rumors run fast in the supernatural world. Everyone knows you're an Immune now. That little ace up your sleeve is long gone."

Well, that was going to make my life difficult. Fuck me, life was just doing its best to sink me lately.

She lifted her hand and pointed a finger at me. "Kill her, pull her heart from her body, and let her bleed out on the ground."

Yeah, me and Daniels, we were going to have it out. Just not today.

The Beast leaped and I spun, running toward the windows, my blades still gripped in my hands. We burst through the glass together, the swirl of red curtains and black panther blending into the sheets of blowing rain.

I rolled across the grass to my feet, slammed my blades into their sheaths, and was running before I truly knew which way I was going.

The sound of heavy breathing and the thump of huge padded feet hitting the ground behind me spurred me on. Legs and arms pumping hard, I bolted, zigzagging to keep the Beast from snatching me. At least that was what I was going for.

"EVE!" I hoped she could hear me. Fuck, I was going to die as a freaking gods-be-damned kitty toy.

Feeling the Beast move up, I dove to the right, narrowly missing the swipe intended to knock me flat. The Beast roared and I didn't wait to see how close he was.

"EVE!"

The pond was to my right, close enough that I might be able to reach it before becoming the Beast's next meal. I knew the cat would be able to swim, but maybe I could swim faster? I wasn't seeing many other options to help me out. Blades wouldn't work, Pamela was out cold, and I was running out of possibilities that would keep my skin intact.

I bolted for the pond and the ten-foot dock that the tiny wooden row boat was tethered to. The Beast pounded down the dock after me, the sound of wood and pilings splintering under his weight. He roared, his breath hot on my neck, as if he were right on me, his wicked teeth inches from my bare skin.

I didn't look back, just pushed harder, reached the end of the dock and leapt, eyes focused on the other side of the pond.

I never hit the water.

"I've got you, Rylee!" Eve crowed as her talons wrapped around me, gripping me tight. My feet just missed the water before she swept us upward, her wingtips skimming along the top of the pond, a rush of air circling around us. The roar of the Beast below us echoed through the rain.

"What was that?" Eve spun on a current in order to look back at the oversized black kitty that paced below us, his silver eyes never leaving me.

"He's a Guardian. But he belongs to that fucker, Daniels, and she's just set him on me."

I stared down at him, a pit opening up in my guts.

"Why do I get the feeling I've just acquired a stalker?" I grumbled outwardly, but inwardly I was trying not to panic. A Guardian coming after me? Shit, I was never going to be on Faris's team, not if this was what I got when people just *thought* I was working with him. Mother fucker, the next time I saw him, and I had no doubt there would be a next time, I was going to . . . to what? He was damn vampire, what the hell did I think I was going to do to him?

"Rylee, where do you want to go?"

I thought about Dr. Daniels and her Beast; there was only one person who would know what the hell was going on.

"Into London. We need to speak to Deanna."

7

Eve held me easily in her talons all the way to London. Not that it was all that far, nor was it all that uncomfortable. But feeling like a Harpy's next meal was not a great addition to how the day had gone so far.

"Do you think the others will be all right?" Eve asked the question I'd been asking myself.

"I think so. I think the Beast is just after me. And while Dr. Daniels is a total bitch, I don't think she's a killer. They didn't hurt Pamela; just knocked her out to keep her from helping me. Besides, the stupid Druid said she swore not to harm anyone in the house." Though she had choked Jack right after saying that. I would call the house as soon as we landed, make sure they were okay. Because regardless of the consequences, if they were being hurt, I had to go back.

At least I'd had the sense to stuff Pamela in the closest, because I had no doubt Daniels still wanted the kid for her own. Hopefully, the Druid left before Pamela woke up.

So much, there was so much swirling around me. But my priority now was O'Shea. O'Shea and staying out of the Guardian's very sharp claws and mouth. Both were rather critical.

Eve made a lazy circle over the roof of the police station we'd worked out of for our last case. Just thinking about why I'd been brought to London made my emotions climb up through me and grief swell up in my heart. So much death, there was so much death in my world. And while I wasn't so stupid as to think everyone could survive, some hurt more than others.

Like losing Giselle.

Eve let me drop to the roof when we were a few feet up still. I took a couple of steps, getting out of her way, and then she landed with a flutter of her wings beside me. The rain was no longer pounding down, but it was chilly and I was feeling the cold, feeling the sharp tang of winter try to get a hold on me.

"Wait here, I may have to make a run for it again." I adjusted my weapons, did a quick count. I was missing my crossbow and my leather jacket, but I could probably get both here. Otherwise, I'd done pretty well at keeping my shit with me this time around.

"Rylee, why do you think you'll have to make a run for it?"

"Remember the Guardians in New Mexico? How they seemed to always be able to find us? I'm thinking they have some ability to Track, maybe even the same way I do. And I have no doubt that the Beast will be on us very soon."

She drooped where she stood, her golden eyes darkening. "That's not good."

"No, no, it's not," I muttered as I went in through the door leading to the stairs into the main part of the building. The last time I'd been here I'd been running *up* the stairs, Agent Valley screaming along behind me. I'd gotten the job done, but Valley and the local SOCA Agent Denning had been pissed to say the least.

I jogged down the stairs, and headed into the main office. There was a mixture of openly hostile stares—I had, after all, caused something of a zombie outbreak during the last case—and a few respectful nods. Those were far less than the glaring angry eyes, but I'd take them.

Will's desk was at the back of the room and though I was no longer jogging, I kept my pace brisk. How long would I have before that damn Guardian showed up? I had to believe it wouldn't be long. I was going to bet less than ten minutes.

Will was working, head down, sandy blond hair messy. Handsome, he was a handsome guy, and maybe if I didn't have O'Shea I would have looked at him as more than just a friend.

Maybe.

I rapped my knuckles on the desk. "William, we need to talk." He'd planned to take time off after our last case, and he had. For about three days. It seemed that, like me, he couldn't, or maybe didn't want to, escape his work.

He didn't lift his head; no doubt he'd smelled me long before I reached him. "Busy right now."

"Oh, pardon me while you're being busy and I deal with the big fucking beast of a Guardian that Daniels has called out on me. Here, let me sit down and wait for him to show up while you be *busy*." I dropped into the chair across from him. His hands stilled on the paperwork he had been writing on just a second before.

"Please tell me you're joking." He slowly lifted his eyes to mine. Yes, he was a looker, our Will. But damned if right now all I wanted to do was shake him till his teeth rattled. Was it his fault that Daniels and her Beast were after me? No, but he'd known about them, his reaction told me that much. And that was enough to rile me. Was this what he'd been holding back? Or was it a reaction to whatever had gone down between Deanna and Daniels?

"That's who roughed you up the night we went to find Deanna, isn't it?" I leaned forward, hands sliding across the desk to steal his pen and twirl it between my fingers.

He let out a low groan. "Yes, the Beast isn't supposed to be used this way, but she's captured him somehow, made him bend to her will. Not unlike the witch did to your O'Shea. And she ousted Deanna."

"Green shit on the walls, this is a mess. But I don't have time to discuss the ousting of your sister. Can the Beast track me?"

"Yes. Perhaps not the same way you Track, but they have some abilities, particularly if they've been set on someone they have been instructed to kill for the betterment of the Destruction."

I threw the pen across the room, wishing I could throw my chair as well. "This is a really bad time for me to be dealing with a Guardian. I assume that he can't be killed?"

"Not that I know of."

"Can Deanna call him off?"

The sounds of footsteps behind me turned me around. Deanna stood there, her coloring and the shape of her face so like Will's. But it didn't look as good on her, like she was trying too hard not to be feminine. She wore a long multi-colored skirt, white button-down shirt, and her hair was tied back with a leather thong.

"Can Deanna call who off?" She pulled a chair up beside me and lowered herself into it with far more grace than I would ever have.

"Daniels and her Beast," I said, watching for her reaction. And boy, did I get one.

Her already pale complexion drained to the point of looking green. She swallowed several times, then finally reached across the desk and took Will's coffee cup, lifting it to her lips.

I lifted my eyebrows at her. "That bad, huh?"

She nodded. "The Beast of Bodmin Moor. He is the phantom cat that protects us in time of need. She, Daniels . . . I can't believe she would set him on you, even though she is the leader now. Are you sure?"

My eyebrows shot upward. "Are you shitting me? The mother-fucking, big black kitty cat that weighs at least a thousand pounds, *chased* me like I was a fucking mouse and you want to know if *I'm sure?*"

"I see," she whispered. "I had hoped perhaps . . . never mind. I apologize."

"Don't apologize, fix this. Can you un-set him?" Gods, I was hoping.

But she was already shaking her head. "I don't know how she did it. For centuries, the Beast has been our protector, keeping us safe. For her to bind him . . . it would take something beyond my ken."

"Well, he's after me now and I have shit that can't wait for me to deal with him." I swiveled in my seat to face Will. "I need a crossbow and a leather jacket of some sort."

"And another set of hands?" His eyes were hopeful. I thought about O'Shea, about how he and Alex had not gotten along when O'Shea was shifting into a werewolf. About the possessiveness around me. Will was an Alpha in his Destruction; that alone was enough to deny him.

"No, I don't think it's a good idea. I know O'Shea, he won't hurt me. But you . . . you'd be competition."

Will stood and Deanna made a move to stand with him, but I put a hand on hers, keeping her with me. "Will, I'll catch up with you in a second." He nodded, jaw ticking as he headed to the armory. I thought about Pamela, thought about going back to get her and take her with me after O'Shea. I might need her something fierce to keep him from killing me. Then again, if he was killing witches she might be in too much danger to keep her safe. Fuck, there was no easy answer here.

"Deanna. Milly used to make me pre-made spells that were contained within a bladder, like a water balloon. Can you do that for me?"

"I think so, what is it you need?"

I took my hand from hers. O'Shea and Pamela might both hate me for it, but it would be something that would maybe keep Pamela out of the line of fire, letting me leave her at home.

"Something that will hold a large werewolf for a good amount of time."

8

The armory was cool, bare bulbs incased in metal screens hung from the ceiling at five-foot intervals making the room overly bright. I squinted and blinked at the sudden glare.

Here was a veritable treasure trove and I couldn't help but stare at all the weapons. Most were too modern for me to use. But there was a good chunk of old school weapons that would work just fine.

Will handed me a crossbow. "Here, this is very similar to yours."

I took the weapon, went over it, letting my hands feel the curve and flow of the grips and the weight of it. Slightly heavier than mine, it was otherwise identical down to the simple firing mechanism.

"This will work," I said, slinging it onto my back. I wore only my long-sleeved shirt and that was still damp from the flight here. I rubbed my arms. "What about coats, jackets?"

He bent down, grabbed a long leather trench coat from a pile. "Here, this is mine; we're close to the same height, so it won't drag." Holding it out for me like a real gentleman, he waited for me to do the girly thing and slip into it. I let out a sigh and turned my back to him, sliding my arms into the coat. The chill of the room disappeared with the weight of the coat. Longer and heavier than I was used to, it would be better than my own jacket when it came to flying.

Will pointed out straps on the inside of the coat. "Those you can wrap around your legs to keep the side panels close to you. Should help when you're up on Eve."

"Thanks. I should get going. I don't think Denning would be too happy with me if every time I visit I drag along some new supernatural creature."

"Isn't Deanna doing something for you?" Crap, his hearing was better even than Alex's.

"Yes, but she said it would only take a few minutes."

Will's eyes softened and he lifted a hand to touch my shoulder, brushing off dirt that didn't exist. "Are you sure you don't want help? I can come with you; Eve could easily carry us both."

The room suddenly felt much smaller than it had just a moment before and I recognized the look in his eye.

Nope, that was so not going to happen. "Yeah, I'm good. I'm used to working on my own. Pamela will be pissed that I left her behind, but I think maybe the Beast did us both a favor. O'Shea's after witches, Pamela's a witch, there's too good of a chance he'll go after her." I was rambling, I knew it, but I couldn't escape the look in Will's eyes, the look that I was trying to avoid.

"What if you can't bring him back, what then?" Will swallowed, looked away and then back at me, his eyes that soft hazel with flecks of green that I had no doubt women swooned over. Shit, Pamela was gaga for him and she was only fourteen.

"I'm bringing him back," I said, my voice firm as I tightened the straps holding my weapons.

"You don't know that. He might not be the man you knew. He's been a wolf for a long time now."

Oh, that's a good kitty, piss off the Tracker.

"Fuck you, Will. I will bring him back one way or another. Alive, dead, still a wolf. Whatever the case, O'Shea is coming back with me." I turned my back on him and left him standing in the armory. I didn't want to question why he was suddenly so worried about O'Shea coming back. Sure, we'd had a few meals together, but that had been all of us: Pamela, Alex, Jack, Deanna, and Will. Not exactly what I would call dating. But shit, if he thought for one instant that I would turn my back on O'Shea, the kitty cat really had no idea—

"Adamson, good to see you here. We need to talk." Agent Valley, his short squat body moving at a speed I still didn't comprehend how he managed with his stubby legs and rotund gut, was just *there* at my side, his fingers tightening around my forearm.

"Well, Agent Valley, I thought you would have gone home by now." Our last meeting hadn't gone so well. A screaming match, a barking werewolf, a young girl ready to light the whole place on fire with her magic. Yeah, not so well at all.

"No, I'm waiting on my best agent."

I cringed and he let out a barking laugh. "Not you, Adamson. O'Shea. You're going after him, aren't you?"

The muscles in my neck and jaw tightened. "You going to be a pain in my ass if I say yes?"

"No. I'm not. But if you manage to bring him back, I want you working with him." He let go of my arm and tipped his head back so he could look me in the eyes.

"I'm not agreeing to that. I don't know why you would even bother asking." I tried to brush past him, but he moved to stand in my way.

"There is a movement for supernaturals to come out to the rest of the world. Do you know what kind of chaos would ensue? I need the best of the best to be working with me on this, to keep a lid on this cluster-fuck that is trying to ensue."

I paused, crossed my arms over my chest, the leather of my new/old jacket squeaking. "Why are you being so open with this?"

"Denning wants the world to know about the super-natural. The FBI does not. Interpol is in the middle, not sure what to do. You can help them decide. I want them to see the chaos that is your world, let them see how very bad it would be and how bad it would get if we humans truly understood."

He was confusing the shit out of me, and to be having this conversation in the open, where anyone could hear us? I glanced around, saw that no one was close enough, at least no one that I knew would be able to hear.

"The zombie attack didn't work?"

"No. Denning brushed it off as a freak accident and panned it to the media as a flash mob gone wrong."

I couldn't help it. I let out a laugh. "A flash . . . mob?" Son of a bitch, Denning was dumber than he looked.

Agent Valley wasn't laughing with me, so I made an effort to pull my shit together.

"Adamson, this is not funny. The world isn't ready for the supernatural, maybe won't ever be ready."

I wiped my hand across my lips as if to brush the last of the laughter from me. "You're right, but you have to admit, it is *kinda* funny. Zombies as a flash mob? I can't believe the media would buy that shit." His lip twitched, but he didn't smile, he didn't laugh.

"Are you with me on this?" His eyes were serious, his lips no longer twitching.

I let out a snort and was about to answer him when the screaming started. Shit, why was it always the screaming that tipped me off?

We spun as Deanna came running around the corner, grenades in her hands. Yes, I said grenades.

"Rylee, run! He's here for you." She slammed into me, shoving the two grenades into the deep pockets of the trench coat.

"What the hell, Deanna!" I dug at them to get them out.

She smacked my hands. "The spells are inside, pull the pin, throw the grenade, and use the ignition word, *Capio*."

I didn't ask any more questions, just bolted for the stairs. The roar of the Beast behind me pushed me faster and made me angry. Denning popped his head out of a doorway, his eyes widening when he saw me, then narrowed with anger.

I ran past him, couldn't resist slapping him as I passed him by. "Denning, you're a fucking idiot if you want this out with the general public!"

Deanna was yelling for people to get out of the way, screaming actually, for them to stand down. No point in getting in the Beast's way, he was only after one thing.

Me.

The stairs flew under my feet and when I reached the top, I careened through the door, slamming it behind me. I ran to Eve and leapt onto her back. I didn't have to say anything. She launched herself into the air as the Beast burst out onto the roof.

His silver eyes followed us as we rose higher, never leaving my face. Eve used the currents to lazily circle upward without much effort on her part. And I warred within myself. I needed to find O'Shea, but I hated that I had to leave Alex and Pamela behind. Jack would protect them as best he could, but I hadn't even thought to ask Will and Deanna to look out for my two wards. There just hadn't been time. Hell, I hadn't even found a phone to check on them.

"Rylee, how high do you want me to climb?" Eve tipped her head so she could look at me.

"To where we can't be seen from below." I needed a moment to think. Or maybe a few moments.

Eve did as I asked, climbing high enough that the air thinned. I fought a sudden wave of anxiety when the breath I took barely filled my lungs. "High enough, Eve."

She banked and dropped down, and the pressure on my lungs eased.

I Tracked O'Shea, felt nothing, knew that I would have to cross over to the mainland to try and get a bead on him. Hopefully he was there and not somehow back in the States. Based on what Milly had said, I didn't think he was in the States. But without an ocean between us, I should be able to track him. Either way, I would find out soon enough.

Then there was Alex and Pamela. My mind kept circling back to them. Logically, it didn't make sense to take them with me, to bring them into danger when it came to O'Shea.

But my gut was telling me otherwise. They were both needed, for some reason, they needed to come with me.

"Keep your blue socks close, you will need them to survive." The memory of Giselle's admonitions cemented my decision, but didn't make it any easier.

Not for one bit.

9

Fuck it all to Hell and back. How the hell was I going to do this?

"Eve, we need to go back to Jack's."

"For Pamela and Alex?"

"Yes. They need to be with us."

Eve let out a screech that made me cringe and the skin on my neck crawl. Even though I trusted her, there had been more than one time that a Harpy had tried to eat me. Even Eve had at one point sized me up for a McRylee Meal.

She tipped her body to the left and I clung to her with my legs. I really, really had to get a harness set up for her. But with the way my life had been going, there just hadn't been time.

There was never enough time, it seemed.

Before long Jack's mansion came into view.

Along with the Beast, pacing below us. Apparently, we hadn't moved fast enough this time around. Damn, I should have asked Eve to fly faster.

"Rylee—"

"I see him." I slipped a hand into my pocket. These were for O'Shea, but if I had Pamela with me they wouldn't be needed. "Land near the pond and then go get Alex and Pamela. Make sure Pam gets my jacket and her weapons."

"What are you going to do?"

"I'm going to slow that big kitty cat down."

The Beast watched us as we circled to the opposite side of the pond. I slid from Eve's back and loosened up my one sword, pulling it free of the sheath. Eve swept across the pond, screeching in the Beast's face as she went by him. But he never even turned her way, his gaze solely centered on me.

"Do you know that you're being compelled?" I asked as the Beast crept around the pond, stalking me. I kept time with him, like a ridiculous game of Ring Around the Rosie. The only thing left to be seen was which one of us would fall down first.

His voice rumbled across to me, surprising the shit out of me.

"Yes, I know I'm compelled. When I am free of the compulsion, I will kill the woman."

Sweet, at least Daniels's death wouldn't end up on my shoulders.

"No chance we could break the compulsion?"

"No. You will die. For that I'm sorry." His black lips rippled back over his teeth and he sprinted around the pond.

I pulled a grenade out of my pocket, yanked the pin with my teeth as I ran and threw it at him.

"*Capio!*"

The grenade exploded in a haze of silvery light and sparkles, blurring my vision. The Beast leapt out of the magic made dust, fog, whatever the fuck it was. Shit, it hadn't worked—or had I missed him? I bolted around the pond, fumbling for the second grenade. If this one didn't work, I'd be forced to stand my ground, and I knew how that would end. Badly, oh so badly.

Maybe Deanna's spell wasn't supposed to work on the Beast; that was possible too. Maybe she'd made it specifically for O'Shea, or a wolf.

I didn't have a lot of time to think about those possibilities. One second I was running, the next my legs were swept out from under me and I was flat on my back, the wind knocked out of me.

The Beast loomed over me, one front paw pinning my legs, the other planted firmly on my chest, making it impossible to breathe.

"I will avenge your death, Tracker," he said as his lips drew back over his pearly white fangs.

My fingers slid around the grenade and I frantically worked the pin with my middle finger. Shit, this had to work, it had to. The pin popped out and as the Beasts head dropped to my face I shoved the grenade deep into his mouth, my hand swallowed deep into his throat.

With the last breath in me, I whispered, "*Capio.*"

The Beast froze, his eyes bugging wide and he stumbled backward off me, and then he collapsed to the ground beside me.

I rolled to my side, stared into his silver eyes.

"Well played, Tracker. Well played." His words were a whisper as his body twitched. "You won't have long before I revive. Perhaps only minutes. Run while you can."

This was too bizarre. I shifted to my knees, then climbed to my feet and jogged toward the mansion.

Movement caught my attention, and I watched as Eve climbed into the sky, two figures with her. I continued to run toward them, glancing back several times to assure myself that the Beast still lay prone on the ground and hadn't snuck up on me on silent pads.

Eve swept down and I climbed onto her back, tucking myself behind Pamela. Eve held Alex in one talon; there just wasn't enough room for him to ride on her back.

"Rylee, I knew you'd come back for us." Pamela glanced over her shoulder, her blue eyes full of trust, and a bruise blooming on the side of her face where Daniels' thugs had knocked her out. Damn.

"I almost didn't."

Her eyes dulled a little, but that was just it. I didn't want her to think I was infallible. Quite the opposite, if you looked at my track record.

Eve flew us across the channel and as dawn broke we landed in a farmer's field on the outskirts of a town.

The Harpy hopped on one foot, flipping a sleeping Alex out of her grip so she could land easily. He tumbled with a yelp, scrambling awake, his eyes round with that look people get when they're startled awake. Like they aren't really seeing the real world yet, but still inside the dream they'd been dreaming.

With a full-bodied shake he turned to glare up at Eve. "Not funny, Evie."

She snorted. "Did you want me to land *on* you?"

He sneezed, scrubbed at his muzzle with a paw, and then shook his head. "No throwing Alex!"

They continued to banter back and forth as Pamela and I slid off Eve's back.

"Rylee . . ."

I glanced over at Pamela, who was rubbing her hands over her arms. "What?"

"Are we stopping here to rest?"

This was the part I'd not really considered. Alex and Eve could keep up with me, but Pamela was still a kid, and a kid who'd been treated pretty shitty-like prior to me finding her. If I was on my own, I'd start Tracking O'Shea and be leaving right away. But with Pamela along for the ride . . . .

"I'm just going to get my bearings, give Eve a chance to rest for bit, and then we'll be flying again. You can sleep in the air, okay?"

She bit her lower lip and nodded. "Okay. I'm kinda hungry."

"Alex hungry too."

The werewolf went from chattering at Eve to scooting himself in front of me, tongue lolling out. "Starving."

I took in the area. The farmhouse would be as good a place as any to grab something to eat. After all, this was France, the land of good food, good wine, and sexy men. At this point, I'd take the first on the list and ignore the other two.

"You three stay here." I pointed at the spot I was standing on and Alex almost shoved me over trying to plant his butt where I pointed.

With a shake of my head, I started off toward the farmhouse across the field. As I walked, I sent out a thread to Track O'Shea. There was a whisper of him, faint, kinda like he was across the Veil that separated the human world from the hidden supernatural realms, but that wasn't quite right, either.

I stopped and concentrated on the feel of him. He was there, but it was like the signal was being blocked. To the east and the north, he was at least on this continent and then it was as if the thread I'd tied to him was cut. Not like he was dead, or across a large body of water, which blocked my abilities, but cut in half. I Tracked him again, or tried to, got nothing, and then the faint thread that was O'Shea fuzzed again. Still to the northeast. Like a crappy radio signal dipping in and out of reception.

But this was weird; I'd never felt anything quite like this before. I started to walk again, mulling it over in my head. I knew we didn't have long on the ground; there was no way the Beast would give up so easily, and I had no idea how long Deanna's spell would hold him for. Food was the first thing, and if I was lucky, the farmhouse would have a phone that I could use to call Jack.

I kept Tracking O'Shea, or trying to. His threads continued to blur in and out of focus. Like one minute he was there, the next he was gone. What the hell was this garbage?

Approaching the farmhouse, I slowed my gait, but walked right up to the front door like I belonged there. No need to go skulking around in the early morning. I tried the doorknob and it turned easily in my hand. Hard to imagine anyone being so trusting in this world anymore.

Stepping across the threshold, I did a quick sweep of the room with my eyes. Nice furniture, older but well kept, a TV and one wall covered in photographs.

Family shots mostly, some school pictures, pictures of people who had nice, normal lives.

If only they knew what had just crept into their home. A shot of embarrassment zipped through me. I made my way through the house, noting the exits, the stairs leading up to the bedrooms. Typical two-story farmhouse. The kitchen was at the back and I hit the jackpot. Rifling through the drawers I found a good-sized paper sack and moved quickly, stuffing it with food. Homemade bread, cheese out of the fridge that looked homemade too by the light coloring, three oversized sausages, a couple of apples, and a glass jug of milk. I'd just have to make sure Pamela ate first or Alex would eat it all, the piggy werewolf.

I slung the sack over my shoulder and looked around for a phone. There on the wall was an older-style rotary phone, which was perfect since I wasn't sure one of the new cordless ones would work for me. I moved to the phone, freezing when I heard a creak of floorboards upstairs and the soft back and forth of voices. Shit, I didn't want to face anyone; it was bad enough I was stealing their food.

I lifted the phone and dialed Jack's number. He picked up on the first ring.

"Got to be you, Rylee, feels like I'm picking up the phone with no one on the other end," he grumbled.

"We're fine, you're okay?"

"Fine, just fucking dandy."

"O'Shea's threads are fuzzing in and out." I spoke in a rush, the creak of the stairs making me talk fast. "Why?"

"Hmm. Not sure."

"Hurry. Time crunch."

Jack took a breath and then coughed. "Could be the wolf has taken too much of him. If he's lost to the wolf, it isn't really O'Shea you're Tracking anymore. If you're getting a bead on him now, that's good. But you might run out of time. Might end up having to Track werewolves in general and hope to hell you can find him that way."

I didn't answer him, just hung up the phone and moved to stand behind the kitchen door, blocking me from sight as the farmer's wife padded into the kitchen. Her gray hair was braided down her back and she wore a calf-length nightgown, white with pink flowers on it. She'd lived her life probably never even knowing the supernatural was real. I didn't want that to change for her.

Denning was wrong. Bringing the supernatural into the open would turn it into a clusterfuck of massive proportions. Even though the supernaturals were stronger and faster, there were far fewer of us than them. If it came down to it, we would be overwhelmed with sheer numbers. Like ants, the humans would swarm and devour the world of the supernatural.

As the farmer's wife bent to pull a frying pan out, I slid around the side of the door and jogged quietly to the front door, slipping through it without a sound. These people didn't deserve to be robbed, or to have some great hulking Beast show up just because I'd been here. Let them live their lives not knowing about the supernatural, let them be in their world of family, farming, and long white nightgowns that would never be used to sop up blood.

I jogged back to my three wards. Three, how the hell had this happened? Jack was right. I had to start saying no. If I didn't, there wouldn't be much time before I was stringing along a fucking circus behind me on every salvage I went after.

I handed the milk to Pamela, portioning out the rest of the food between her, Alex, and myself. Eve took one of the sausages, but nothing else.

The three of them chattered away at each other and I stood back, watching them. They interacted easily, as if they'd known each other for years, and for a split moment it was as if I saw them ten years from now. Older, wiser, still working together. They would make an amazing team, and when that time came, I knew they wouldn't need me anymore.

This was their training grounds, and I was their mentor as Giselle had been to me. More than ever before, I felt the weight of that on my shoulders, the responsibility I had to them and to the world, to make sure they were trained up right. To make sure they didn't end up causing more harm than good.

The last thing the world needed was more supernaturals like Faris.

Or worse yet, more supernaturals like Milly.

10

Eve announced she was ready to go not long after Alex had polished off the last of the food.

As we rose up into the clouds, I looked down, expecting to see the Beast below us. What I wasn't expecting was the blow from above.

The only warning we had was a rush of air, the back draft of a wingspan that dwarfed us. Glittering, scaled talons struck hard and deep; they buried themselves into Eve's body, pinning my legs to her. I expected a Harpy, thought maybe we'd crossed into territory that was already taken. I looked up, shock snapping along my nerve endings.

Pamela screamed, Alex barked, and the noise only added to the confusion of what I was seeing, of what my mind—so used to the supernatural—struggled to accept. Scales of green, silver, and blue rippled in the dim sunlight and the leathery wings that spread above us obscured my vision from anything but what I was looking at. Triangular head, four legs, big fucking wings, long tail that cut through the air like a rudder. And scales. Lots and lots of scales.

A dragon, fuck me, an ever-loving dragon had us in his talons. Teeth that looked as though they were shards of steel glistened just above us, but no fire escaped him. Or maybe it was a her, I had no way of knowing. Either way, we were royally fucked. I didn't think for one instant this was going to be anything other than a fight to the finish.

Eve struggled and then went still below me, the calm in her voice surprised me. "Rylee, I can't break free and I think my wings are broken."

Without a sound the dragon banked hard to the right, taking us south, away from O'Shea. Though at that particular moment O'Shea was the least of my worries.

I couldn't take my eyes from the beast above us, knowing that even if my swords bit into the dragon's skin and he dropped us, we were dead in the air without Eve's wings. "Yeah, this could be a problem." We were going to have to wait until we landed. I gave Pamela a light shake. "Screaming isn't going to help, and it could attract more attention from other supernaturals. Which would be . . ."

She sucked in a sharp breath and let it out in a rush. "Bad." She finished for me, her eyes full of unshed tears.

She bit her lower lip and muffled the sounds escaping her. Fear, pure and simple. Alex hung below us still, Eve clinging to him, and he was still barking like a mad man, but again, that was the least of my worries.

I whispered into Pamela's ear. "When we land, you and Alex run for it. As far and as fast as you can. Got it?"

"What about you and Eve?"

"We'll be right behind you." Lies, I was lying to her and we both knew it. This was going to get ugly and the best thing I could do was send her away. The best thing I could do was try to protect her, even if that meant Eve and I didn't make it. What the fuck had I been thinking bringing them with me? I should have gone after O'Shea by myself. I was a fucking moron.

"I can help," she said, her eyes wet with tears.

Eve answered her. "Your magic will fail on the dragon. They are Immune like Rylee. You cannot help us; do as your mentor says."

Oh fuck, Immune? We were done, toast. Maybe in the most literal of senses.

The dragon let out a roar and suddenly we lost altitude with a speed that yanked Pamela out of my hands. She screamed and I reached up, grabbing her as her ass floated above Eve's back. I yanked her back down, the leverage I had with my legs pinned to Eve's side working in my favor.

"I gotcha." I held her tight against me, my heart in my throat. I Tracked O'Shea, feeling him in the north, then Tracked Berget, feeling her closer, here in the south. She was happy, ecstatic about something. I held tight to Pamela.

This felt like goodbye to me, felt like there would be no more after this. How did you fight a dragon who was an Immune like me? You didn't. You ran or you died. Eve couldn't run, so neither would I. Which only left one option that I wasn't particularly happy about.

Dragons were rare, something you didn't hear about anymore, their numbers cut by disease and the use of their body parts for powerful spells. All I knew was that they killed intruders of their territories without mercy, and that they didn't bargain with their captives.

Ever.

The dragon sped toward the base of a mountain, and I grit my teeth against what I knew was going to be a sudden stop.

With a back wash of leathery wings our downward descent stopped and again Pamela was jerked out of my arms, despite how tightly I held her.

"Rylee!"

I managed to snag the back of her pants. "Get ready to run, you got that? Alex, you too, you look after Pamela. Protect her, got it?"

His reply was a shaky, "Yuppy doody, Rylee."

There was no cave, just an indentation in the mountain, like a half-assed box canyon. At the back there were piles of bones, corpses of animals both natural and supernatural, in several stages of decomposition. At the front 'entrance' of the canyon were piles of boulders, each one at least the size of my Jeep back home. They partially blocked the canyon, giving the illusion that there was nothing beyond them.

"I'm sorry, Rylee," Eve said, her voice trembling, the fear leaking out with her words.

"Don't be sorry yet, Harpy. We aren't done until the blood spills and we aren't breathing anymore," I said, trying to figure out a way to get our asses out of this mess.

The dragon touched down and I pushed Pamela off Eve's back. She hit the ground with a grunt, rolling with the fall, cradling her left arm. Eve dropped Alex and he herded Pamela away, the two of them running as fast as they could. Pamela glanced back as they reached the edge of the indent in the mountain, a determined look on her face. Ah, shit, apparently she was as bad as me when it came to taking orders.

"No!" I shouted, but I was too late. The young witch threw one hand in the air, lifting three massive boulders from the entrance and then, with a flick of her fingers, flung them one by one at the dragon's head.

The first one caught him on the side of the head, smashing him sideways. He roared, but more importantly, he let go of me and Eve.

The Harpy crashed to the ground, the puncture wounds from where the dragon had pierced her oozing blood. Her wings were crumpled, as if they'd been made of tinfoil and flexi straws instead of bone and cartilage.

"Run, Rylee," Eve yelled, dragging herself across the ground. She wasn't going anywhere.

"I'm getting mighty pissed with all this running. Freaking Beast of Bodmin Moor and now a dragon? Nope, no more running," I said, loosening my swords. Above us, the sky lit with a crack of lightning followed by a ridiculously close boom of thunder, the clouds bursting open as if the lightning peeled away whatever held the rain back.

"It's the dragon," Eve said, dragging herself along the ground. "He is controlling the weather." Oh, that was just fucking peachy.

The dragon turned to face us, hatred burning in his eyes, which was really not an encouraging feeling. Seriously, what had we done to piss the dragon off?

Pamela continued to hold the boulders up, her whole body shaking with concentration, her lips tight. I stood there, swords in hand as the rain cascaded down on us.

And then things went from bad to worse. As in really fucking gods-be-damned worse.

The air around the canyon shifted, the whirlwind weather stirred up by the *other* dragons flying in, perching on outcroppings of rock along the mountain.

The dragon that'd snatched us out of the sky let out a long, low growl, but he didn't move toward us. I settled into a fighting stance, putting myself between Eve and the dragon, and trying not to think about the newcomers. There wasn't anything I could do about them anyway. One dragon at a time, thank you very much.

"Are we going to do this, or are you just going to stand there and think about how badly I'm going to kick your ass?" I shouted, my words punctuated with several flashes of lightning.

His head snaked backward and he let out a roar, lifting his head to the sky and baring his throat. I drove my two swords into the ground at my feet and yanked my crossbow forward, slamming a bolt into the channel. The idiot continued to roar as I lifted the crossbow up, aimed, and pulled the trigger. The bolt flew straight and true, burying itself deep into the flesh between his jaw and his neck. He let out a strangled gasp of air, blood spurting past his lips.

You have drawn first blood. This battle will be true to the rules laid down centuries ago. The voice in my head was not my own and I did my best not to stare up at the other dragons, where it 'felt' like it had come from.

"What?" I shouted, popping another bolt into the crossbow as the dragon in front of me clawed at his own neck. A lucky shot, a perfect shot. One I doubted I could duplicate again. Already the bolt was being pushed out as the dragon's body healed itself. Damn supernaturals and their talents with healing.

The battle must now be between the two of you. If you best him, you will be free to go. If your friends help, we will destroy you all. We have waited for this battle, sensed its imminence since the dawns arrival. This has been foretold since Blaz's birth. A battle of blood was seen, as much as he might not agree, it is what we knew would come. It is why we are here, to witness this.

Well shit, I didn't like the sound of any of that.

"Pamela, lift Eve up and you three get the hell out of here. If you help me, the other dragons will be shitting witch, werewolf, Tracker, and Harpy tomorrow."

I didn't have the luxury of making sure she did as I asked, I had to trust her. Only one other time had I faced such a big reptile, and that hadn't gone so well for me. Giselle had saved my life, and if she hadn't been there, I had no doubt I would have been swallowed whole and slowly digested while I still breathed.

But that was then, this was now. I had no other choice but to fight to win. To kill him or at the least make him beg for mercy.

Right.

I lifted the crossbow and aimed at the dragon's head, aimed for the glittering eye. I hit the trigger, watched the bolt bounce off the side of its head. Unfortunately for me, it not only didn't do any damage, it reminded the big fucker I was still there.

Oops.

His breath came in raspy belts, blood trickling out his mouth and over his steel-colored teeth as he advanced on me, ignoring my three wards. Guess he got the same memo I did. One-on-one or not at all.

I dropped the crossbow to the ground and grabbed the handles of my swords, pulling them free of the dirt. Fear bounced along my spine and down my arms, but I pushed it back. There could be no panic, or I'd lose whatever edge I had. Assuming I had an edge against him.

His body was easily twenty feet long with at least another ten feet of tail and though he was big, and injured, he moved *fast*.

He swiped his front claws at me, one after another, reminiscent of a bear swiping the dirt in order to scare an intruder, to show how tough it was.

I backed up, let him advance, and as he began to raise his right claw for another pass, I raced toward him. Bolting between his front feet, I slashed his underbelly with my sword, felt it stick hard in between the scales. I let it go rather than fighting with it. The dragon squealed like a stuck pig, the squeal turning into a bellow of rage that was echoed back to us by the other dragons.

I ducked out from under him and, without another thought, used his back haunches to climb onto his back. Each protrusion along his spin made for a perfect handhold. If I could just get to his neck, I could drive my sword—

He bucked hard, sent me flying through the air to slam into the ground a second time. I rolled with the momentum and scrambled to my feet. But not before the dragon was back on me, his head swinging toward me like a club. I took the blow, tried to roll with it again, but fuck, he had a hard head.

For the third time I hit the dirt, blood coating the inside of my mouth, mingling with the dirt and sweat, and I was getting seriously pissed off. Could I take a dragon on my own? Probably not, but I was angry enough not to care anymore. When he swung his head at me a second time, I was ready for him. Holding my sword handle at my ear, I braced for the impact, driving the tip of my blade into the soft tissue of his jaw. He jerked away from me and the blade cut even deeper as it slid free. Blood splashed all over my hands, the warmth of it a morbid relief in this chilled weather.

Blood ran from a gash over my eye, partially blinding me, but I barely noticed it. Tomorrow I'd be sore, bruised, and battered. I just had to get to tomorrow. No problem, right?

Lightning cracked over our heads once more, darted between us, and struck the ground at my feet. I threw my arms up and stumbled backward, blinded by the flash of light.

"If he gets to use magic, so do I!"

Let it be done, the rules of the blood battle are all in fairness given.

Perfect. "Pamela, keep him off me till I give you the okay."

I kept moving away from the sound of the dragon getting pummeled by boulders. A thud of flesh meeting stone, a grunt, and then a yelp from him. I blinked furiously, tried to clear my vision. A peal of thunder rippled through the mock canyon, my teeth rattling with the vibration of it. Far too slowly for my liking (though it was less than thirty seconds) my vision came back to me.

The dragon had his back to me and again, I ran for him, jumping over his lashing tail and scrambling up onto his back. Uncoiling my whip, I snapped it loose. "Hold off, Pam!"

The shower of boulders on his head eased as I fought my way up to the juncture of his shoulders and wings. He turned his head, a shocked look rippling over his face, and then his eyes narrowed. I cracked the whip forward, the length of it wrapping around his neck, the handle giving me something to hang on to.

I smiled at him. "Come on now, let's see what you've got, you big mother fucker."

He snarled, a hiss of blood and spit splattering me. I didn't even wipe it off, not caring anymore what happened as long as the others were safe. His blood was hot and stung the cuts in my face, making me grit my teeth against the sharp pain.

With a powerful launch he shot himself into the air. I gripped the handle of my whip as the dragon rolled in the air and found myself hanging from his back, the ground hundreds of feet below us already. Eve was fast, agile and talented in the air, could have tossed me a hundred times with ease.

She had nothing on this big boy.

He flipped back around, slamming my body into his back. As much as I wanted to ram my sword through his spine and end this, part of me held back. One, we were so far up, the fall would kill me. Two, I just couldn't explain it, maybe it was some ridiculous Tracker trait or maybe it was just me, but I just couldn't do it. Not yet.

11

Fighting the dragon really wasn't as scary as my brain was telling me it should be. And believe me, my brain was screaming at me that this thing below me was a big fucking monster and I should end it as fast as possible.

But, if I was being honest with myself, as he spun and bucked in the air, scales sparkling when random beams of sunlight hit him, I was kinda having fun.

Fun. Fighting with a dragon shouldn't be fun. What the fuck was wrong with me?

On a brief respite between rolls, I slid my sword back into my sheath. "This isn't going to end well for either of us. I don't suppose you want to call a truce?"

Fuck off, Tracker.

I leaned my head back and laughed into the wind. While the other dragon had been polite, reserved, and exactly as I would have thought a dragon would sound and feel inside my head, this one sounded a bit more—gods help us—like me.

He rolled again and I did everything I could to hang on, keeping my legs tucked in between his shoulder blades and wings. Power, there was so much power in him, and I could do nothing but hang on for the ride . . . .

Hours, maybe minutes, passed—I don't know. We flew through winds and lightning and thunder, clouds, and even hail. He took me so high black dots danced in my vision and my breath came in gasps, then he dropped to the earth skimming the edges of a lake at the last instant, rolling so that I was plunged into the water. But I hung on, my fingers wrapped around the handle of my whip. I refused to let him win this. But how the fuck I managed to stay on, I couldn't tell you.

Finally, after what felt like days, he flew back to the mock canyon, landing in a stumbling heap. I was still on his back and I wasn't sure I wanted to get off. At least from my perch I was relatively safe.

"You ready to call a truce?" I fought to keep my voice steady, to keep my body from shaking with exhaustion. Every muscle I had was starting to cramp from clinging to him.

Get off my back.

"Do you mean that literally or more in a figurative way?"

His head spun around so he could stare at me, mouth dropping open, and I thought this was it, he was going to roast me.

Instead he laughed, a deep boom of a laugh that rolled out of him in a wave of sound.

Get off my back, you crazy-ass Tracker. Now.

"You don't seem to get it, I'm pretty comfy up here. I kinda like it." I smiled at him, gave him a wink. Shouldn't I be stabbing his eyes out with my sword? Hell, he was close enough that I could do it.

With a groan, he sunk to the ground.

The other dragon, the one with the commanding, grown up voice, spoke to us.

I believe you two are well matched. Otherwise, one of you would have made the killing blow.

I blinked and tightened my grip on the handle of the whip. "If I could have killed him, I would have."

The dragon gave his head a sharp jerk up and down, agreeing with me, apparently. *Same here. I'm hungry and the Tracker would make a great appetizer. If I could have killed her, I would have.*

The dragons sitting around us chuckled, laughing and exchanging looks I didn't like. The kind of condescending looks of a parent seeing something the children couldn't. Suddenly I wanted to be off his back. I untangled the whip from around his neck and slid off, stumbling on my numbed and cramping legs.

His tail whipped around, propping me up on one side, helping me gain my balance. What the hell?

I shook my head and looked up at him. His eyes widened and he snatched his tail away from me as if it burned him. Maybe it did. All I could see was that if I wasn't careful, I was going to add to my circus act.

"Oh, shit. I can't take on any more juveniles!" Jack was going to kill me.

I am NOT a juvenile. His lips curled back over his teeth.

Blaz! You will not disgrace us.

The dragon, Blaz, hunched his shoulders and let out a suspicious hissing sound, not unlike a kid muttering under his breath.

Blaz turned his eyes at me and glared. *I'm not going to protect you.*

"Who the hell asked you too?" I snapped, limping toward the last place I'd seen Pamela. Somewhere in the fight, I'd gotten my right leg thumped hard and already the muscles of that thigh were tightening up, banding into a Charley horse that was going to be a bitch to deal with.

ENOUGH!

The word was followed by a roar that made Blaz's bellows earlier seem small in comparison. I fell to my knees, clapped my hands over my ears, and then something hard and warm wrapped around me, sheltering me from the wrath of the older dragon.

I glanced up to see Blaz over the top of me, facing the other dragons, his teeth bared and his tail curled around me.

Piss off, old man, I will deal with this. Blaz's voice was distinct, deeper and more gravelly than the other dragon's.

She carries the blood of the lost, she spilled your blood and you spilled hers, both mingled. The binding is complete. You are hers until the final storm comes. Do not forget this, Blaz. Do not disgrace our kind with your reluctance to be what you are. With those words, the other dragons lifted off their perches in unison, into the sky, with a swirl of sparkling colors and wings, disappearing within seconds as if they had never been there.

I put a hand on Blaz's tail, feeling something shift between us, and he let out a long sigh, rolling onto his back away from me.

Go to your friends and do not come back here. Ever. Or I will eat you.

That was clear enough for me.

"Nice meeting you too, Blaz." I gathered up my weapons and ran to the front entrance of the mock canyon. There, peeking through the other side was Alex, his golden eyes taking up his entire face.

"Rylee hurt?"

"No, I'm okay. Where are Eve and Pamela?" Alex led me through the strewn boulders to see that the two girls were crouched in the 'V' of a boulder and the side of the mountain. Eve's eyes were pain filled, but cognizant.

"How bad is it?" I knelt down beside her and moved her feathers so I could see the puncture wounds in her sides.

"I'll live, the wounds will heal quickly, but I don't know about my wings. I've never had broken wings before so I don't know for sure."

I closed my eyes and took a deep breath. "The Beast can't be that far behind with this delay; we have to find you a place to stay and either Alex or Pamela is going to have to stay with you."

Pamela swallowed hard, her blue eyes as serious as I'd ever seen them. "Alex isn't going to be able to help her much. And I think my arm is broken. I can stay with her."

Already she was more grown up than Milly, a better person than Milly. I put a hand on her shoulder and gave her a smile, then eyed up her left arm. Broken for sure. Shit, this was bad. "Let's go. Can you lift her again?"

With Pamela holding Eve up in a spell, we moved her down the edge of the mountain. We walked for close to an hour, moving slowly so both Pamela could maneuver Eve, and so I could help Pamela manage the downed logs and other obstacles. This far south, it was a lot warmer than where we'd come from, and it didn't take long to work up a sweat in my lined leather pants. Suddenly they weren't feeling like such a good idea as I slowly broiled in my own sweat.

We found a small grove of trees where, thank the gods, there was a run-down shack that would provide some cover for Eve and Pamela.

I slipped out of the trench coat and laid it over a low hanging tree branch, then turned to Pamela. "Let's get you out of that coat and take a look at your arm."

I helped her out of the short leather coat, working it carefully down over her arm. Pamela's face paled even more, and she swayed on her feet. I helped her sit down and then ran my fingers lightly over her arm. Broken, but clean. She sucked in a sharp breath as I prodded it.

"I feel like you're always leaving me behind," she said softly as I helped her out of her long-sleeved shirt.

With a flick of my knife, I sliced her shirt and twisted it into a sling, tying it around her neck in a loop we carefully settled her arm into.

"It won't always be like this. There are going to be days when we go on a salvage that you'll wish you were back here with Eve, hanging out in a piss poor shack." I grabbed my short leather jacket and zipped it up, then slid the long trench coat over Pamela's shoulders.

Eve bobbed her head in agreement with me. "Rylee is right. My mentor, Eagle, he told me much the same.

We are young yet, we will not always be in the midst of the battles. Not until we are ready. If we try too soon, we put not only ourselves in danger, but those that are there to teach and protect us."

Damn, and why again had I brought the whole crew with me? Gut feeling . . . right. Slowly, I was learning that sometimes I had to just run with things. Even when I turned out to be wrong. Then again, Pamela had saved my ass with Blaz. Or maybe I just needed to meet him? Maybe our paths wouldn't have crossed if we hadn't gone back for Pamela and Alex? In my world, there was little in the way of coincidences. For some reason this was all happening as it was. I just had to figure out why.

"Eve, what was that all about, with the dragons? Do you know?" She'd lived in Europe in her early years and had more knowledge about the creatures specific to the area than I did.

Her beak stuttered with several sharp clacks before she answered me. "My mother told me that the dragons were too tied in their prophecies. That instead of living each day, they were always looking to the future."

"And the blood mingling? How problematic is this going to be?"

She settled onto the ground just inside the shack. "According to what my mother told me, I would think not that big of a deal. They see signs and prophecies in the smallest details. In things that don't really matter." Eve attempted a shrug, then winced as her wings shifted.

I pushed all that away, had to. Whatever 'mingling' of blood Blaz and I had, it was clear he wanted no part of it, or me. Which was just fine. And if Eve was right, it probably meant nothing anyway.

Pamela moved to my side, her eyes serious. Crap, she wasn't going to let this go.

"Alex gets to go with you," Pamela said.

"You volunteered to stay, remember? And Alex isn't a child," I said, adjusting my weapon straps. "He might act like one, but he isn't. Whatever his life was before, he was a grown up when he was turned into a werewolf."

Alex nodded his head along with my words. "Alex grown up."

I lifted my hands in surrender. "See?"

Pamela gave me a smile, a small one, but a smile nonetheless. "So as I get older—"

"I'll take you with me until you beg me not too. You take care of Eve; that is just as important as me and Alex going after O'Shea. We're a family; we take care of each other. No matter what kind of shit is thrown at us."

Her grin grew and she carefully put her good arm around me. I hugged her back. Alex hugged our legs and Eve reached out a talon, which I took in my hand. Though I'd said the words on a whim, they were no less true.

We were a family, messed up, supernatural, getting chased and hurt, but a family no matter what.

Fuck, that was sappy.

"Alex, let's go." I untangled myself from Pamela's arms, pushing her gently toward Eve.

We left them behind without a backward glance. Worst case scenario, they would have to wait for Eve to heal up and then they could fly to Jack. He would help them.

We, on the other hand, were most definitely on our own. I picked up a jog, and Alex kept pace with me easily, sometimes stopping to bite at a bush or a wayward stick. He was, as always, oblivious to the danger we faced, to what was coming behind us. That was, as always, a part of his charm.

For two hours we ran, not full tilt, but close to it.

Just before noon, we stopped on the outskirts of a town, or more accurately, a big city.

From the signs, we were still in France.

From the sounds of the ocean, and the heat that was making me sweat like a pig in my lined pants, Blaz had brought us all the way to the southern region. Shit, this was not going to help when O'Shea was in the northeast. I Tracked him to be sure and got nothing back, not even a fuzzy signal.

Jack was right, we were running out of time.

"Alex, we've got to get a car," I glanced down at him, and he rolled his eyes up to mine.

"Yupsies. Feets are pooped." He waved a paw as if cooling it off.

It didn't take me long to find a car I wanted to drive. The black 911 Porsche was pristine, just sitting there waiting to be snatched off the side road it was parked on. Fast, sleek, it would have us moving at a clip that would no doubt have our time cut in half. I slid my hand along the body of the car.

"Too flashy," I muttered, hating that I was right. A car like that would get noticed and the last thing I needed was the *politzia* looking for a missing Porsche.

Three blocks over, I found the car that would do the job, though I cringed at the sight of it. An older mini, painted white by hand, with perfect rust holes added for depth to the areas where the white paint hadn't peeled away to show the original red color.

Ugly.

But it was easy to break into and easier to start, seeing as the keys had been left in the visor. Maybe someone didn't want the piece of shit car anymore and had left it out to *be* stolen; that I could believe.

Alex piled in, all two hundred pounds of him, awkward limbs, and seemingly endless tongue. There were mere inches between us, hardly enough room to breathe. The engine started after I pumped the gas pedal several times and begged it to turn over. With a sputtering cough, it revved up and we were off. Not as stylish as a Porsche, not as fast, but less likely to run into trouble along the way.

"Stinky," Alex said, about an hour into our drive.

What was he talking about . . . the stench of dog fart filled the small space in a matter of seconds. I gagged, frantically rolling the window down. "Warning, you have to give me some warning."

"Sorry."

With the window down, I did my best to ignore the steady stream of gas erupting out of the werewolf. What the hell had he been eating? Nothing I'd fed him smelled like that. Unless you count in the milk and cheese. Shit on a stick, I was never feeding him dairy again.

Tracking O'Shea, I finally got a bead on him. He was even further north now, which could just have been because we were so far south. But I knew better—he was moving steadily further away from me.

"Just stay where you are, O'Shea," I whispered.

"O'Shea stay." Alex whispered back to me.

I could only hope that the man left inside of the wolf O'Shea had become would hang on just a little longer.

Stay with us, Liam, just a little longer. I'm coming for you.

12

The wolf slept easy, the taste of witch blood thick and sweet on his tongue.

Tonight, his dreams bled red with vengeance, soothing the beast raging inside him. More than wolf, less than man, he only knew that to kill those who had chained him would bring him peace.

The crack of a twig snapped his head up, a distant memory recalling a woman with dark hair and green eyes sneaking up behind him. When he'd been weak, when he'd still let the man rule his actions.

His eyes narrowed as he watched a figure approach. He lifted his nose to the air and breathed deep. Not a witch; something else.

Something more dangerous than a witch; a rival for his territory. Steel-gray hair floated on the breeze and golden eyes stared down at him. Lean and wiry, the old man—who the wolf somehow knew was like him—stared at him from the shelter of the trees where he stood.

"Wolf, you hunt the witches, but do you know what you are?"

His lips curled back in a snarl, a rumbling growl warning the old man to back off.

Gray hair came forward, though, not back as the wolf had expected.

Closer with each step, the old man came to within leaping distance. A single leap and his throat would be in the wolf's jaws. Crushed.

They assessed each other, and finally the old man gave a slow nod. "You must go. The witches come in a force even you won't be able to stop. You endanger us all. Go to the north. Your mate will come for you there. She will save you. But, the witches will destroy her if you bring them together. Her death would be on your hands."

His words stirred something in the wolf, a buried thought, a broken memory. Tri-colored eyes, auburn hair, and a sharp tongue that was sweeter than any witch's blood.

Lover. Fighter. Mate.

He shook his head and the old man was gone.

As if he'd never been.

The wolf slowly raised himself up and stared to the north. There, she would find him. If the witches came, he would end them. But no longer would he taunt them, hunt them. Not if her life depended on it.

Turning his muzzle into the wind, he headed north.

We made it to Warsaw, Poland with very little problem. No Beast, no cops, seriously relentless wolf farts, but otherwise, we didn't have much issue. Nearly eighteen hours on the route we'd taken and I was done in. I had to sleep, no matter how much I wanted to keep going.

The car stuttered to a stop in front of a midsized hotel. Good enough for me. I told the front desk Alex was a therapy dog. It had worked in London and seemed to go over well in Warsaw too. Perfect.

I checked into my room, glanced over it quickly. We were four stories up, and while I didn't think it would stop the Beast, I still checked to make sure the window was locked.

The bed was lumpy, and I didn't turn the sheets down, just crashed on top of them, Alex curling up beside me. I passed out in a matter of seconds.

A few hours later, I woke up with a jolt, sitting bolt upright. I didn't know what it was, but something woke me up. Blurry-eyed, fuzzy-brained, I acted on pure instinct. I rolled from the bed and landed on one knee as I pulled a sword free from its sheath.

A voice spoke from the darkest corner of the room. "You know, I could have taken your blood ten times over, you were so deeply asleep. And your wolf there, he isn't much better."

Faris stepped forward, the light from the city through the window illuminating him.

"Do you ever make appointments, you know, show up when you're supposed to?" I didn't lower my sword, though I suspected I probably could. He made a good point; if he'd wanted to kill me, he could have on several occasions, not just that night.

I couldn't see it, but I knew he was smiling at me by the way his voice lilted as he said my name. "And would you make an appointment with me, Rylee?"

"Nope."

"Well then, it seems that this is the way it must be done." He continued forward, pulling the only chair in the room with him, sitting down in it.

"Are you aware that your Milly is pregnant?" He laced his hands together in front of him.

"Old news," I said, wishing I could get to the light switch. Alex snored lightly, rolled over and burrowed his face into the pillows.

"Quiet, Alex sleeping," he grumbled. What a guard wolf he was.

I shifted my stance, lowering the tip of my sword to rest in the thin carpet. "You know I have people trying to kill me because they think I've aligned with you. Now why would that be, why would they think I'm on your side?"

Faris stared at me, his eyes visibly blue even in the shadowed light, like they glowed in the darkness. The freaky-ass vampire.

"Am I wrong to assume you don't want the supernatural world announced to the humans?"

Fuck, this was not how I wanted the conversation to go. I did *not* want to agree with him on anything.

"Don't assume you know me."

"Am I wrong?" He bit out the words.

I let out a huff of air, once more aware that my level of fear around the vampire had dipped considerably since the first time I'd met him. "No. You aren't wrong."

There. I'd said it. The words tasted a bit like bile, having to agree with him.

He spread his hands in front of him. "So whether you like it or not, we are on the same side. I do not want to have the world know about us, and neither do you. The Child Empress wants the world to bow to her. That is a fool's way of thinking, one she learned at her parents' feet."

Again, I agreed, but I didn't say as much. Since I had him here, I was going to see about getting some of my questions answered. Much as I hated to admit it, Faris knew a great deal—and much of it, I had no doubt, could help me survive. He was in the center of all the supernatural politics and I was barely on the fringes. Which meant I could use what he knew.

"Speaking of the Child Empress, what's her beef with Pamela?"

Faris blinked several times and I realized that I'd caught him off guard. Score one for me.

"Pardon?"

So damn proper. "The Child Empress sent Doran after Pamela, why?"

"Did you kill him?" There was just a tad too much eagerness there for my liking.

"Never mind that. What beef would this kid have with Pamela?"

Faris pursed his lips, and his eyes dropped to half mast, cloaking the brilliant blue. "Perhaps jealousy. The Child Empress has been spoiled beyond belief, and now she is prepped to rule the world. Your Pamela, if my understanding is correct, once she matures, will put Milly to shame. That makes her a threat. What better time to wipe out a threat than when it is young and defenseless?"

My jaw tightened and I gave him a nod. "Point taken."

Silence then, as he sat there and stared at me, and I stared back, not sure what exactly was going on.

"What are you doing here, Faris? I doubt you're just stopping in to chit-chat."

He answered me with a question of his own. "Aren't you even the least bit curious how I found you? You are, after all, one of the last Trackers in the world; I'd think this would be of interest to you."

I shrugged and leaned back on my bent knee. "Milly had some of my blood. I know she has the spells it would take, plus the strength to use them to find me."

Faris leaned toward me. "I've tasted your blood, Rylee. I can find you anywhere now. Anywhere at all. A particular talent I've honed over the years."

Ah, fuck, that is not what I wanted to hear. But I acted like I didn't care, though my heart tried to leap up my throat, making my next words come out a bit strangled. "Whatever, anything else? A particular reason you wanted to wake me up in the middle of the night in the middle of Poland? Maybe you came to apologize for setting Milly on me, to have her try to kill my friends?"

He stood and started toward me. I rose to stand, facing him. I refused to back down, to give him the pleasure of seeing him push me the way he wanted me to go.

"Rylee, Milly and I were partners—of a sort. What she did to you and yours was nothing I had anything to do with, though no doubt that is what she told you. I wish you could see things as I do." He reached out, put one finger under my chin and tipped my face up. I batted his hand away, and he just chuckled.

"Spit it out. I have only a little more time to get some piss poor sleep before I have to leave."

He nodded, his face suddenly drawing tight, as if he had bad news for someone he cared about. But that was ridiculous, because one, I knew he didn't really give a shit about me. I was just a tool to him, and two, regardless of how bad things were for Milly, I wasn't helping her.

"Are you aware that your sister is in mortal danger?"

That I hadn't expected. My heart lurched hard, and sweat beaded up in an instant on my lower back. Every moment of my life since Berget had gone missing, I'd dreamed of going back in time and saving her. Of making right the one thing in my life I could never take back. Son of a bitch, even while my head explained that Faris knew that about me, if he knew nothing else: that my sister was the key to making me do what he wanted. Even knowing that, my heart was screaming at me to move, to get to her, and save her, screw the rest of the people around me. With everything I had, I forced myself to hold still, to remember that it was Faris I was dealing with.

"You can't know that." I struggled to deny him, to get the words out, old fears waking up with a vengeance as his words hit me.

"But I do know it. Her death is scheduled. Tomorrow at sunset, her blood will be spilled into the canals of Venice."

I fought to keep my legs from buckling under me. There was no way he was telling the truth. I Tracked Berget, felt her happiness and laughter, she was finding something very funny. Her life coursed through the thread that connected us once more now that we were on the same side of the water. A faint hint of uncertainty lay there too, but no fear. "You lie, I can feel her, she isn't afraid. There is nothing that would—"

"She knows it comes and she believes it is a thing she must do. She believes it is for the best. That it will save lives."

He reached for me again, and this time I didn't pull away. Not because I wanted him to touch me, but because I literally couldn't move. He had to be lying, there was no other answer. This was just a manipulation on his part. A way to make me do what he wanted. There was no way he would have come here just to help me—just to save my little sister. There had to be some angle, some benefit to him that I just wasn't seeing. He was a vampire, not some gods-be-damned saint.

His hands settled on my shoulders. "You could stop them, stay the hands that would slay her. But you would have to come with me. We would have to leave now."

Berget's life danced inside my head. I felt her as surely as if she were standing in front of me. Faris could be lying—in fact, I was almost certain he was. This was a ploy, a way to get inside my head. A way to control me, to get me to do what he wanted.

Faris had never been straight with me, and he *knew* that Berget was a card I would have a hard time ignoring if he played it. Fuck, I couldn't deal with this right now.

I took a deep breath and knew that I had to call his bluff, as hard as it was. "I don't believe you." I stepped back from him, watched the unexpected sorrow fill his eyes. Sorrow, not anger.

"Then your sister will die—tomorrow."

Panic clawed at my throat. If I was wrong, I was sentencing Berget to death without even lifting a single finger. I closed my eyes and Faris spoke from across the room.

"I would save her, if I could. But I can't. It is outside my abilities to stay a death such as hers, at least not without help."

"Then what makes you think I can save her?" I opened my eyes, stared at him as if somehow I would gain the answers I wanted from him.

"Because you are the Tracker. The catalyst." His eyes never left my face. "You will blame me for her death when it happens."

"She isn't going to die," I said, finding the strength to push the doubts away. "This is a game, an elaborate fucking game to you. You think I'm going to Venice? You're wrong. I'm not. I don't believe you. Berget is fine."

"Then the Child Empress wins."

I blinked and he was gone, the room empty of his blue eyes that were becoming all too familiar to me.

"Fuck," I snapped, grabbing my sword and driving it into its sheath with perhaps a little too much force. Alex snorted and rolled over, a jaw-cracking yawn splitting his muzzle.

"Going now?"

I paced the room, Berget's threads strong inside my head. Happy, healthy, not a drop of fear in her, a small hum of sadness and uncertainty flickered from her to me, but it was gone in a flash. Almost like it had never been. How could Faris think I would believe him?

I Tracked O'Shea, felt the fuzzing of his mind, the blip as he went off the radar, and then back on.

I didn't have time to check on Berget, to prove Faris wrong.

O'Shea was slipping away from me, faster with each passing moment, and that was if I discounted a team of witches going after him to end his life. But what if Faris was telling me the truth? What if this time there was no game in him?

I put my hands over my face. What the fuck was I going to do?

13

The road ahead of us was clear, even though the farther north we got, the more the skies darkened with snow-filled clouds.

I had my foot jammed on the gas pedal, pushing the little car as hard as I could. While I drove, I clung to Berget's threads, feeling what she felt. Even though she was happy, joyous even, I couldn't completely push Faris's warnings away. Was he going to try and kill her, was that what he'd been doing, threatening her? Fuck, I just didn't know. All I knew was that O'Shea needed me first, and I had to go after him before anyone else.

After Faris's visit, I hadn't been able to sleep. No point in sticking around anyway. Who the hell knew where the Beast was behind us? That, combined with my irrational fear that Faris *had* been telling me the truth, had stolen any chance I'd had at resting.

I eased my foot off the gas pedal as I had a literal moment of wanting to bash my head against the steering wheel. Blaming my stupidity on my sleep-deprived brain.

"Why the fuck didn't I think of this earlier?"

Letting go of Berget's threads, I Tracked the Beast. His proximity made me suck a sharp gulp of air and hit the gas with my foot.

Less than two miles, directly behind us. Mother of God, we were up shit creek with holes in the boat and no fucking paddles. Between my fight with that stupid dragon, Blaz, and the few hours sleep, the Beast had gained an amazing amount of ground on us.

"Alex has to pee."

I turned to glare at the werewolf. "You have to hold it. We can't stop."

"Peeing!"

"No, no peeing in the car!"

His bottom lip stuck out and he fiddled with the window crank. "Have to pee bad."

Two miles. The Beast was two miles behind us. I Tracked O'Shea—and felt nothing. Fuck, what else could go wrong? No, I didn't want to know.

Alex was scrambling at the door handle, actually getting the door open, leaving me no choice.

I cranked the wheel over and slammed on the brakes. "Pee and come back, hurry it up."

Alex fell out of the car, bounding through the deep snow drifts. Not peeing at all, just playing.

"Alex, fucking well pee or get back in the car." I Tracked the Beast, feeling the distance between us tighten like a noose around my neck. Less than a mile and a half, closer to a single mile in the time it was taking for Alex to take a leak—fuck, we were in trouble.

The werewolf finally cocked a leg on a tree, then bounded back to the car, tumbling in. I reached across and yanked the door shut.

Trying not to panic, I pulled back onto the road and again, putting the gas pedal all the way to the floor. More and more I was regretting my 'smart' decision when it came to my choice of cars. Right about now, a Porsche would be mighty handy. As it was, we were having difficulty getting the speedometer up over forty miles an hour.

I Tracked the Beast, Berget, and tried to Track O'Shea all at one time. The Beast came through loud and clear as he continued to gain on us. Berget was fine, same as before, and still, there was nothing from O'Shea.

"Damn you, Liam. Where the fuck are you?"

"Finding Boss?"

"Trying, I'm trying," I whispered, sweat trickling down my spine even with the steady stream of cool air slipping through the car's vents.

I was going to have to do a group Track, looking for a werewolf instead of O'Shea in particular. I thought about the characteristics, good and bad. Loyal, blood thirsty, pack-bound, and wild.

Of course, the first thing that came up was Alex sitting right next to me. I pushed his Threads back and reached out further, away from him.

There, to the northeast, in the same direction I'd last felt O'Shea came the hum of a werewolf, strong and clear.

Bingo.

I hung onto those three threads, did my best to ignore the Beast's, did my best to not worry about Berget's, and headed straight for O'Shea. A headache began to throb just behind my eyes, no doubt from hanging onto so many threads at the same time. Shit, just add it to the list.

The next half hour passed in a white-knuckled drive that had nothing to do with the weather or the road. Each minute that passed, the Beast cut the distance between us down, until, in my rearview mirror, I caught glimpses of his black body just as we'd round a corner. We had run out of time.

"Fuck, fuck!"

Alex barked, excitement spilling off him. "Yay! Fuck! Fucking rabbits?"

"No, no rabbits. Bad kitty."

The werewolf frowned. "Will?"

"Not Will, bigger kitty."

The engine took that moment to splutter, to fucking *splutter*, when I knew it wasn't out of fuel. I pumped the gas pedal, "Come on, you bastard, you can't do this to me."

Harder, I jammed my foot up and down, begging the car to keep going. Coughing and hacking like a fifty-year smoker, the car shuddered, speed falling as it gave up the last of its life.

Oh, we were so screwed.

I jerked the wheel to the right, pulling the car over to the shoulder, made sure I had all my weapons and jumped out of the car. Alex leapt out beside me, almost pushing me into traffic.

From behind us, I could feel the Beast, feel him closing the gap faster now, as if he knew we were on foot.

"Let's go." I bolted off down the side of the highway running as fast as I could, Alex loping along easily beside me. How the hell were we going to get out of this mess?

"Big truck!" Alex howled, pointing and dancing as a big rig with a flat deck piled high with strapped down containers came around the bend, going in our direction. The Beast was a hundred feet behind it, maybe less.

"Get on the big truck," I yelled, and Alex wasted no time, bolting after the rig, leaping up onto the flat deck. I ran full out, arms pumping hard and fast, and I leapt toward the truck, outstretched hands just catching the edge of the flat deck. The wood splintered, old and rotten, under my hands. My legs were pulled along the pavement, dangling out behind me as the wood continued to break away.

"Alex, help!"

The werewolf inched toward me, eyes glimmering with fear as he stared out behind me, whimpering. "Big, bad kitty."

"Help me up!" I couldn't get my feet under me, and in about three seconds I was going to lose my grip. Which wasn't really my biggest problem as I could feel the Beast less than a few feet behind me, within swiping distance.

Alex reached down, his claws digging into my forearms, pinching me hard even through the leather jacket. I wrapped my hand around his forearms as he yanked me up onto the flat deck. We tumbled backward and the Beast let out a roar, the sound of it so close that I could smell his breath, the tangy scent of blood and old meat. Obviously, he hadn't been stopping to eat . . . probably just waiting on me.

I rolled to the side, bumping into one of the containers and looked back. The Beast was not being left behind. Shit, this was about to get ugly. "Alex, try to stay clear of him."

The werewolf whimpered again. "No want kitty to come on big truck."

"Me neither, buddy." Not that we had a choice in whether or not he joined us. I looked at what was strapped down on the truck. Five feet by five feet, the square wooden crates were stacked two high and were held on by thick canvas straps, three straps to each double stack of totes. There was no telling what was inside the wooden crates, they could be empty, or there could be fucking bombs inside. I was hoping for bombs.

I yanked my sword, and sliced through the canvas tie downs. "Alex, push it!" I pointed at the tote and he didn't question me, just shoved the tote off the end of the truck.

With an ease that did not bode well for me, the Beast dodged the falling tote, which exploded in shower of brilliant red ceramic tiles. Maybe the move had gained us a few seconds, a few feet, but the Beast made it up in a matter of heartbeats. So much for that idea.

We backed away from the edge of the flat deck.

"Alex no like kitties."

Yeah, I wasn't real fond of them either right at that moment.

The Beast's muscles bunched and he launched himself toward the rig, landing on the flat deck.

"Alex, hide!"

I ducked in between the cargo, knowing the space was small enough that the Beast couldn't get in after me. He leapt up on top of the containers, his eyes staring down at me. Huge, silver orbs, full of a sorrow that made my heart ache in response, even with the fear he inspired. He was being compelled to do this, to kill someone.

His eyes narrowed and a snarl of frustration slipped out of him, then he was clawing at the straps that held the big containers on. I slashed my sword toward the big cat, cutting through the flesh of its flank, the skin peeling open and then closing back up as I expected it would. He roared and clawed again at the heavy straps holding the cargo containers down. The containers wobbled, sliding toward one another, dangerously close to pinning me between them. I sidestepped and put myself between the next set of containers. I only had two more groupings before I was up against the cab of the truck, so this trick wasn't going to last long. Shit, what the hell was I going to do?

My mind raced. I knew I couldn't kill the Beast, like the other Guardians I'd met, I didn't have the ability to kill them. I didn't really know if anyone did.

But could I maim him? Slow him down?

The Beast's paw swiping at the straps flicked in and out of view with each blow, giving me the only idea that I had. Timing it, I swung hard on his next swipe, my sword slicing through the bone and flesh connecting his paw to his leg. It came off cleanly, the Beast roaring with pain, a gush of blood flowing out for a brief moment before the wound closed over.

I held my breath. Would it grow back, or would—

The containers I hid between suddenly jerked and slammed me between them. I screamed and then could do nothing, my chest compressed between the two sets of cargo, arms pinned.

Beside me, I saw the other containers the Beast had been working at slide all to one side of the flatbed, and the truck rocked as we took a corner. Oh, fuck, this was about to get ugly.

I had to get out from between these containers. Like now.

Pushing myself sideways, grimacing with the pressure on my body, feeling as if my skin was going to peel from my body, I gained a few inches toward the next set of cargo. The Beast was still here, but I didn't know what he was up to. The truck lurched again in the other direction and the containers holding me loosened up. I scrambled to get out from between them, diving to the next set of containers as the ones I'd just been between slammed together.

With no warning, the Jake brakes on the truck came on, screaming as the driver lost control of the big rig. The rig flipped as we hit a corner, and for a split second, gravity no longer held me as I floated in the air between the two containers.

A clawed hand shot out, yanking me from the death trap, and Alex jerked us both off the truck as it tumbled down the embankment. The twisted shrieks of metal competed with the roar of the beast as we sailed through the air, hitting a snowbank that seemed more gravel and dirt than snow.

There was no graceful roll. We hit the snowbank hard and our bodies flipped over it, sliding down a good ten feet before we stopped. I pushed myself to my knees and did a quick check of my weapons.

"Alex, we've got to move." I yanked him up, running before I even really got myself balanced, feeling the bruising in my chest and legs already tightening up my muscles. I Tracked the Beast, but he stayed where he was, not moving. He was alive, but . . . maybe that was the trick? Maybe you had to de-limb, or detain the Guardians in order to hurt or stop them?

Fuck, that would be messy. But at least it was something. Maybe.

We ran, Alex and I, deep into the forest, using the paths the local wildlife had created. The feel of the werewolf that wasn't Alex hummed in my head, closer now than ever before. Maybe O'Shea had started back toward us. Not that he knew we were coming, but maybe his roving pattern had changed? But what was I going to do when I found him? Now that I was this close, I had to figure out a plan. I still had the Beast behind me, and I had no way of holding O'Shea if he was unreasonable. No way of binding him.

No time, there was just no time to even plan. I would have to deal with O'Shea when we found him and hope for the best. We hopped a frozen creek, scrambled up the other side of the embankment, and emerged out onto a wide path, wide enough for a car at least, though it was covered in a thin layer of frozen snow.

A shadow of movement at the far end of the trail stopped me, stilling my mind and body.

"O'Shea?"

Alex lifted his nose to the breeze. "Wolf."

"Good enough for me." I jogged down the trail as fast as my stiffening body would allow, the trees around us hanging low with the frozen snow. Our breath misted out in bursts of steam in the cold air. Alex tried to bite his.

We reached the spot where I'd seen the movement, where I'd seen O'Shea.

A low growl rumbled off to our right. Shit, I'd really, really hoped that O'Shea would remember a little about me. Just enough that he'd know we were here to help him.

"Liam, it's me, Rylee. I'm going to take you home." I kept my voice even and as soothing as I could.

The growl eased off and a black nose emerged from the heavy underbrush followed by a gray muzzle, gray head and huge golden eyes. The werewolf stared up at me, his wolf body dwarfing Alex's by at least a hundred and fifty pounds.

Staring into his eyes, I knew only one thing.

This was not O'Shea.

I yanked my sword out and slid into a crouch, holding the blade steady. "Who are you? And don't you for one fucking second try to tell me you don't understand."

The werewolf tipped its head to one side and then withdrew into the bush, disappearing as if he never had been there. I glanced at Alex, not wanting to take my eyes from the werewolf in front of me. Alex's eyes were wide and he pointed with one claw at the bush. "Old man wolf. Not Boss."

His explanation was a little belated, since I'd already figured out it wasn't O'Shea.

There was a rustle in the bush, the sounds of a person's steps cracking branches underfoot as a tall, gray-haired man emerged from where the wolf had peered only moments before. "You must be his mate, yes?"

At first I thought he meant Alex. "No, I'm not Alex's mate."

"Rylee is Alex's Boss," Alex said, his tongue lolling out as he grinned up at the gray-haired man.

"And she shall teach the submissive to stand." He murmured, smiling at me. "No, I meant the black wolf who hunts the witches. He is your mate. He waits for you."

Chills swept through me, my body twitching with the desire to run after O'Shea. I couldn't deny it, we were bound, he and I, had been for years.

"Yes, I am."

"I am Peter. Your mate waits for you in the north, near the wolf stone. The witches are almost on him, you must hurry."

I slid my sword back into its sheath, Tracked the Beast, and found with a sigh of relief that he hadn't yet stirred from where we'd left him. He must have been pinned under the rig. Yay for big-ass trucks.

"Yeah, that's the plan. How far is this wolf stone?"

"Twenty-five miles northeast. Stay on this path, it will take you most of the way there." His golden eyes traced over my body. "And when you are ready to know the truth behind him, come back to me. I will share with you the legend of what he is becoming."

With those words, he melted back into the bush, without a sound.

I spun and ran down the path, grateful at least that we wouldn't be slogging through the forest. The legend of what O'Shea was becoming? Wasn't he just a werewolf?

What was I missing?

I shook it off, no point in freaking out about something that I wasn't sure would even matter in a few hours. Twenty-five miles, the Beast on my ass, O'Shea dealing with witches. All bad, so very, very bad. And we were running straight toward it with open eyes.

14

Sweat stung my eyes, the run taking more out of me than I thought it would have. The combination of lined pants, slippery footing, and packing all my weapons made the distance seem twice as far, regardless of all the training I did. The day was waning, and I knew that we were getting close to sunset. Close to Berget's supposed death sentence. Still, though, her threads were sweet and happy. Vibrant and without fear, not even that small glimmer of uncertainty I'd felt earlier. She was fine. Faris was a fucking liar.

I sent a thread out to Track a werewolf, again pushing the feel of Alex aside. There were three ways I was being pulled. To the north and then there were two werewolves to the east.

O'Shea was being hunted by witches though. I Tracked for a group of witches and hit a bingo. They surrounded one of the werewolves to the east of me. The path didn't take us that way, so I jogged into the bush, pushing my way through the dense foliage. Alex helped, breaking branches with his paws and mouth with a vigor that told me he had no idea this was a salvage.

"You having fun, buddy?" I panted, hopping over a downed log.

Alex leapt it beside me, curling his paws tight to his body, as if he were an Olympic jumping horse.

"Alex funny!" He bolted ahead, tucking his tail under his butt and scooting around in a mad dash. Yeah, he didn't have a clue.

"Alex, this is serious." I could feel the witches, and they were less than a quarter mile away. The werewolf I was Tracking, the one that had to be O'Shea, was full of rage and bloodlust. And maybe even a little bit of fear. Shit.

"Alex, O'Shea is in trouble. Witches like Milly are going to kill him. We have to stop them. Got it?"

Alex's eyes went wide, and he shook his head. "No kill Boss." After that, he stayed close to me, peering into the woods, cocking his head from time to time. Once focused, he was actually pretty good back up. The deal was just trying to get him to focus.

"Rylee, Alex hears." He grabbed at my leg, slowing me down.

"What?"

"Bad witches. Talking bad to Boss."

I let out a slow breath, running my hands over my weapons, the comfort of having them easing some of my anxiety. I had to assume these witches we were going to be facing would know about my Immunity. So we had to take care of them fast. I could still so easily feel the crunch of cannonballs slamming into my body from the last time I'd been attacked by a group of witches. Rather unpleasant all around and not something I was keen to repeat.

I pulled my crossbow from my back and slid a bolt into the channel. More and more, this was turning out to be the best addition to my repertoire in a long time. We crept the last two hundred feet until we reached a clearing that sat on the edge of a frozen creek, a huge stone jammed into the middle of the ground. It did look like the nose of a wolf tipped to howl at the moon, the base of the neck buried into the ground. Around the stone stood four witches, and two more lay still on the ground, the snow around them bright crimson instead of white.

A massive black wolf stood with his back to the stone, hackles standing up, pale golden eyes narrowed, and a deep snarl erupting from his mouth in a continuous stream as spit dripped off his canines. Shit, he was intimidating, and I'd been dealing with the Beast for the last few days.

I Tracked O'Shea and felt the faintest of flickers now that we were this close to him. His eyes drifted to mine, and I gave him the slightest of nods. I lifted the crossbow, aimed at the closest witch's head, and pulled the trigger. The witch dropped without a sound, giving me a chance to reload and shoot a second witch in the base of the neck. That one, a woman, gave a gurgled screech and went down to her knees with a thump. The remaining witches, two men, spun toward me. I lowered the crossbow and pulled my swords free.

"You have a choice, you can either leave now and I won't gut you like the fuckers you are, or you can stay and I'll feed what's left of you to my boys."

Alex hopped around beside me, claws scrabbling on the frozen ground. "Witchy fuckers."

They said nothing, just raised their hands. The snow from the trees and the ground lifted into a swirling vortex, effectively blinding me.

"Tricky, very tricky," I grumbled.

I went to my belly, flattening myself out as lightning danced amongst the vortex. Alex mimicked me, army crawling forward. "Follow Alex."

We shimmied along the ground and Alex led me to the first witch. From my belly, I slashed upward, my blade sliding into his groin, slicing his leg three-quarters of the way off. He fell backwards, and the swirling vortex faded as he screamed for help from his friend in what sounded like French. I crawled the few feet up and over him, driving my sword through his heart, silencing his screams.

The swirling snow fell still, and the last witch standing stared around him. His eyes were not wide with fear as I'd thought. They were full of rage. He screamed a death spell at us, and I rolled over Alex to take the brunt of it, feeling the black aura dissipate over my skin. I stood up, gave the witch a smile.

"You done?"

"What are you?" His accent was heavy, laden with deep French undertones.

"Does it matter? You're trying to kill my wolf. Which puts you in a piss-poor position when it comes to us getting along." I stepped toward him and he stepped back.

"I may leave, but I will come back—"

O'Shea hit him from behind, teeth snapping closed over the screaming witch's neck. There was the sharp snap of bones breaking, and silence reigned. O'Shea dropped the witch, then glared up at me. Very slowly, he backed away. I Tracked him, felt nothing that was O'Shea.

What if Milly had been telling me the truth? What if O'Shea was completely gone?

"Liam." I went to my knees and reached out to him. "Liam, please."

He snarled at me, and then the snarl left his lips as his nose lifted to the breeze. From my knees, he stood over me, dwarfing me with his bulk, his black fur rippling in the wind.

With no response to me, he spun and loped away, back into the forest.

I bowed my head, fought the loss that kept me on my knees.

The cold seeped into me, even through my lined pants, but I didn't move. I knew the Beast was on the move again; we maybe had half an hour before he was on us. Maybe.

Thirty minutes to do what? Liam wasn't responding, was maybe gone completely. I lifted my head and looked at the sky. The sun had set and the final glow of the day was fading. Berget was still alive, though I felt a sudden confusion off her, she wasn't afraid. Faris had lied to me, though I wasn't sure any of it mattered. With a deep sigh, I pulled myself to my feet and slid my swords from their sheaths. We, I, would have to make a stand here against the Beast and hope to all that was holy that I could maim him bad enough. Fuck, just thinking about how I was going to have to lop off each limb while somehow keeping my own body intact—

The shattering inside my head, the burst of pain and the threads of Berget's life untangling in a flurry of emotions froze me in place. Stunned, I felt her heart slow as her life slipped away, felt her breathing ease a sudden shard of fear piercing her as the last of her life faded. I tried to hang onto her threads, as if my will alone would keep her alive.

"NOOOOOOOO!" I grabbed my head, fell to the ground, could barely connect the animal noises I was making with the person I knew myself to be.

This was not happening.

I couldn't have lost her, not like this, not without even trying. Not when Faris had tried to warn me, had tried to get me to help her.

What had I done?

The wolf stood on the edge of the clearing, feeling the woman's pain as if it was his own. Why should he care that a human was hurting? She wasn't a witch, so he wouldn't kill her, but her pain should be of no concern of his.

Her screams echoed through the air as if she'd been wounded, as if her life blood leaked out onto the snow. He paused, smelling the air again, trying to discern who she was, what she was.

Mate. Rylee.

He didn't question the voice, only knew that it was right, and so he obeyed it. Stepping back into the clearing, he moved toward the woman, his heart thumping with anticipation. How could a human be his mate?

On her knees, she was bent forward, rocking with whatever pain it was that clung to her. The wolf sniffed the air, didn't smell her blood. That didn't make any sense. The scent of another wolf snapped his head around and he glared at the half creature in front of him.

"Alex no hurt," the half creature said, and the words made sense, which disturbed the wolf even more. He snarled at the creature, and the submissive fell to his belly, putting his paws over his head. That would do; he would prove no fight for the wolf. His eyes flickered over the clearing and the bodies strewn about. More witches would come. But for now he couldn't leave, not with the woman, his mate, inconsolable.

There was nothing the wolf could do for the woman but stay by her side until the pain passed, until the hurt was gone. With a heavy sigh, he felt something twist inside of him at the sight of her tears, her strange eyes clouded with whatever wounded her.

He carefully curled his body around her, sheltering her from the biting wind that coursed through the trees as night fell.

And for the first time since he'd been freed from the witch, he felt at peace.

This was his mate, his heart.

She was his home.

Warmth surrounded me, and the world went black with dark fur. A heavy head lay across the back of my shoulders and a low-pitched whine broke through my own keening. Distantly, somewhere in the recesses of my mind, I knew that O'Shea had come back, had somehow known who I was. But a part of me had almost hoped it was the Beast. Let him have me, let him tear me apart.

For the second time in my life, I'd failed Berget, failed her completely. In the instant of her death, I was thrown back to losing her the first time, the guilt compounded by years of blaming myself and now . . . now to know that I'd had a chance to go and find her. To bring her home. I'd known she was alive for weeks, but I'd avoided going after her because I'd been afraid that what I could offer her wouldn't be good enough. That she would be in danger if I brought her into my life.

And now she was dead. I couldn't stop the tears, couldn't stop the sobs that erupted out of me. There was no reason, no way to take back what I'd done. No way to make it right. Her death lay squarely on my shoulders; Faris was wrong, I didn't blame him. I blamed me.

Berget's death was my fault.

O'Shea let out a low warning growl, one I could feel through my bones. I lifted my head to see a man standing on the edge of the clearing. He limped toward us, his one arm at a bad angle, his face swollen and cut. His blue eyes pierced me through to my heart. I let out a groan and buried my face. Faris had tried to tell me, to help me save her.

"I tried, on my own, to stay her death." His voice reached me, but I could tell he'd stopped moving.

"Did you come to gloat?" I could barely muster up the strength to speak, to lift my head and look at him.

"No. But there is more now to this story than a simple death. Far more. Come, we must be gone from here, the Beast is close." Faris held his hand out to me, and O'Shea snarled, leaping to his feet, stalking toward the vampire.

Faris chuckled. "I see that he does remember some things."

I sat there, staring at them, knowing that I should do something. Anything. I struggled to my feet, swayed once, and then I was up.

Faris and O'Shea squared off, but it was Faris that took the first swing, smashing O'Shea on the side of the head, sending his body flying through the air.

I didn't even think, I just let my training take over. I pulled a sword and rushed Faris. His eyes widened first, and then narrowed into a glare.

"Rylee, this is not a wise move."

I slashed at him, cutting into his shirt, but not actually hitting him. Not that I wasn't trying.

"Fuck you, you did something to O'Shea."

Faris kept a few feet ahead of me. "Why would you say that?"

"Because the only other people he's attacked are witches. Milly held him. You did something to make him hate you."

He shrugged, and then he was just behind me, like I had closed my eyes and let him sneak up on me, but that wasn't the case. Faris was just that damn fast.

He pinned my arms to my sides, and then called over his shoulder. "We're going to have a little chat.

Wait for us like a couple of good doggies. We'll be back in a minute." O'Shea let out a snarl, Alex howled, and then I heard nothing.

With a gut-wrenching twist, the world shifted, bending around us, and my only thought was that *this* was how he travelled, how he showed up wherever the fuck he wanted to, not unlike a Necromancer; he cut his way through the Veil, using it to travel wherever he needed to go.

He stepped out of the Veil, still holding me against his chest. Faris lowered his mouth to my ear. "I'm going to let you go; you need to put your sword away or I will take it from you and you won't like that."

What did I care if he killed me or if I had to lower my weapons? I nodded, numb from the onslaught of emotions. I scrabbled at the threads that were Berget, at her life that was gone. I could still pinpoint her body, of course, but what made her Berget was gone.

Dust in the wind. I closed my eyes as Faris let go of me, not really caring where we were . . . I blinked and looked again. We were on the other side of the Veil in a place I knew all too well. The castle O'Shea and I had found India in.

Maybe he saw the recognition in my eyes. "This place is a turning point on this side of the Veil. It opens into a myriad of places and allows me to move freely to where I need to be."

So not quite like a Necromancer. But still handy, useful. I knew that I was focusing on the stupid things to avoid thinking about Berget. Knew it and didn't care.

"Rylee." He let out a heavy sigh, dropping into a chair against the wall. He slid a hand over his face, a very human gesture that seemed odd on him.

"What? You want to say you told me so? Neener, neener, neener?"

"No."

"Then why the fuck am I here?"

Again, he scrubbed his hand over his face before answering. "Because you do not understand the situation, and while I am somewhat loathe to tell you all our secrets, I realize now that I must tell you some if I am to gain your help. You remember the memory I showed you? Where I knelt before the Emperor and Empress?"

"Yes." I trembled where I stood, but knew if I sat down I might not get back up. So I stayed where I was, hoping that what Faris had to tell me was actually of importance. And for the moment, it kept me focused on something other than Berget's death.

"There are two factions of vampires. Those of us who wish to remain in the shadows. To control the humans as we do, puppeteers with tasty little puppets jumping with our every wish. And then there are the others, those like the Emperor and Empress."

"Who you killed."

"Who I killed quite happily and would have killed their child, who they have raised to believe as they do. That the vampire nation should be unafraid of the world and should show themselves."

I stared at him, forcing the words out. "What has this got to do with Berget?"

"I'm getting there."

He stood and started to pace, his hands clasped behind his back. His blond hair was blood crusted, but otherwise the wounds he'd carried when he'd first entered the clearing had healed. Vampire perks at their best.

"The Child Empress is a jealous creature, and not prone to realizing the ramifications of coming out to the world. Not just for us, but for the entire supernatural community."

I closed my eyes and did my best to follow. "I get it and I agree. The humans aren't ready to know what they've been living next to. Maybe one day, but not yet. There is too much violence in them."

"The Child Empress is not the only one who feels that way. There are factions of witches, Druids, and shifters who would agree with the Child."

"Still not seeing how this affects me, Berget, any of it." I looked up at him, felt the hollow emptiness of everything in my heart spill into my eyes.

"Rylee." He stepped closer, lifting his hands to place them on my shoulders. "We all lose the ones we love. You are no different than any other supernatural."

The hollowness continued through me, cooling the pain of my grief, making me hard. "That supposed to be a fucking pick-me-up?"

"No. It is the truth. The Child Empress will take everything we love in an attempt to break us, to make us fear. That is the goal."

I pushed his hands off my shoulders and backed up, feeling strength sweep through me with the emptiness. I would feel nothing and that would get me through. If I felt nothing there could be no grief, no pain, no guilt and hurt.

"What are you saying?"

His perfectly sculpted face saddened. "The Child Empress brought about the death of Berget. With her death, the Child Empress sealed the throne and took control of the vampire nation and is preparing to announce to the world that the supernatural exists. If we'd stopped her death . . . ."

"Don't lay the fucking guilt trip on me," I said, my words icy. I stared over his shoulder at the darkened hallway, remembering too clearly being here for India, wrestling a demon, O'Shea helping me.

Life had gone downhill fast since then. I had a moment of understanding. The problems had started when the Black Coven had called up the demon.

"Rylee, will we stand together on this?"

"When we first met, you tried to kill me." I slid my gaze across to his. "What has changed? Now you want to be my ally, but you have never been a steady constant. Kill me or don't, you can't have it both ways."

I wasn't taunting him, I was being serious. I didn't understand him and his motives, which continually confused me.

"I have watched you for some time. Years. You side with the humans, finding their children. Keeping them safe. From what I know of Trackers, I assumed you would be on their side when the decision came down to this."

I snorted. "You tried to kill me based on a fucking assumption?"

He stared at me. "I've killed people for less. It was not so much of a stretch combined with the information I gained from your so-called best friend."

Ahh, now that made more sense. Before I could say anything, Faris went on.

"I want you to trust me; we need to trust one another to survive this." His eyes were deadly serious. "I acted on my assumptions and information from Milly. It is obvious to me now that she was not being truthful. But I did what I did, based upon my knowledge of Trackers and her assessment of you. She fed my assumptions with her lies, padding my already skewed understanding of who you are. I realize that I, too, bear guilt for Berget's death. For if you'd trusted me, we would not be here now. We'd be celebrating with your sister in Venice."

"And O'Shea would be dead," I whispered.

"Which would you rather lose?"

Fury lit through me, an anger so bright and intense I shook with it all the way to my fingertips. "I would lose neither! They are my heart!"

Faris's icy-blue eyes widened and he gave me a slow nod. "I see."

I took a deep breath, but didn't try to still the anger. Better than that empty hollowness that had been quickly consuming me. I glared at Faris, but he didn't seem bothered by my anger.

"The Child Empress has done this. Will you stand with me against this threat?" He stood in front of me, his eyes searching my face. There was no question, not really.

No, that wasn't entirely true. There was one question I needed answered.

"Are we going to kill the Child Empress?"

Faris gave a slow nod, his eyes full of sorrow that seemed out of place. "Yes, that will be the plan. Kill the Child Empress; prove that I am the better leader. Take the throne and seal vampires and the supernatural away from the world."

"And the memory you showed me? What of that? You need me to prove you are the one to lead the vampire nation, right? I have to find something for you, don't I?"

Again, he nodded. "Yes, but once I take the throne, that will be the last step."

"So doesn't this Child Empress need me too?"

He closed his eyes and slowly shook his head. "You are not the only Tracker left alive, Rylee."

What was left of my strength slipped out of me and I dropped to my knees.

"Jack."

15

Faris took me back to the clearing, but only after a huge argument. I needed to get my two wolves, regardless of what the vampire thought. He suggested going back to London via the Veil first, to start planning. I was still arguing that we should strike now, while the Child Empress might still consider herself safe because she'd only just been set on the throne.

My argument won, at least the part about going back to the clearing where O'Shea and Alex were frantically pacing. One wolf was fucking terrifying, the look on his face enough to scare the piss out of anyone. The other, just . . . well, just looked like a lost little boy waiting for his mother to find him.

I stumbled out of Faris's hands and toward the two werewolves, catching O'Shea around the neck and burying my face in his fur. Alex shuffled forward and I put a hand on him too, felt him sigh under my fingers. O'Shea sniffed my hair and then stepped toward Faris, a low growl rumbling through his chest. I held him back, with difficulty. "No, we're working together now. You have to play nice, Liam. You have to."

He snorted, stopped straining against my hold, and glared at the vampire, who just stood there, hands clasped behind his back.

"Are we quite done collecting your pets?"

"Really, you think today is the day to piss me off?" I spat over my shoulder.

Faris chuckled. "Yes, yes I do. You need to be reminded that death is not the end. Not to mention that you fight better when you're angry."

I clenched my fingers into O'Shea's thick fur. His cold nose slipped under my chin and he pushed my head up. He was right. Chin up, we could do this.

I would avenge Berget, save Jack, and then . . . then I would grieve. Just like with losing Giselle, there wasn't time to breathe, never mind feel sorrow over the loss. I didn't have the fucking luxury.

I didn't realize that I was staring into O'Shea's eyes; he gave me a lick on the side of my face. At least I had him back in my life, even like this was better than nothing at all.

"Let's go."

Faris opened up the twist between this world and the Veil. Alex made a move as if to go first until O'Shea growled at him.

"Sorry, Boss. Alex forgets." He settled in behind O'Shea, letting the Alpha wolf go first. Except that O'Shea paused at the threshold, staring into the scene beyond him. Maybe he was remembering our time there? The demon we'd fought?

No, that wasn't it at all. He made a move as if to go forward, but stopped again with a grunt.

He couldn't cross the threshold. Shit, this was going to make things interesting.

"Perfect." Faris muttered, and again I was struck by how very un-vampire-like he seemed.

"Looks like we're going the long way." I turned away from the opening to face the other side of the clearing and saw what was waiting for me there. We were upwind, which explained why the two wolves hadn't smelled the Beast.

"Oh. Shit." I pulled my sword out and the Beast roared, running toward me on three paws, its balance off. That's why it had taken so long to get here. Three legs left to go. That was the key, take his limbs and he could be killed, or at least maimed like any other creature.

But before I could reach him, O'Shea leapt in front of me, tackling the Beast to the ground even though he was only half the size of the panther.

They tumbled through the snow, but the Beast wasn't interested in O'Shea; he didn't even try to fight back. He just wanted to get to me.

Faris grabbed my arm. "We have to go, we have to get you out of here."

"I'm not a fucking China doll!"

He shook me, hard enough that my teeth snapped together. "That is a Guardian; you might be able to hurt it, but we can't kill it."

The vampire let me jerk out of his hands so I could see the battle raging behind us. Alex had stepped up, working with O'Shea to keep the Beast at bay, yanking its legs out from under it repeatedly. Again, though, the Beast wasn't fighting them.

His silver eyes met mine, and I could see that this was not what he wanted. This was not his choice.

He was bound by oaths and a spell that even Deanna didn't know how to break.

Your blood is a catalyst, Jack's words floated through my brain. My blood, taken from my body, would break the spell that held the Beast. Maybe.

"Faris, if I'm wrong, please save Jack. Pamela needs someone."

Faris grabbed my wrist. "What are you talking about?"

"Let me go. I know what I'm doing."

"Then why would I have to save Jack?" The vampire's eyes snared me, and I looked away, toward the battle. The Beast was still fighting to get to me, essentially allowing O'Shea and Alex to pummel him.

"This could stop him, you have to trust me."

There it was, that word again between the two of us. Faris let me go, his fingers sliding from my wrist. "I don't think this is a good idea."

I didn't answer him, just ran toward the Beast, knowing that Faris was fast enough to stop me, but he didn't. He didn't try to interfere. I drew close enough that the Beast couldn't help but catch me up with his remaining paw. O'Shea snarled and leapt onto the Beast's back, Alex howled, his head thrown back. Confusion in his eyes, the Beast bit down into my side. My leather jacket was no protection from his four canines, which slid through the coat like it was just another layer of skin. I couldn't help the scream that passed my lips; the pain of four enormous daggers being driven into my body at the same time was more than even I could handle.

My blood spilled out of the wounds, spread along his lips. The confusion in his eyes faded. We stared at one another, and I knew that even if I died from the wounds, I'd done the right thing. Pamela would be proud. Berget would be proud. Maybe I'd done it because I wanted to die, but even so, it was still the right thing.

Tears slipped from my eyes as the Beast lowered me to the ground. Alex and O'Shea stumbled away from him, uncertainty written all over their faces as the Beast took great care to lay me down gently.

"Are you going to kill Daniels?" I whispered, struggling to breathe around the wounds, but I needed to know that my death wasn't in vain.

The Beast shifted, his man form crouching at my side. Blood trickled from his lips, my blood, but his blood also trickled from his back. Great gouge marks where O'Shea had lit into him. How was that possible? Guardians didn't bleed . . . .

"Yes, Daniels will die. Then I will go back to being nothing more than a ghost on the moors. Thank you, Tracker. Your wolf, he will be a Guardian of a sort, a Great Wolf, but there is very little left of the man he was. Do not hope too much for what cannot be." He looked over his shoulder at O'Shea, who stood there, seemingly confused by the Beast's sudden shift into human form, and his suddenly gentle manner with me.

His words barely registered, but I managed to ask. "Is that why he could hurt you?"

The Beast nodded. "Yes."

He touched the spot over my heart, then his fingers drifted across to the demon mark I carried on my chest, the black snowflake that had almost killed me.

"You have the heart that will save us all. When you have need of me, I will stand with you against the darkness."

He touched my throat, and then bent and kissed me softly. Standing, he turned and walked into the forest, disappearing as the old werewolf had done, as if he'd never even been there.

I wished in that moment that I could see the look on Daniels's face when he showed up for her. The thought made me smile despite the pain.

O'Shea lay down beside me and I reached over, slid my hand over his face. It didn't feel the same as when he'd been human, yet it was still him, my fingers still recognized him. My heart was slowing down; the sluggish thump was that of a mortal wound leaking my life out. The Beast hadn't pierced my heart, but his fangs had gone through my lungs and, by the black blood creeping out of the lower wound, my liver. That was the bad one, all the toxins floating through my system and shit like that.

A pair of blue eyes hovered over me. "Rylee, you need to be healed. I can think of only one person strong enough to do so, but you must trust me as I trusted you."

I groaned, knowing exactly who he meant. "I don't want her help; she's a horrible person. Bitch, I hate her."

"But she can save you." He was scooping me up in his arms and I couldn't stop him.

"No, I'd rather die."

Faris snorted. "Stop being a child. She'll heal you, probably for some small favor."

"She wants me to be the godmother to her demon spawn."

The vampire held me tight against his chest. I could see his mouth moving, could sense something happening, but then there was nothing. Nothing but blessedly sweet darkness.

No, that wasn't true. There was something else, a soft voice I recalled, a sweet girl I'd held in my arms when she'd had bad dreams, a child I'd pushed on the swings and had loved more than any other.

"Rylee, what are you doing here?" Berget was there, but it wasn't the little girl I remembered. She was all grown up, her long blonde hair flowing around her face on a breeze I couldn't feel. Blue eyes sparkling as she saw me, reached for me. She had grown into a beautiful young woman, long-limbed and softly curved. Her face had thinned, the baby fat gone and the lines of her cheekbones highlighted her eyes.

I pulled her to me; she felt so real and it occurred to me that perhaps it was because I was dead too, like her.

"Fuck, Berget, I'm so sorry, I should have come for you. I should have been there . . ."

She pushed me away gently, her face a like that of the one I remembered, only now there was a sculpted perfection to it caused by the loss of her childhood.

"This is as it's meant to be. Rylee, you are not to blame. Everything happens for a reason. You know that. I know you do."

Gods, how could one so young be so wise?

"You don't blame me for not saving you?"

She threw back her head and laughed. "Rylee, you are my sister, and you will save me yet. Of that, I have no doubt. Do not grieve me, for death is never the end, not with us. I know you will save me; you will save us all. Things are not as they seem, not in our world. Do not believe your eyes, believe your heart."

I held her hands, stared at her as if I could somehow soak her in. Keep her with me and take back her death.

"You must go now, the wolf calls to you; I can feel his ties to you as strongly as if they were ropes tangled around your limbs. He will save you, I think. Save you with his love, as you will save him with yours." She squeezed my hands and then let go, fading into the darkness.

Voices swirled around me. "Rylee, you have to pull back your Immunity. I can't heal you if you don't."

Milly's voice. Fuck, if that wasn't the worst way to come to.

But she was right, and she knew all my tricks. I pulled my Immunity off my hands, exposing myself to her. Her fingers were warm as they circled around mine, her magic rushing through me. I'd been healed once before and this was the same. Not painless, but a reversal of the damage as my body stitched itself back together, fueled by magic.

I groaned, my innards writhing as they came to-gether, became whole again. And just like the last time I'd been healed, I lay there on the floor, drained of anything but the desire to sleep.

"Rylee." Milly's voice again. I kept my eyes closed. Maybe she'd go away. I wanted to kill her; fuck and she'd just saved my life. I settled for hurting her.

"You know that it's your fault Giselle is dead?" I bit the words out, slowly opening my eyes to see her face pale.

"Giselle? No, I thought she was at home—"

"We went after you, you stupid bitch, and your friends put a truth spell on her. To make sure we were telling the truth about your crazy ass. It drained what was left of her life."

She covered her face with her hands, sobs shaking her shoulders. "I didn't know. I didn't ever want her to be hurt. I didn't, you have to believe me. I only ever did what I did to keep you two safe as best I could."

With great difficulty, I pulled myself to my feet and reached for my swords, but my hands found nothing.

"I took your weapons off you," Faris said from behind me. I turned to glare at him and he shrugged. "Her only request."

"Doesn't mean I can't still kill her." I glared at her, crouched on the floor. In my head I did the math; she was about four months along and her belly was just starting to show. She saw where my gaze landed and she cradled her stomach. I snorted and turned away. Even I wasn't so cold as to run her through when she was pregnant.

I looked around, wobbled, and Faris reached out to balance me. "Why didn't you just fix me up?"

An exasperated sigh slipped out of him. "You had already lost a great deal of blood, and if I'd taken more in order to make the bond between us work—for the limited time it does with you—you would have died. As it was, we barely made it here."

"Where is here?" I couldn't make sense of the place. I could hear water, I could smell flowers as if it was spring and not November, and it was warm. Quite warm, actually.

"You don't need to know that. Now, I've done my part." Milly slowly stood, brushing off the loose flowing skirt that swirled around her legs. Green and brown, the dress was cut to flatter her changing figure while still giving her the trademark sexy girl look that she had perfected over the years. Her deep brown hair was tousled and her makeup was flawless. Next to her, I had no doubt I looked like a complete wreck, not that that was anything new with the two of us. Already, she had put aside her tears for Giselle, showing me once again just how fucking cold she really was.

"Let's go." I didn't know where we had to go, only that we needed to leave. And since Faris had brought me here, I needed him to take me away.

Milly stepped so that she was in front of me. "You owe me, Rylee. I saved your life."

Ah, fuck it, I knew this had been coming. "What do you want?" I asked, but already knew the answer. Hated that it was going to be forced on me.

"Promise me you'll protect my son, at all costs."

Gods that was a loaded request. "If I do this, it doesn't absolve you. The next time we meet . . . ." I turned and stared at her. My former best friend, the one person I would have trusted over all others.

Her eyes welled with tears and she gave a slow nod. "I know where you stand, Rylee. I always have, I think. I'd just hoped that you'd understand why I've done what I've done. Maybe someday you will."

"Whatever."

"Swear an oath, Rylee. One you'll keep." Milly said, her voice soft with tears.

I took a deep breath, thinking about the best way to word an oath that would satisfy her. "I swear on the souls of all those I love, of all those who stand in need of my abilities, that *if* your child needs protecting, and *if* I am able to, I will protect him at all costs. Even to the loss of my own life."

Milly let out a breath, her shoulders slumping. "Thank you, Rylee. Thank you."

I couldn't look at her any longer. I flicked my fingers at Faris. "Are we going?"

"Now?"

"Yes, now. Seriously, we have people to kill, a war to start. A rescue to make happen." I shook my head at him. "All those things aren't going to go on by themselves."

Faris's lips twitched. "Good to see you have some of your old self back."

His hand went to my lower back, guiding me through the sea side house. I could guess where we were, but I didn't really care.

"Yeah, talking to dead people will do that to you. Make you smarten the fuck up."

He jerked me around to face him. "What dead people?"

I knew I couldn't break his grip on me, so I didn't try. Besides, I was exhausted. "Berget spoke to me, when I was . . . dying, I guess."

His eyes were deadly serious. "What did she say?"

I squirmed like a kid caught with my hand in their mother's chocolate stash. "That she didn't blame me, that death wasn't the end."

Faris relaxed his grip on me. "That's all she said?"

Shrugging, I pulled myself from his loosened hands. "What else would she say to me?"

He didn't say anything else, just went back to guiding me through the house and out into the backyard. Blossoms and plants covered everything, filling every inch with bright sprays of color under the light of what looked to be hundreds of candles. The whole place was stunning. The smell of roses, lavender, and jasmine sat heavy on the night air and I breathed it in, wishing for a brief moment that this was our destination.

"Why did we have to come out here?" I turned to face Faris again, but he was turned away from me, watching the way we'd come.

"Milly is trying to learn how to jump the Veil like I do. I have done my best to keep her from seeing me jump the Veil. I do not think she can learn it, but if anyone can—"

"She can."

He gave me a nod, took my hand and yanked me hard to his chest. "Hang on." He leaned in, as if to kiss me, but I ducked my head down so his lips hit the top of my head.

"Sorry, I've got a thing for a wolf."

"We shall see about that."

Faris stepped backward and the Veil parted, and we fell through the twist, jump, whatever the fuck he wanted to call it. The thing was, the Veil wasn't magic, it was real and solid as anything else. And the ability to manipulate it apparently wasn't magic either, or it wouldn't work with me and my Immunity. Did that mean *I* could learn how to do it? Shit, now that would be brilliant. Faris seemed to be reading my mind.

"Perhaps if we work together, I will show you how to jump the Veil. If I can."

His unspoken words spoke far louder than the ones he whispered. Perhaps if I let him have what he wanted from me, he'd show me how. Fuck that, I wasn't like Milly.

"Yeah, sure." I grunted as we stepped out into the castle that acted as the way point between places for the vampire.

I strode away from him, wanting to get back to where O'Shea and Alex waited, but not having the means to do so on my own. Faris had explained it to me. There were some jumps across the Veil that just didn't work. He couldn't take me from the forest directly to Milly; he'd had to come here first, then to Milly's. No rhyme or reason, just the way it was.

"You say that like you don't want to learn." Faris came up behind me, sliding his hands up my arms and I was suddenly reminded that Faris had taken my weapons off me in the clearing before he jumped us to Milly, and I was alone with a vampire who'd mentioned on several occasions how much he'd like to sink his fangs, amongst other things, into me.

"I do want to learn." I squirmed away from him. "But not at the cost of my body."

His eyes widened. "You think I would bargain that knowledge for a piece of ass?"

"Yes."

He barked out a laugh. "Perhaps, but I'd much rather see if I could bind you to me permanently."

"Nope, that ain't going to happen, either." I put my hand on the wall closest to me, feeling the coldness from the stone numb my hand in a matter of heartbeats.

"We shall see."

I glared at him. No fucking way, there was no fucking way I'd ever let him bind me to him. "You don't know me so well, do you?"

He took my hand and we jumped the Veil. He smiled at me, eyes sparkling. "Ah, but I plan to."

16

Problem number one: O'Shea couldn't jump the Veil. Problem number two: Faris thought he was in charge.

Problem number three: I had to deal with two incredibly alpha males, neither of which seemed willing to work together. Just fucking peachy.

Faris handed me my weapons when we came back through, and O'Shea immediately shoved himself between us, a low growl on his lips.

"Do not test me, wolf," Faris snarled.

O'Shea snarled back, and I put myself between them. "Listen, we have to work together, so knock it the fuck off. Both of you." I strapped on my swords, knife, crossbow and bolts, and whip back onto my body. It felt good to have my weapons back where they belonged.

Faris smoothed his face and gave me a barely there nod. O'Shea didn't move, didn't lift his eyes from the glare he'd pinned on the vampire. Well, at least they weren't fighting.

Alex all but glued himself to my side, the tension obviously stressing him out. He panted with anxiety, drool dripping in great gobs from his tongue, but he said nothing. Faris paced the small clearing as the night grew thin and the not so distant dawn lit the tops of the trees with a dim glow.

I'd had enough. I needed to get Pamela and Eve, phone Jack, and pray that Faris was wrong about the Child Empress taking him . . . .

On impulse, I Tracked Jack. His threads tugged me toward the south, way south, instead of west toward London, as I'd really been hoping they'd be. Shit sticks, again Faris was telling me the truth. Damn. I did not want to trust the vampire, I just didn't. There was a saying that Giselle had been fond of, before her mind had gone.

"The devil will tell you nine truths, so that you'll believe one lie. Lots of supernaturals are like that too."

The thing was, Faris was a vampire. I knew what he was capable of, or at least some of what he was capable of. But discerning the truths from the lies with him was going to be tough. Had already proved to be tough.

I stood, stretched, and turned away, heading back into the forest. I Tracked Pamela. She was roughly where I'd left her; it felt like they may have moved a little to the west, but not far.

O'Shea ghosted to my other side, pressing his flank up against my leg. Alex grinned across at him. "Wanna play?"

O'Shea snorted, shook his head and Alex visibly drooped, kicking at the snow.

"Where are you going?" Faris shouted from behind us.

"Collecting my wards and going after Jack."

The vampire was suddenly in front of us, eyes blazing with anger. "You tried things your way and it got your sister killed, remember?"

"Fuck off and . . . well, I'd say die, but that seems redundant, don't you think?"

His eyes bugged out. "I saved your life, and this is how you would thank me?"

O'Shea gave a low rumble that sounded suspiciously like a snicker. I glared at the top of his head. "Who asked you for your opinion, wolf boy?"

Tongue lolling, he turned his head up and gave me a wink with one pale golden eye.

Faris reached out as if to grab me, and O'Shea put himself between us, forcing the vampire back. I lifted my hands up. "Listen, you want to plan this, plan that, whatever. When I find Jack, I'll find the Child Empress. I will kill her, and take Jack with me back to London. You either do it my way, or go the fuck away."

His jaw tightened as he glared at me. Finally he gave a slight nod of his head. "When you are ready to see things my way, you can call me."

He turned, a slash appeared in the air and he stepped through, disappearing to wherever the hell he went. Probably the castle, not that it mattered to me where he was.

Exhaustion nipped at me. The last twenty-four hours had been rough, as rough as I'd ever had. And I wasn't really any further ahead. Sure, I'd found O'Shea, I glanced at him as we walked. But he was trapped, stuck in the wolf body as surely as Alex was stuck between wolf and human. Which was better? At least O'Shea seemed to have a more adult view on the world, more so than Alex, anyway.

Then there was Berget . . . no, I shied away from thoughts of her. I couldn't deal with her death, not if I were to rescue Jack. I felt him, inside my head there in the south. He wasn't well; his heart was not strong and a steady thread of apathy hummed through him. Jack had stopped caring, which meant he'd stopped fighting and that was a bitch of a bad sign.

As the sun crested high, and the forest lightened up, I called a halt to our walk. We'd only been at it for a couple of hours, but I was done. Since walking into a hotel—with two werewolves at my side—would be, to say the least, difficult, I opted for a tree to sit against. Alex and O'Shea curled up beside me, O'Shea surprising me with his willingness to let Alex be so close to us both. I leaned my head back, closed my eyes and drifted in and out of sleep as the day passed.

Berget's death.

O'Shea trapped as a wolf.

Jack kidnapped.

The realities I couldn't escape kept me from resting fully. Kept me from being able to ease the ache in my mind, body, or heart. Groggily, I opened my eyes, stared at the canopy above my head. The ground was cold, but I was warm, my werewolf blanket doing a damn fine job of keeping me from the cold.

"All right boys, time to go." I shoved Alex from my lap, or at least tried to. He lifted his head, yawned, and then let out a gust of hot wolf breath right into my face. Nice way to wake up.

I waved my hands in front of my face, stood, and headed toward Pamela and Eve once more. Though I hadn't rested, I had come to a decision.

First, we had to get Jack away from the Child Empress. That had to come first, no matter how badly I wanted to help O'Shea. And I was going to need all the help I could get, as fast as I could. Pamela, if her arm was healed—which it should be, since witches healed almost as fast as werewolves—was going to come with me, though again we'd have to leave Eve behind. The Harpy was going to be pissed.

Second, we'd take Jack home and get O'Shea to Doran. Doran, and maybe Deanna, would be able to bring him back. I had to believe that. There was no room for any other options inside my head.

Last, I'd grieve for Berget. And maybe, finally, for Giselle too.

Step one required me to get my ass all the way to France. At the first truck stop we came on, early that evening, I stole a pickup truck. This time I went for something middle of the road, big enough to take two werewolves in the back, not nice enough to be noticed missing. I hoped.

O'Shea and Alex seemed more than content to ride in the back, winter wind blowing through their fur. Alex was howling and hopping around the back so much that he actually rocked the whole vehicle.

I cranked the side window down. "Knock it the fuck off, Alex! You're tipping us."

He slapped his paws over his muzzle, eyes as big as saucers. O'Shea nipped him on the shoulder and Alex lay down, flat out on his belly. Good enough.

After that, he settled down and we had no more problems.

Until we crossed into Italy.

At first, I thought it was the police behind us, dark-colored vehicles coming up fast, boxing us in on the highway.

Nope, far worse than the police.

Witches.

"Really?" I yelped as the vehicle to our left slammed into us. I fought the steering wheel to keep the truck steady. A glance in the mirror showed Alex still flat on the deck, but O'Shea was staring at the people, witches, in the cars, his gaze not wavering even when we were rammed.

I hit the gas pedal, smashing into the bumper of the car in front of us, pushing it hard. "Out of my way, prick!"

The car spun to the right, taking out the vehicle on that side of us too. Pushing the truck hard, I took us through the opening, using the other vehicles around us as blockers. Shit, the last time I'd been in a car chase had been with O'Shea too; the irony didn't escape me. I yanked the wheel to the left, jerking the truck around a semi as it lit on fire in a burst of flames. Yes, on fire.

The witches were brassy to be throwing spells at us in the open like this. Brassy witches were the last things I needed. The rig next to us swerved, blowing its horn, the tires coming dangerously close to us. Behind us, a pickup truck like the one I was driving, came up fast. Fuck this. I hit the brakes and swerved to the left using the edge of the road as a new lane.

Foot back on the gas pedal, I punched it hard, the truck shooting forward. Thank the gods someone liked speed in their big boy toy.

O'Shea and Alex scrabbled to stay upright, but only O'Shea looked concerned. Alex was grinning like a fool, barking and laughing every time he wiped out as I swerved or jerked the wheel to avoid a car.

An explosion erupted in front of us, the ground shattering, and chunks of concrete flew everywhere. A chunk landed on the hood, bounced into the back of the truck. Alex gave a yelp. I assumed he'd been smacked by the block. He started mouthing off at the top of his lungs.

"Sons of bitches, stupid witches!"

I wanted to laugh, it was his best rhyme yet, but I was too busy focusing on the road as it continued to explode, and I fought to keep the truck from doing a header into one of the magic-made craters.

Then one of the witches got crafty and blew out my back right tire. The truck wobbled and jerked to the right, slowing down way too much for my liking. I grit my teeth, knuckles white on the steering wheel. Then the other back tire blew and the truck was literally dragging its ass along the road.

If they'd wanted to, they would have just flipped the truck, but they'd held back. I was betting they were just after O'Shea and were, in their own way, trying to get me to just hand him over. Of course, that wasn't going to happen.

I hit the brakes hard, turning the wheel sharp to the right, turning the truck sideways across the lanes in order to block the road as best I could. The slam of two large bodies hit the back of the cab. With a jerk on the handle, I shoved the door open and leapt out.

"Time to go, boys!"

They jumped out of the back of the truck, one graceful, the other, not so much. Alex's legs seemed to go every which way, tangling him up so that he landed in a heap. O'Shea grabbed him by the scruff of the neck without missing a beat, yanking Alex out of the way of a black spell that slammed into the truck where his head had been.

I didn't look back, just bolted down the side of the highway, the pileup from the craters, flaming rig, and all the humans running around were a perfect diversion. Sure, the witches continued to lob spells at us, but they were inaccurate and sloppy. I was freaking happy that Milly wasn't with them. Her aim was almost as good as mine.

We ran for about an hour before I dared to Track the witches as a group. From the distance between us, I could tell they hadn't moved from the highway. Maybe they were just putting the run on us, pushing us out of their country?

The next day, and one more stolen truck later, we crossed into France. Pamela and Eve were a few hours south of us if we didn't have any more diversions of the witchy sort.

Reaching the town by the ocean that I knew was only a short jog to where Eve and Pamela had holed up, I pulled over. We were in a no-driving zone, pedestrians only apparently in this section of the town, so we would have to walk from here on out. I left the keys in the truck for someone else to take. That was the least I could do after all my thefts of vehicles over the last few days.

There was only one small problem. Alex was wearing a collar that hid him from the world of the humans. O'Shea had no such collar and it was very apparent that he was not a dog, but a big-ass black wolf.

"What the hell are we going to do?" I muttered, staring at the two werewolves in the back of the truck. Shit, this was not really something I'd thought about. This was what I got for doing things by the seat of my pants.

The best thing I could do would be to find something that I could use for a leash. Sure, people would wonder what the fuck kind of dog/wolf hybrid O'Shea was, but if he was on a leash, at least they would know he was tame. Right, a tame werewolf. Behind the seat of the truck was a long coil of rope, the edges frayed and smelling slightly of fish.

"Okay, come on, let's go." I motioned for them to jump out of the truck, looping the rope around O'Shea's neck as he jumped. Not thinking for one fucking minute that there would be a problem.

My bad.

He hit the ground and spun, knocking me over. I landed on my ass, hands clenching the end of the rope. "What the hell was that about?"

His eyes traced the rope from close to where it looped around his neck, along the ground to my hand clutching the end of it. Realization dawned and I stared at him, frozen with what could happen. He was becoming a Guardian. If that was true, I couldn't kill him, even if he attacked me. Not that I wanted to fight him, but . . . .

"O'Shea, we have to get through town." I held up my hands as his lips curled back over his enormous teeth. "We have to make them, the humans, think you are safe. As soon as we get to the other side I'll drop it, we can take it off."

O'Shea didn't ease up, but instead he stepped forward, his eyes no longer soft and full of recognition. I didn't dare move, knowing that the second I tried, he'd be on me.

Alex scooted forward, putting himself between us. "Hiya Boss, Alex holds it."

The submissive wolf scooped up the rope in his teeth and grinned at O'Shea around it.

O'Shea stilled, eyes flicking once over Alex, then back to me, then he deliberately turned his face away from me.

I slowly stood, afraid to make any fast moves. Holy shit, that could have gone bad in a fucking instant. And here again, Alex had saved my stupid, sorry ass.

"Alex, come on." He trotted to my side and I gripped his collar. O'Shea followed him, and like a bizarre parade, we cut through the last few blocks of towns. Yes, we got some double takes, some stares and a few sets of fingers pointing. But we avoided any catastrophes. For once.

As soon as we entered the edge of the trees, Alex dropped the rope and O'Shea shook himself out of it.

But neither wolf would look at me. Like I'd done something wrong in putting the rope on O'Shea.

What the fuck was I going to do with Pamela? I had a witch with me, and a werewolf who wanted nothing more than to kill witches.

"You two stay here. I'll go get Pamela and Eve." I needed time to think, to process this situation. There was no way I could let Pamela get hurt, but I needed her with me; I already had an idea of how to get Jack away from the Child Empress, but I would need Pamela working some pretty heavy magic to make it happen. I jogged through the trees, winding my way to where the girls were. When I stepped out to where I could see the shack, Eve was the one who saw me first.

"Rylee! You're back already! Where is Alex?" Her face softened with horror.

"He's fine, don't worry about him. I've just left him back at the edge of the woods."

She fluffed up her body, and clacked her beak several times. "I was afraid—"

"No, I won't let anything happen to him, Eve. I promise." Dangerous to promise that, but I had to because it was the truth. If there was anything I could do to save him, I would.

Pamela came running around the side of the shed, blonde hair flying back from her face. "You're back!" She ran toward me, smiling, happy, her arm no longer in a sling. I lifted my hand in greeting, feeling both the need to protect her and how badly I needed her help. The two feelings warred within me. I was about to take her into a nest of vampires in order to save Jack. How the hell was I going to keep her safe?

Turns out, I should have been more worried about the then and there.

The crack of a twig behind me spun me around. O'Shea stared across at Pamela, who still hadn't seen him.

Fuck it all to hell and back.

I bolted toward Pamela, knowing it would be close. Her eyes widened, flicked to look over my shoulder, and I saw her raise her hand with a spell.

"No magic!" I slammed into her, tackling her to the ground, covering her body with my own.

O'Shea was on top of me, his teeth sinking in around my shoulder in an effort to pull me off.

He bit deep, but didn't break any bones. He lifted me and I clung to Pamela. "Hang onto me, whatever you do."

She let out a sob, her small arms clinging to my waist. O'Shea shook us from side to side, trying to dislodge her. Eve let out a hunting screech.

"No, Eve, let me deal with him." The words didn't come out in a nice smooth sentence, but she didn't interfere.

O'Shea finally dropped me. Gods, it was as if my body had been strapped to a jackhammer, the inside of my skull still buzzing with the vibrations. I lifted my body up, so that I was crouched over Pamela.

"She is mine, and you will not hurt her. Got it?" I glared at him, meeting the challenge of his eyes full on. He snarled and lunged at me; I snapped a fist out and punched him in the nose. He shook his head and circled around while Pamela cried silent, terrified tears.

"O'Shea, she is *not* Milly."

His ears flattened to his skull. Not quite the reaction I was going for.

"Alex likes Pamie." Alex slunk forward, being submissive as always, but putting himself close enough that he could reach out and touch Pamela. "Boss no hurt Pamie. Please."

I wasn't sure if it was Alex, me, or the combination, but O'Shea backed off, growling still, but nothing more, his hackles slowly lowering.

"That was not pleasant." Eve hobbled toward us. O'Shea gave her a glance, but again, nothing more, seemingly dismissing her. "Are you sure that is the agent?"

"Yes. But whatever . . . whatever the other witch did to him was bad enough to make him hate them all." I carefully got to my feet, and then reached down to take Pamela's hand. She stood, wiped her eyes, and choked back the rest of her tears.

I put one hand on her shoulder, and with the other I tipped her chin up so she had to look me in the eye. "If he comes at you, you do what you have to do. Got it?"

"I can't hold him forever."

"I know."

Her eyes were still dilated with adrenaline. "Do you think he will attack me again?"

I looked over at O'Shea, who stood on the edge of the clearing, glaring at us.

"Yes, yes I do."

17

How could his mate stand for a witch? Had he been wrong? No, he was sure the one with the three colors in her eyes belonged with him, but she did things that he hated. Put a rope on him, cared for a child witch. The desire to run free and wild coursed through him the second his mate left with the witch child. To escape the confines of the human world.

But he couldn't leave her. Whatever bindings were between them were too strong to fight, even for the wolf in him. Which, for the first time in many days, he saw as separate. He was two, made one.

He shook his head and laid down, head on his paws. The other wolf—the half creature—played with the large bird, some sort of game that involved touching her and then bounding away when she squawked. Her feathers would puff up and she'd dance around as if to try and catch the half creature.

Perhaps she would be worth killing; a large bird like that would provide much meat. His stomach rumbled, reminding him it had been too long since he'd had any sustenance.

But the bird seemed to belong to his mate too. Perhaps this was her pack?

Yes, that much was clear. This was her pack. The thought stalled him, made his head tip to one side. Her pack. Could he accept them, accept even the witch child? Because if they belonged to his mate, and were hers to protect, then they were his to protect as well.

They were his pack by rights too.

He rose to his feet and gave a soft bark at the half creature, stopping him mid-game. The bird screeched a victory, smacking the half creature first, knocking him over on his back.

"There, you take that!" She clacked her beak and the half creature laughed, rolling onto his side.

The wolf barked again, a deeper, commanding call. The time to hunt had come. And even though this was surely the strangest pack he'd ever seen, it was his.

And he would care for every part of it.

His eyes narrowed. Even the witch child.

Pamela went with me to see Blaz. I'd left Eve with Alex and O'Shea, and while O'Shea was not happy, he at least didn't follow me this time. I didn't tell Eve where we were going, since I wasn't even sure Blaz would help. No need to get the Harpy all riled up.

"I thought the dragon threatened you?" We were picking our way through the boulders toward the mock canyon Blaz inhabited.

"He did."

"Then" —she placed her hand on a large outcropping of rock and swung her legs over— "why are we going back there?"

I let out a sigh. "We need someone to get us to Venice and then back to London. Eve can't fly yet, though she looks like it might only be another few hours before her wings finish healing."

I lifted my head to the breeze that blew toward us. Smelled like a charcoal BBQ, and my stomach growled. Pamela's stomach answered mine. She ducked her head, but acted as though it hadn't grumbled at all. "But that doesn't explain why we need Blaz."

"Even with her wings healed, Eve can't carry all of us. O'Shea is too big. She'd have to make multiple trips, and if we need a quick getaway . . . ." I let her fill in the blanks. We'd be royally screwed if we had to move fast. Or at least O'Shea and I would be. Because I would send out Pamela, Alex, and Jack first if it came to that, and I would stand with O'Shea against anything that was coming at us from behind, covering the others' escape. At least, that was the plan in my head, if it came to that.

We made our way through the rocks and I peered around them to see Blaz passed out on the canyon floor, the remains of something still smoking to one side of him. I knew I was hungry when the sight of it made my mouth water. Pamela licked her lips.

I blocked her with an arm, stopping her from going any further. "Stay here. I don't think I should need your help."

"You just didn't want to leave me with the were-wolf. I know." She backed up, putting herself against the flat of a big rock. Again, she was showing just how mature she was for her age. Taking everything that had come at us, pretty much in stride. No hissy fits, no tantrums.

Taking a deep breath, I stepped out into the mock canyon and strode toward Blaz like I owned the place.

Please don't let me be wrong about him.

Yet, as I drew closer, my confidence grew. He was watching me, one eye tracking my steps.

I thought I told you I'd eat you if you came back. His voice rumbled through my head.

I shrugged, and then pointed at the carcass. "Looks like you already ate. Besides, I'm quite sure I'd taste like shit."

His eye widened and he let out a bellow of a laugh. *Yes, you're probably right. You'd taste awful. You're far too scrawny for me.*

I made my way to the carcass, pulled my sword, and hacked a piece off. The meat was still warm, lightly charred, and smelled a-fucking-mazing. I bit into it and groaned, the juices flowing down my throat, coating my tongue with a perfect blend of savory tang. "Fuck, you're a good cook for a lazy-ass lizard."

His head swiveled around to mine and he picked at his teeth with one long claw, and then pointed to the rocks where Pamela waited. *You going to invite your little friend to eat too?*

"You going to try and eat her?" I didn't think he would, but shit, I had to ask.

Nah, too young. Besides, she's got a deadly aim with those rocks.

"Come eat, Pam." I gave her a wave and she made her way cautiously to my side. I hacked her off a piece of the carcass.

"What is it?"

I was already shaking my head. "Don't ask, just eat."

Blaz grinned and by the look on Pamela's face, she was hearing his words as clearly as I was. Apparently he could project to more than just me. I wasn't sure if that was good or not.

It is a Harpy. Seems that when you flew through with your nestling, you stirred up the whole fucking continent of them. Which is just fine by me.

Maybe not so good. Crap, I swallowed hard. "Don't tell Eve."

Pamela shook her head, eyes wide. "I won't."

We sat for a few minutes, stuffing ourselves with Harpy. I tried very hard not to think about how good it tasted, but by the look on Blaz's face, he knew.

Best thing you ever ate, isn't it?

Pamela nodded, as did I, but I wouldn't agree out loud. I just let the juices flow down my throat, hacked another piece off, and ate it too.

"I've had better," I said, slicing off another piece.

Why are you here? Blaz's back leg stretched forward and he scratched at his head with a back claw. His tail flicked at the end, like a nervous twitch. Like he was trying to play it cool.

"I need a hand with something. I'm hoping you would consider a trade."

You have nothing I want. No, that's not true. I would take Harpy off your hands; she's young and tender. He gave an evil grin that Pamela reacted to.

"I'll smash you with those boulders if you even touch Eve," she said, popping another piece of meat in her mouth.

Blaz's head snaked forward. *Little witch, you perhaps do not realize that I could eat you quite easily. One bite would do it.*

She put her hands on her hips and I just watched, wanting to see how much piss and vinegar the kid had.

"I'll crush you with boulders, you can't stop that."

I'll fry you with lightning.

Her lips thinned. "I'll pull down your mountain on your fat, stupid head."

Blaz laughed in her face and what happened next was one of those things that I will never forget.

Pamela glared at the dragon, lifted one hand, and the ground began to shake, the rocks and pebbles rattling and dancing across the earth. The shaking intensified, except for where she stood; the earth heaved, throwing Blaz backward. Along the edges of the mountain, the cliffs where the other dragons had perched crumbled, cracked, and fell to the ground. This had gone far enough.

I scrambled to her side, grabbing her arms, nulling her magic.

"Hey, so you know that being a show off will make you a target?" I stared into her eyes, didn't let her miss the fact that I wasn't going to let this pass without saying something.

"He thinks I'm weak."

No, I don't think you're weak. Blaz moved closer, a wary eye on the witch. *But I had no idea you had those kinds of abilities.*

"You aren't going to try and hurt my family?"

He blinked several times, as if her words had been a foreign language. His eyes slid to mine.

I shrugged. "We are tight-knit. I won't apologize for it."

I won't make any such promise. Now what kind of trade do you want?

I put Pamela behind me, just in case. Though to be fair, I already knew that he wouldn't hurt us. He would have killed us by now if he'd been going to.

"Round-trip flight. That's it. Done. You'll never see me again." Which I knew without him saying so was what he wanted. Whatever binding had happened between us, he didn't want it. Didn't want to be responsible for me. Which was fine by me. If Eve was right, it was just a bunch of stupid ridiculousness anyway.

His eyes narrowed and he drew a line in the dirt between us. *Where are we going?*

"You would take me, Pamela, and one werewolf to Venice. We're going to pick up someone there, and then you would take us all back to London."

Sounds simple.

"It isn't."

His tongue flicked out and ran along his teeth. *And I get what out of this?*

"I'll owe you a favor, to be cashed in when you need it."

He laughed, his sides heaving with mirth, scales glittering in the dull sunlight. *What could you possibly do for me?*

"I could Track for you."

Blaz went very still, and then slowly nodded. *Done.*

For some reason I suspected I should be more worried about making a deal with a Dragon than I was. He'd agreed far too quickly.

Yes, I had a feeling I should be much more worried. *Let's go. I have other things I could be doing.*

I motioned for Pamela to step up and I lifted her up onto Blaz's back. This was happening faster than I'd planned, but I wouldn't get another chance at the kind of help I would need to get us all home in one piece.

As I mounted up on Blaz's back, I Tracked Jack, his life throbbing dully in the south. Like he was being hurt, or maybe like the cancer was making a resurgence. I wasn't sure, had never Tracked him before and this—what I felt inside my head—was more of an ache than an actual pain.

I settled in behind Pamela, then flicked my whip out and around Blaz's neck for a handhold. He turned around to stare at me, arching his darkly scaled eyebrow.

I'm not going to try and dump your ass this time.

"You say that now. I know how fast I can piss people off. I'd rather have something to hang onto."

He chuckled and the muscles underneath us bunched. With a shot of power, he launched himself into the air, wings driving downward, and he actually used them to push off the ground as well. A few sharp wing beats and we were high in the air, circling around the mountain. I pointed out the direction where Eve, Alex, and O'Shea waited.

Pamela's hands clutched my wrists, and her blonde hair streamed back around me. And for a moment, I could think that she was Berget, that I hadn't failed my little sister again. A heavy ache spread through my chest, like the weight of one of the boulders crushing me.

Tracker, I do not want to know, but I will tell you this: if you go into battle with a grief like the one coursing through you, you will put not only yourself in danger, but that of your family.

"You always spy on people's thoughts?" I snapped, giving the whip a jerk, wishing I could tighten it around him enough that he would actually feel it.

Your emotions come through to me. Just one more reason that you need to be far away from me. Far, far away.

I wanted to ask him what the other dragons had meant when they'd spoken about the binding, what had happened to him and I?

Then again, maybe I didn't want to know. Yeah, at this point in my life, with all the shit I had going on, that was probably better.

18

In order to pick up O'Shea, Blaz had to land, and that meant crushing trees. With a glee I could *feel* as if I were Tracking him, Blaz went to work, hovering just above a cluster of trees, taking them out with his claws and tail, a grin stretching across his face so wide I could see the corners of it from his back. Leaves, mud, rocks, and branches flew as he cleared a patch large enough for him to land.

Pamela turned to face me. "Kinda destructive, isn't he?"

"Yeah, kinda. But he is a dragon. I'm not sure they're known for being quiet and humble."

Humble, yes. Quiet, no.

Tucking his wings in tight, Blaz dropped into his cleared area. I slid off his back first and then caught Pamela as she slid down his scaled side.

"We'll be right back," I said as we turned and headed toward the shack where we'd left the others.

Please let them all still be there and not fighting. Even taking Pamela with me, I'd been unsure of how O'Shea would handle being alone with Eve and Alex. As we stepped out of the thick bush and into the smallish clearing, a spurt of relief washed through me. Which, considering what was waiting for us, was kinda weird.

O'Shea stood between us and Eve and Alex, who huddled back against the shack. O'Shea's hackles were standing straight up, making him look even bigger, and his teeth were bared. As we came into view, he lifted his head, took a sniff, and relaxed. With a shake of his head and shoulders, the tension was broken.

He'd been protecting them.

Eve let out a squawk, flapping her obviously just healed wings as she ran toward us, bumping into O'Shea as she ran by him. O'Shea gave a grunt, but didn't make any move toward her.

"Rylee, what was that great crashing noise? It sounded as if the forest was being destroyed." She bobbed her head several times, golden eyes watching me intently.

"Blaz brought us here." Soon enough, I would have to tell her that the dragon who'd wanted to eat her was going to be with us for a little while. But not yet.

"Who is . . .?"

"The dragon," Pamela said.

Ah, fuck, I hadn't counted on the kid.

Eve squawked and let out a screech that made my skin crawl.

I held a hand up to her. "Eve, stop it. He's not here for you, he's here to help get us all to Venice, get Jack, and then he'll take us home. There are too many of us for you to fucking carry."

"He wanted to *eat* me!" Her wings were spread as wide as they would go and her feathers were most certainly ruffled.

I let out a sigh. "Fine, then you can take Alex with you back to London and wait for us there."

Alex let out a whimper. "Stay with Rylee."

The Harpy flapped her wings a few times, stirring up the bush around us. "I don't like it."

"I know." I stared up at her. "I *can* do this salvage without you, Eve. It'll be quick, you can—"

"No. I will come. You are my mentor." She seemed to pull herself together. "I can take more than Alex, though."

"You may have to, on the way back. Depends on how Jack is doing." I led the way back through the trees to where Blaz waited, sprawled out on his back. The dragon was snoring lightly, eyes shut against the light mist that fell, but it was a ruse. I could sense that he was awake. Bugger, this blood mingling thing on top of my Tracking was making my head hurt. Too much of other people's feelings inside my head at once was not a good thing.

O'Shea took one look at him, glanced at me, and then looked back at the dragon.

"Yeah, I can hardly believe it, either." I reached over and slid my hand along the top of his head, the tension easing out of me as I did. He gave a soft woof, shook his head, and plunked his ass down beside me.

Eve was not so subtle. Her body fluffed up, wings spread with alarm that she couldn't seem to contain. Her eyes tracked every breath the dragon took, and her beak clacked together in fast, rapid clicks.

I've already eaten Harpy today. I'm quite full. Blaz rolled to the side to stare at our group. He moved slowly, and I could tell, without knowing why, that he was worried about freaking Eve out. It didn't work. Eve hopped from foot to foot, wings flapping, lifting her a few feet off the ground.

His eyes flicked to me and gave me a slight nod, maybe confirming what I was suspecting? This bond thing was weird; I didn't like it. Blaz gave me a grin and a wink, but then he lifted his head and stared out behind me. Like there was someone there.

I spun, yanking a sword from its sheath to see Faris standing ten feet behind me.

"Quite the army you've put together."

"Fuck, don't sneak up on me—us—like that."

He spread his hands in front of his body. "Hardly sneaking up on you. Tell me, how *do* you acquire all these creatures? I don't think I've ever seen anyone with a grouping quite like this."

"What do you want?"

"I'm here to help. I told you that you can't do this on your own. There's no way you will be able to get in and out without help."

I slid my sword back into its sheath. "I'm going after Jack."

"And the Child Empress?"

I said the only thing that I could. The truth.

"I'll do what I have to, Faris. From everything I've seen, this Child Empress is one problem our world doesn't need."

Faris' eyelids flickered ever so slightly. "And you would swear an oath on this?"

"What the fuck would I need an oath for?" I glared at him, trying to figure out what he was up to. Because even though he hadn't lied to me about Berget, I still didn't trust him.

I just couldn't shake the feeling that he was maneuvering me into whatever position it was that he wanted.

"You need to be committed to this path. Completely. Or I will not help you—and you won't be able to manage this without me." His eyes never left mine, as I continued to glare at him.

"She doesn't need you." Pamela said from behind me. "She has us." I didn't turn around, but I had no doubt her hands were on her hips as she stood up to the vampire who, I knew without a doubt, terrified her. Gods, she was going to be a strong woman when she got older. She was already stronger than most adults now, at fourteen.

Faris gave me a small smile. "You will be facing vampires and their pets, who happen to be imbued with their master's strengths. Rylee, you know you aren't fast enough."

Fuck, he was right, but I had to find a way around this. I wracked my brain, but no way that I looked at it could I see around the fact that we were outclassed, speed wise at least, when it came to the blood drinkers.

Maybe Faris saw the uncertainty in my eyes, because he smiled and stepped closer to me. "If we go back to London, if we re-group, then I can pull together those of my brethren who would stand with me—*then* perhaps we can make an assault on the Child Empress."

"And Jack?" I already knew the answer though, at least what Faris would say.

"He will die. But there are casualties in war. And make no mistake, Rylee, this *is* war."

Be very careful, this one is a tricky bastard. Even the Dragons have heard of him. But he is better than the Child Empress; anyone would be better than that one and her twisted mind.

"We don't have time to go back to London," I said, a plan already forming in my mind, though I hated what it would take to make it happen. Gods, if it meant I could bring Jack out safely, if I could keep the others safe . . .

"Faris, I need to speak with you." I motioned for the others to back away, to give me some room. O'Shea was watching me closely, his eyes narrowing ever so slightly. He would understand, he would have to; I had no other choices left to me.

Lesser of two evils, that's what I was doing, or at least, that was how I soothed myself.

"You are ready to swear the oath?"

My jaw clenched of its own volition, irritation and a little bit of fear trickling through me.

I kept my voice low. "I will swear it, if you will do something for me."

He leaned in close, his mouth next to my ear, cool breath tickling along my neck. "What would you have of me . . . Tracker?"

I closed my eyes, reminded myself that Jack needed me, and I'd promised him I would come back to London so that either he wouldn't die alone, or I would make sure if he'd died that he was taken care of. This was no different, only now it wasn't London, it was Venice.

"When we get close to Venice, I want you to bite me." I lifted my eyes to his, just as his widened.

"Rather inappropriate timing, don't you think?"

"Your bite just before the zombie attack, when you . . ." Gods, what was it that he'd done?

"I invoked the bite in order to heal you." His voice was soft and his hands had found their way to my waist. I pushed them off.

"Knock it the fuck off. Bite me now then, and invoke it when we get close to Venice. That work for you?"

The grin that stretched across his face said it all. "You're going to enjoy this."

I snorted. "Nope, I'm not. I've told you, I've got a thing for a wolf."

Faris frowned and from behind us Alex gave a woof.

"The troops are getting restless," I said. "So either do it or don't."

"Swear the oath."

I gave a growl, which O'Shea echoed back to me. Clearly he had been getting the gist of what was going to happen and wasn't happy about it, either.

"I swear to you that I will do all I can to kill the Child Empress."

"Swear it on the blood of the lost."

A chill rippled through me.

I swallowed hard, suddenly nervous. "I swear it on the blood of the lost."

He didn't give me any warning and I reacted even though I had asked for him to bite me. I tried to jerk away from him, one hand pushing him away even as his arms snaked around me, and his mouth slammed into the side of my neck. His fangs dug in deep, and

I knew I was going to have bruises after this. The bite was not like the one Doran had given me, but there was again a memory that wrapped me in it and sucked me down deep, even though I felt Faris fighting it alongside me, a hum of pleasure sharp and sweet singing along my veins, distracting me.

Whatever the memory was, he didn't want me to see it. My interest piqued—maybe I'd finally find out what he'd been hiding from me all this time.

I wasn't disappointed.

I recognized where we were—where the memory took place—almost immediately.

Deerborn Park.

Laughter circled up around us, Berget's six-year-old laughter. Fuck, fuck! How was it that this was Faris's memory? Was it somehow mine and he'd been pulled into it? Was that even possible?

No, I stood in the shadows of the trees on the edge of the park, staring out over the heads of two vampires as they watched Berget play.

She was on the swings, legs pumping hard, stretching out her toes, reaching them as far as she could. Blonde hair streamed out behind her in two long braids as she pushed herself higher and higher.

"Rylee! I'm going to flip over!"

"No, you aren't." That was my voice, but I hadn't said a word. My eyes fell on my teenage self, long auburn hair hanging down around my face as I lay on my belly, reading a book next to the swings. I knew without seeing it that the book was *Of Mice and Men*, and I knew even the part I was at, what exactly I'd been reading. Lenny had pet the puppies too hard and was about to get busted. Bile rose in my throat. I'd never been able to finish the book, though I knew how it ended. Just like life. Badly.

The two shadows I stood next to worked their way closer, the one on the left a woman.

"Do we take them both?"

The other vampire turned his blue eyes toward her, his face the same then as it was now. "No, we take just the child. Only the child."

I screamed, fury lighting me up like nothing I'd ever felt. Faris had been the one, he'd stolen Berget, he'd been the one to take her away to Venice, the one to lead me on to make me think he would have saved her. To make me feel like I'd been the one to blame, to then lull me into trusting him.

I snapped out of the memory, screaming and punching. A wild rage that I couldn't control spun through me. Faris's mouth was covered in my blood and his eyes were locked on mine. He was trying to enthrall me; I could feel it pulsing against my skin, his power drawing at my soul, trying to get to me through my eyes.

"You fucking piece of shit! You stole her from me!" O'Shea went from being across the clearing to at my side in half a breath. I buried my hands into the thick fur of his neck, clinging to him like a life raft in a stormy ocean. Calm slid through me and I knew without looking that Blaz was using whatever bond was between us to mellow me out.

"Don't, Blaz. I want to be fucking angry."

Anger can be used, you know that. Use it to find your friend, to kill the Child Empress. There is more good in those things than in fighting with one vampire, or losing your life to him.

I glared at Faris, who was breathing hard, but he wasn't coming after me. Nor was there any sign of shame in him. Not a drop.

"You're an asshole." I spun on my heel and strode across to Blaz. No one said anything, not even Alex. Pamela sat in front of me on Blaz, and O'Shea jumped onto the dragon's back, wedging himself between two of the dragon's back ridges as if he'd been flying by dragon all his life.

Eve gathered up Alex and the two winged creatures launched into the air, one right after the other.

We'd been flying for about ten minutes before anyone said anything. And it was the Dragon who decided to try and draw me out.

Once we are in Venice, where are we going?

"I'll tell you when we get there." I bit the words out, gripping the whip handle. How the hell could I have ever thought Faris was on my side? That he was here to help me? I closed my eyes and tipped my forehead down until it was pressed into Pamela's shoulder. Faris. My whole world had been turned upside down because of him.

"Rylee? Do you have a plan this time?" Pamela's voice made me open my eyes.

"Jack is first. When we find him we'll send him home with Eve right away."

"And after?"

She knew that I was going to try and kill a child, which went against every oath I'd ever made. Then again, a vampire child would look young, but that didn't mean she would be young. Probably hundreds of years old, trapped in a child's body.

"I don't know, Pamela. If I can, I'll find the Child Empress."

She twisted around to look at me. "And?"

Pamela had no idea, had no fucking idea what was being asked of me. "You know the answer to that."

Her eyes watched me, like she was trying to see if I was serious.

"Fuck, kid. This isn't a gods-be-damned Disney movie. You can't save everyone, and not everyone deserves to be saved."

Her chin trembled, but she nodded, her jaw tightening and stilling the tremble.

Yeah, good job with the mentoring there, Rylee. My own voice in my head mocked me. Then again, it was the truth. A hard truth that she would have to learn at some point. Better that I tell her, than she learn it firsthand.

Fuck. What a mess.

Yes. A mess for fucking sure.

I rolled my eyes.

Don't roll your eyes at me.

I clamped my jaw shut, since I had a sneaking suspicion that Blaz was only speaking to me.

I am only speaking to you.

I wished that I understood how the bond worked, or if it was just a pain in the ass.

Yes, it is a pain. But it means that no matter how far you are from me, we can communicate like this. It means that what you feel in terms of pain or strong emotions, I can feel them if I'm close enough. Fortunately, the bond doesn't work both ways, at least not for the most part. You can only get some emotions from me, but you can't read my mind as I can read yours.

I wanted to groan and cover my face. Just . . . fucking fantastic.

My thoughts exactly.

19

We flew through the night, stopping every hour or so for Eve to give her wings a rest. They had healed, but were still weak from the damage Blaz had inflicted on them. However, she wouldn't stop unless Blaz stopped first, much to his displeasure.

"What does it matter who stops first?" I grunted at the third stop, stretching my legs.

Eve glowered across at Blaz, but wouldn't say anything. Maybe it was some sort of code of conduct. Who the fuck knew?

The eastern coast of Italy, at the top of the boot, stared out across the Adriatic Sea and the so-called 'floating' city of Venice lit up the sky. We stopped there just before sunrise. Eve was sucking wind hard and landed in a heap, her legs buckling under her.

"Shit, Eve. We could have stopped earlier." I ran to her side, but there was nothing I could do to help the thousand-pound Harpy.

"I'm fine." She pushed me away with her beak and I considered that again, this had more to do with some code I was unaware of. I shook my head. Pride and supernaturals went together like peanut butter and chocolate. I should know, I was as bad as the rest of them.

"We'll wait here until the sun is fully up; if you can find something to eat without resorting to eating one another, do so." I looked around, giving them each a hard look.

The beach wasn't far and I found myself working my way down to the water's edge. Waves rushed up over the sand and rocks, the sibilant whisper of the tide pulling at the earth. I sank down, dropping my knees to the soft wet sand. I trailed my fingers in the water and lowered my chin to my chest. I was about to go into battle with a bunch of young, half-trained supernaturals. But they were all I had and I needed their help to get Jack out. For one of the first times in my life, I wished that I'd been cursed with a better ability. Something that could save lives, rather than just find them.

A warm body pressed up against my side, O'Shea coming to sit beside me, as Alex went spinning by me like an out-of-control top into the water. So much for a moment of contemplation.

"I wish you were here. Really here, Liam," I said softly. He put his chin on my shoulder and stared out across the water with me, watching the sunrise over Venice. Beautiful, haunting, surreal. All those words applied and yet, they seemed damn inadequate.

Jack was in the city, his life threads hummed alongside my own. Not strong, but not dead. With Jack that was as good a sign as any. I reached up and curled my arm around O'Shea's neck, holding him to me. What if this was all I'd ever have of him? What if Milly was right and there was no bringing him back? Fuck, I wouldn't let that happen.

Alex was doggy paddling out into the deeper water, oblivious to the cold and the severity of the situation.

I held O'Shea tighter. He wasn't like Alex, even though he too was trapped inside a wolf body. O'Shea was still . . . O'Shea. Even if he was stuck, even if he couldn't talk, he'd retained so much of his personality.

I closed my eyes and O'Shea let out a low whine.

"I'm still here."

Gods, what I wouldn't give to have his arms around me.

There was the crunch of sand and gravel, and then Pamela sat on the other side of me. "I'm sorry, about what I said up there."

"Forget about it."

"I can't, I just . . . ." She brushed her bangs off her forehead. "I know there are people out there who are bad people. But you saved me. What if this Child Empress isn't a bad kid, what if it's the people around her?"

Now that was not a question I'd even considered. "Shit. Well, I guess I'll deal with that when I get close."

"And how is Faris going to invoke your bite if he's asleep? It will be daylight when we go in, won't it?"

I let out a groan. "Damn it all. I hadn't thought of that."

O'Shea gave a grunt and pushed me with his nose. Like an "I told you so."

Screw this.

I stood up. "Come on. We've got Jack to rescue and a vampire to kill."

Pamela scrambled to her feet, and Alex came sloshing into shore, looking like a drowned rat. He was grinning from ear to ear. His body was thin under all that hair; no wonder he was hungry all the time. Next to O'Shea's bulk, Alex was a scrawny, gangly teenager.

I strode back to Eve and Blaz. Blaz let out a bone-cracking yawn, and Eve glared at him from where she sat, feathers all fluffed up. At least he wasn't trying to eat her.

I said I wouldn't.

"Stay outta my head, Blaz."

You don't want me listening in on your lusting after the wolf? He grinned at me, a big, lecherous grin and gave me a wink. Fuck, that was the last thing I needed. I took a deep breath.

"Shut your pie hole, dragon. Before I turn you into a pair of new boots."

Eve let out a cackling laugh and flapped her wings. "I want a purse if you get new boots."

An image of Eve packing around a Blaz-colored purse flitted through my head, and he frowned at me, scales catching the morning light.

Not funny.

We mounted up again and Blaz launched into the air first, Eve close behind him. I tapped into Jack's threads and, through me, Blaz quickly honed in on the Tracker. That was fucking handy, I had to give him that.

Yes, I suppose there are a few benefits. But not enough to be warranted other than on this trip.

"And whenever you decide to have me do some Tracking for you."

That too.

Across the water we flew, skimming close to the ocean. Eve flew higher than us and I could see her labored efforts, see the strain of holding not only her own body aloft, but Alex too. Shit, this was going to get bad if she had to—

Eve stumbled in midair, her wings just giving out.

Blaz cut sideways and the three of us clung to his back as he grabbed Eve out of the sky. Like plucking an apple off a tree, it was just that easy for him.

Now we had a problem.

Yes. I will drop you, the witch and the wolf off and take the Harpy, and the other wolf back to the forest, then I will come back for you.

There was no other way to make this happen.

I leaned over the dragon's side. "Eve, Blaz is going to take you and Alex back to the shack."

"I'm fine, just tired."

I can feel her wings, they are still fractured, probably just the strain of flying too soon.

Damn it, I shouldn't have let her come with us so soon.

Not your fault. She knew and she let you believe she was better. Harpies can be like that. Stubborn and prideful. Not like Dragons. It's why we kicked them out.

"What?" I couldn't help the question that popped out of me.

Pamela cranked around to look at me, her eyebrows raised. I shook my head, clearing it of everything but Jack. We were just coming up to the first canal, and with Blaz feeling what I was feeling he flew straight toward Jack.

We kicked them out of the Winged. That is partly why they hate us and we hate them. Or in my case, eat them.

Banking up, the dragon flew about a hundred feet above the tops of the buildings.

"I can't believe people don't see him, he's bloody well huge!" Pamela pointed at the people moving about their business below, and I shrugged.

"Most humans never see what's right in front of them, though some do." I pointed to a single person who stared up at us from the street, his hand in the air pointing at us.

"And they're the crazy ones. Aren't they?"

"Yes. The people who believe in what's truly out there, the masses label them squirrely as a bag full of fucking nuts."

Blaz let out a chuckle as he spun lazily in a downward spiral toward the top of a huge building that, for some reason, filled me with an undeniable sense of dread. Shaped like a 'U', the rooftop was flat with pikes around the edges. There looked to be enough room for Blaz to land, which was a perk. On the far side was what looked like a church . . . .

That is the Basilica of St. Marks, and where we will land is the Doges Palace. Not only is it the seat of power for the humans, it contains the seat of power for the vampires. You are going into a nest of them, you know that, right?

"Yeah, kinda." Shit, a nest of them? I was hoping for less than three.

I cannot help you once you are inside.

"That wasn't part of the deal."

Just making sure you understand, Tracker.

The courtyard between the Palace and the Basilica crawled with tourists. I mean like a freaking ant hive of activity.

I can help with that.

Before I could say 'yes thanks,' or 'fuck no,' a bolt of lightning forked out of the sky and danced along the courtyard. It didn't touch anyone and didn't cause any damage, but as the light show continued all the humans drew closer to watch. Idiots.

"Don't they know that lightning is dangerous?" Pamela stared at the humans, her mouth hanging open.

"Yes, they know. But they're drawn to it, like they're drawn to so much that is dangerous."

Like you should talk. Walking into a nest of vampires.

Pamela slapped a hand over her mouth, stifling a giggle; obviously, that had been audible to everyone. Blaz landed and the light show continued. I slid from his back, O'Shea leapt off, and Pamela scrambled down his side. I caught her partway and helped her to the ground.

"Eve, we won't be long. Then we'll just wait until you're healed."

"I don't want to go," she said, her eyes flicking toward Blaz almost imperceptibly.

"This isn't a choice. You have to trust me, and in this, I trust him." I put a hand out and touched the arch of her wing. "You are a liability when you're hurt like this."

She let out a shuddering sigh. "I know."

"Alex, you look after Eve. Okay?"

He bounded over to me, his big eyes tearing up. "Sending Alex away, always away."

I bent and gave him a hug, squeezing him hard. "I love you, Alex. And you can't stay with me this time. It just . . . it just isn't good, buddy."

"Alex loves Rylee too. Pamie too. Evie too. Boss too." He whispered into my arms, sniffling. Gods, I'd barely spent any time with him since we'd been in London.

"Listen, after this, we'll go home. Back to North Dakota. No more being sent away."

His head jerked up, eyes lighting with eagerness. "Home? Yuppy doody! Home, home, home!" He barked and then spun on the spot, chasing his tail, finally grabbing it and yelping with pain. I touched him on the head.

"Easy, you go with Eve, and then we'll go home. We'll all go home." I only hoped that I was going to be able to keep this promise.

Because if I was being honest with myself, I wasn't sure that any of us were going to make it out of this alive.

You are right to be wary. I will be back as quickly as I can. You can call for me, if you need me.

I put a hand on his leg closest to me. "Thanks."

A heartbeat later, he launched back into the sky, the lightning still dancing in the courtyard. The humans surrounded it, staring and pointing where it struck, where it burned the ground and scorched the stones.

Locking onto Jack, I headed toward the closest door. Pamela and O'Shea walked on either side of me. For all his animosity earlier, O'Shea seemed to be able to control himself now. Although he watched Pamela warily, there was no lashing out, no growling.

We reached the door and the handle turned, but it was locked. Before I could grab my sword, Pamela put her hand to it and the door melted. Like hot wax dripping, the whole metal door melted right down to the hinges.

I stared at her, knowing I was going to hurt her feelings, but knowing I had to. I pointed at the puddle of metal at our feet. "Much as that's a nifty trick, and would be amazing in certain situations, it is going to be fucking hard to hide that we've come this way."

She blushed. "I didn't think about that."

"Yeah, learning curve." I stepped through the doorway and over the metal. Pamela followed, and O'Shea brought up the rear. The door opened into a storage room, coated in dust, cobwebs and scurrying things. Pamela gave a squeak and jumped into me.

I spun and grabbed her by the arms, again, knowing that this was not going to seem nice. But she was going to get us killed. "Vampires. If you see a vampire or some other fucking nasty supernatural, then you can scream, pee your pants, whatever. But bugs don't get screamed at. Got it?"

Her eyes welled up, but again she nodded, and I could feel her spine stiffening. I gave her a smile to soften my words and she smiled back, tremulous and uncertain. But she was trying.

O'Shea was the one who found the trap door leading down and out of the storage room. He dug at it, his nose pressed against the dusty carpet covering the large ringed handle.

Pamela put her hand out and I shook my head, pressing a finger to my lips. I wrapped my hands around the ring and pulled. The hinges were well oiled, and the door lifted easily. With it open, I could peer down to see where we were. Kinda.

The room below looked like it had been closed off to the public, which was perfect. I took Pamela's hands and lowered her down first. Next went O'Shea, and I went last, dropping lightly to a crouch. The walls were covered in oil paintings, as in the walls themselves were painted and accented with gold gilt scrollwork that was fussy and overdone.

"This is beautiful," Pamela whispered, and then slapped her hand over her mouth.

I pointed to the only door in the room. The next ten minutes, I spent trying to get closer to Jack, but only managed to get turned around. We would head toward him, and I'd think we were getting somewhere, and then we'd hit a dead end. Like a fucking maze, the Doges Palace twisted and turned, rooms, hallways, and more just kept blocking my way. Shit.

Inside yet another dead end room, I stood staring at the wall, knowing that if I could get through it Jack wasn't that much further away.

I narrowed my eyes and used my second sight, hoping there would be a hidden door. There wasn't, but other things became very apparent.

Like the warnings scrawled in blood on the paintings in the wall.

Dying is a blessing.

Death is a curse.

May your bowels be filled with blood and mercy.

Nice. Real classy.

But better than that . . . I lifted my hand and traced the bloody arrow pointing toward the door. Rather obvious and it was one of two things: a marker system for new vamps needing directions or a fucking trap.

I was going with a trap, for five hundred, Mr. Trebek. If I was right, and it was a trap, it would lead us where we had to go. We just had to ready for the trap to spring. Yup, *no problemo*.

Pamela grabbed my hand and frowned at me. I pointed at my eyes, then at the wall. We'd been practicing using her second sight, but she struggled with it.

Her eyes widened and she pointed. Apparently she got it this time around. We followed the arrows out into the hallway, down a set of narrow stairs, and onto the main floor.

Where all the humans were hanging out, taking pictures and staring at the walls like the tourists they were.

Crap.

The arrows led straight across the main entrance. We were going to have to bolt for it if O'Shea wasn't going to get noticed. I snorted softly to myself and glanced over at him. Yeah, who was going to miss a five-hundred-pound jet-black wolf running across the palace entrance?

His slowly silvering eyes flicked up to me, as if he knew what I was thinking.

I'd wanted to avoid the humans as much as possible, they were just cannon fodder, and had a tendency to get killed when supernaturals rumbled.

"Pamela," I whispered. "Can you block off the entrances to the main room, so people can't go in and out?"

She nodded, stepped out, and lifted her hands. A tingle of energy trickled along my skin and I watched as the humans were slowly corralled into one doorway or another. Then Pamela darkened the blocks so they weren't clear, but murky and shadowed. So they couldn't be seen through.

"Brilliant. Good job."

She grinned up at me and I grinned back. Score one for the witch.

We jogged down the final flight of steps and started across the main entranceway. A roar of defiance shocked the shit out of me. I spun, and in the main doorway leading into the palace stalked a fucking, I'll-be-damned, Gryphon.

A lion with wings, he was easily as big as O'Shea, maybe even bigger. Hard to tell with the wings. Shit, he must be some sort watchdog for the vampires. Tawny hide rippled over thick, powerful muscles, his darker mane waved in the breeze as he walked, and his wings were the color of honey. Stunning, he was a truly incredible creature. But he was still going to try and kill us, of that I had no doubt. Which left me no choice.

"I thought you blocked all the entranceways," I said as I pulled my swords free.

"I did, he must have broken through," Pamela said.

That meant one of two things. Either he was another Immune like me, or he had some sort of magic of his own. I was hoping he wasn't Immune.

Pamela snapped a hand forward and the Gryphon ran through what she tossed at it. Immune it was then.

"Leave this one to us," I said as I stepped sideways, cutting down through the Gryphon's wings with my sword. Feathers and blood spurted out, and the Gryphon roared. But before he could spin and tackle me, O'Shea was on his back, his jaws sinking in around the Gryphon's neck.

The huge cat reached up and yanked O'Shea off his back, tossing him to the floor, leaving his back exposed to me. I ran forward and sliced downward and lengthwise as I passed the Gryphon's side, cutting though his ribs and opening up his guts. Viscera spilled out onto the tiled floor and the Gryphon slumped, his last breaths slipping out of him in a matter of seconds. Fast, so fast, and a trickle of remorse skittered through me. Gryphons were rare, kind of the endangered species of the supernatural world, and we'd cut him down in a matter of minutes.

Jaw clenched, I went to one knee and put a hand on the tawny hide, felt the heat from his body fading already. Son of a bitch, of all the things the vampires could have used for a guard animal, why did it have to be a Gryphon? And one that obviously had no real fighting skills for us to take him out as fast as we had. Just one more reason to go after the Child Empress. This death shouldn't have happened either, didn't need to have happened.

I stared around us. The whole set up had seemed too easy. O'Shea's eyes caught mine. Yeah, too damn easy, indeed. Like they were testing us, to see if we were worth bothering with. My hunch that this, and the arrows, were a trap increased—like a tightening noose around my neck. Not a good sign.

"Let's go, they know we're here."

20

We found our way down into the lower levels via a panel in the wall that the oh-so-helpful bloody arrows pointed to. Once inside the walls, I could see where they'd been opened up and made to look like a reflection of the true palace. If I hadn't known better, I would have thought that I was in the regular section with the oil paintings directly on the walls, the scrollwork, even the gold laid into the floors was the same.

"Why would they go to all this effort?" Pamela asked softly, her voice barely above a whisper.

"I don't know. Now be quiet." I suspected I did know the reason, but I wasn't going to go and try to explain it right then. I'd save that for later, when we weren't walking into a nest of vampires who knew we were coming.

Vampires were one of the few supernatural creatures that had once been human. They had all started out normal at one point. From what I understood, it was a big part of why they were such assholes. Werewolves were the same, and the two groups were some of the most difficult to deal with. The rest of us had never been human, even if we thought we were, we had always been different. I suspected that this attempt at 'normalizing' the insides of the walls was to make the vampires feel like they were still a little bit human. Even though there wasn't a drop of humanity left in them.

We worked our way through, toward Jack who was close now; there were no longer the dead ends when it came to trying to pin him down.

The next corner rounded into an intersection of hallways; I could feel Jack, closer now. Where we stood, six branches led off from the intersection. Dark, long tunnels that no doubt held creatures we wanted nothing to do with. From what I could tell, Jack was at the end of the branch on our right. At the end of it, there was a single, flickering light above a heavy wooden door. Iron slides that banded across the wood were an added strength over a simple lock. It made me wonder what the fuck they kept locked up down here.

If it hadn't been for Berget, I never would have even thought about going down any of those hallways, except for the one Jack was at the end of. But down one of those dark tunnels was the Child Empress. I hesitated, staring at the hallway across from me, and found myself Tracking vampires as a group. No one close, everything was all still and quiet; the only vampires I could feel were about a mile deep. How the hell was that possible in a floating city? I shook my head. That didn't matter, at least not yet.

I pointed at Jack's door and took a step forward.

And that's when the trap was sprung, and all hell broke loose.

From each of the dark hallways came a vampire. They could have moved faster, but by the grins on their faces, they wanted to see our fear. Wanted us to believe we could break free of them. How the hell had I missed them?

We were so fucked.

O'Shea managed to grab one; Pamela nailed another with a fireball, which did far more damage, and the others gave her some room.

The other four advanced on me, as if I were the dangerous one, which I freaking well knew I wasn't compared to O'Shea, or even Pamela with her fireballs. Yet they tackled me, pinned me to the ground, and there wasn't a thing I could do about it. My muscles strained against their hands, fought them, but there was no comparison. Their strength and speed wasn't legendary for no reason. I knew why they were at the top of the food chain.

"Get her out of here, O'Shea," I yelled, my words echoing against the painted walls.

He snarled at me—defiance I could feel dancing along my skin—and snatched one of the vampires by the leg and threw them against the wall. From the corner of my eye, a vampire reached from the darkness toward Pamela, his mouth open with glee. Shit.

"Get her the fuck out of here!" There was nothing I could do, my body completely controlled by the vampires who held me tight.

O'Shea spun on his haunches, and I saw him take everything in. There were just too many of them, we wouldn't win, and he finally got it. Time for a retreat and a re-group, if wanted any chance at saving me, he had to leave. His claws scrabbled across the uneven rock, and then he bolted past me, grabbing Pamela as he went. Down one of the corridors they ran and disappeared into the darkness.

The vampire closest to me leaned down and put her mouth close to my ear. "Our Empress is waiting for you, Tracker. But don't worry, we'll find the girl, and her little dog too."

"Fuck you."

"Umm. I'd like that, but I heard you prefer your wolves to women." She licked my cheek and I went very still, turned just my eyes to her.

"Perhaps your girl would be more to my liking."

I stared up at her, knew that the three colors in my eyes would be shifting wildly with my anger. "Touch her and I'll stop playing nice, you fucking piece of shit."

She laughed, but there was a touch of fear in her laughter, like she was trying to convince herself.

They lifted me, one vampire on each arm and one on each foot, holding me above the ground as they took me down the hallway toward Jack's door. The last vampire stripped me of my weapons as they walked. Everything went—my two swords, knife, whip, crossbow, and bolts.

The door opened, and I was thrown into the cell, landing flat on my back on the hard floor. It knocked the wind out of me, and I lay there, waiting for my breath to come back. What a freaking mess this was.

Finally, I rolled to my knees and squinted into the darkness, knowing Jack was in here somewhere with me.

"Jack?"

"What the fuck, Rylee." He was in the corner on a low pallet, a blanket over him. I made my way to his side and sat on the edge of the pallet. His skin, what I could see of it, was gray and sallow, his eyes were sunken into his head and his bright red hair seemed to have dimmed in the short time since I'd seen him last.

"Jack, shouldn't the vampires have been sleeping?"

"They are, you idiot. Those were the mother fucking pets. How the hell did you get this far, anyway?" He'd barely finished speaking when a series of coughs wracked his frame, the wet, awful sound of fluid on his lungs. Fluid or blood, one or the other.

"What happened to Doran, why didn't he try to help keep you out of their hands?"

He spat a gob of something against the wall, and we watched it slide down for a moment before he answered.

"There were too many of them, no need for the fanged fuck to get taken too. He was all but shaking in his boots, didn't want to be taken to the Empress again."

I put a hand on his shoulder, hoping I was right about him and the fact that they would have thought him defenseless when they took him. "Jack, they took all my weapons."

"That surprises you?"

"No, but did they take all yours?"

He gave a chuckle. "No. They didn't even check me. I'm just a dying old man. It's between the pallet and the floor."

I slid my fingers along until I felt the handle of a weapon. I pulled out a short sword, about half the length of my two, but it was a hell of a lot better than nothing at all.

"It is spelled to cut deep, like yours, so watch the edge," he muttered.

"They're going to take me for an audience with the Child Empress."

"You think you've got it in you?"

I took a couple of swings with the sword, feeling the weight of it, how it cut through the air.

"If I don't, we're all dead. So yeah, I guess I do."

"Good. But don't come back for me. Stupid bunch of idiots, you shouldn't have come here in the first place."

I ignored him and checked the door over, but it was too solid, even for a spelled blade.

"Rylee, I have a few more things to tell you. If you're ready for it," Jack said, coughing again after he spoke.

"Is it bad? Cause honestly, I'm full up with bad shit right now."

I went and sat beside him, found my hand wrapping around his, knowing that again, I was going to lose someone I cared about. Yet he'd only been in my life a few weeks. Not long enough to get this attached, surely. Especially not since he'd avoided and pissed me off at every turn.

His fingers gripped mine. "I should have let you read those damn books."

A shiver of fear tiptoed up my spine and sat on the back of my neck, but I still had to know. "Why?"

"I lied to you."

Dear gods, not again. Men and lies, lately they seemed to be fucking joined at the hip.

He leaned back on his bed. "There is a prophecy that I would train the last Tracker, I've always known that it was true. You are the only one I've ever trained, even a little bit. I don't have much to offer you, only the knowledge of what we are, of how to not get used up. But that doesn't matter.

"You are the last of us, Rylee. You are the one who will stand between the world and the darkness that comes. I've known it from the minute you walked into that fucking hospital room with that bedraggled werewolf. I saw it in both of you, the start of the prophecies coming to light. Even though I couldn't Read you, I knew."

I tried to pull away, but he held my hand tighter than a dying man should have been able to.

"Jack, you are fucking delusional. Just rest." The fear on the back of my neck dug in deep, just like Faris's fangs.

With effort, he sat up until he was looking me right in the face. "I can't Read you. But I can Read all those around you. And their stories, what I see there, all of it points at one thing. You are the center of it, the center of where all the stories sit. Like a bright spot that keeps me from Reading you."

What the hell was I supposed to say to that? Anything?

"Just listen to me, kid. You have so much coming your way, but just follow your heart. That is what you have to do. Hold to what you know is right, no matter what anyone else says."

"Even when it means rescuing an old, stubborn, dying Tracker?" I lifted an eyebrow at him, wanting to change the subject. Needing to. I couldn't be the last Tracker, that wasn't possible. But hadn't I for years thought I was the only Tracker?

He shrugged and slumped back to the pallet. "Perhaps, but was it your heart that brought you here or your need for revenge?"

My jaw tightened. "Did you meet the Child Empress?"

"Briefly. I saw a lot around the kid, even though she was covered up. Death, lots and lots of death and manipulation, but that is true for any vampire no matter how young they are. But you are trying to change the fucking subject. Right now, it's about prophecies. You need to read them, understand them, so when the time comes you have at least an idea of what you're going to be up against."

I scrubbed a hand over my face, thinking that perhaps Jack had a fever, and that he'd lost his marbles in the last few days locked away inside the palace walls. Fuck, anything was possible. But what he was saying couldn't be true. I was no legend in the making. Trackers were just that—Trackers; nothing more.

I stood, and Jack let me go. Pacing the small room didn't help, only made me feel more freaked out. Fuck, this was bad.

"Rylee, the endgame is going to be played out, and you are central to it. Many of your friends are central to it."

"How the fuck am I supposed to take this, Jack?" I shouted, feeling an unfamiliar wash of anxiety sweeping over me.

"Like a fucking Tracker," he shouted back. "You do what you must, you keep your oaths, you save the goddamn world. Stop whining. This is your life, learn to fucking deal with it."

Was he right?

Yes, fuck it all to hell and back, Jack was right. At least about dealing with my life, and probably about the rest too.

But at that moment, I just couldn't handle more shit about the prophecies. I had to worry about saving my ass, Jack, Pamela, and O'Shea. Kill a Child Empress and escape a nest of vampires.

Yeah, I was kind of tied up.

"Later, Jack. Can we talk about this later?"

He threw his cane at me, and I dodged it easily. "You don't fucking know if there will even be a fucking later."

I blew out a sharp breath of air. "If the prophecies are right, there will be a later and we can talk about it then."

With a mutter of some choice expletives, he lay back down on the rough bed. He couldn't really argue with my logic and we both knew it. If he was right, I would have a later. If he was wrong, well, we'd find out soon enough.

I leaned against the far wall, watched Jack slip in and out of sleep, knew that I should probably sit with him, hold his hand. But I couldn't because he would start in on me again.

Why do the prophecies scare you so bad? The words weren't from Blaz, or any other person. They were my own thoughts, scrambling through my head.

Yeah, good fucking question.

More than anything, I wanted to believe I had control over my own life, that fate wasn't forcing me into situations. Manipulating me. Fuck, I hated that more than anything else, and that's what the prophecies felt like, a complete and utter shit-hole of a manipulation.

The day waned, or I assumed it did. I was thirsty, hungry, and tired. I didn't dare close my eyes, and I could do nothing about the other two issues. I wondered about Pamela and O'Shea. Please, gods, let them get out of here. I Tracked Pamela, but she wasn't far away, certainly not as far away as I would have liked. Damn, they were still down here. My guts clenched. I had to believe O'Shea would protect her. Had to.

Late in the day, I knew that they, the guards, pets, whatever the hell they were, would be coming for me soon. Bringing me out for an audience with the Child Empress. My last stand.

When the footsteps echoed to me down the hallway, I went to the door. I tucked the short sword into one of my sheaths and shoved it so that the handle was hidden by my jacket.

The door was flung open and I stepped back, letting them take me. At least this way I would be right in the presence of the Child Empress. This way I had a chance to kill her.

I looked over my shoulder. "I can't be the one the prophecies speak of, Jack. I know I can't be."

He lifted his eyes to mine. "You don't know that."

But I did know that. Because I knew there was no way to fill any prophecies when I was dead.

another hallway to the left. I was very well-behaved, said nothing, and didn't try to get away. I kept track of where they were taking me, memorizing the turns so I could make my way back to Jack.

Assuming I was in one piece after this audience and could make my way back.

The hallway dipped down on a slope, running water trickling along in a miniature river on each side of it. Wall sconces were lit with pitch-covered torches, the droplets of fire and pitch hissing as they fell into the water.

We passed a kitchen and, out the corner of my eye, I caught a glimpse of golden eyes and black fur. Something in me eased, knowing that they hadn't caught O'Shea. And if they hadn't caught him, they hadn't caught Pamela.

Better and better.

My handlers didn't speak, and I didn't try to engage them. Wasn't sure I wanted to. What would I say? Had any good blood lately? So what's it like being a slave to a psycho?

No, none of that would help me, and for once I managed to keep my damn mouth shut.

We dipped lower and lower, and more water trickled along the side of the hallway. Fuck, what would happen if Pamela pulled a power stunt like she'd shown Blaz? She could sink this entire place.

A chill swept along my spine. Yeah, that would be a last ditch effort, used only if we had to.

One more corner and the hallway opened up into a gilded ballroom I'd seen before, in Faris's memory, the first one he'd shown me.

They let me go and shoved me forward. Around the room stood an array of vampires, some I recognized from Faris's memory, though their clothes were far more modern—not so much lace this time around. I dusted off the front of my jacket.

"So, where's the snot-nosed brat that runs this shit hole?" I lifted an eyebrow. "Or is it past her bedtime?"

The general reaction was not one of outrage, but of fear. They pulled back, as if by stepping away from me they wouldn't get caught in any backlash.

I laughed. "Oh please, are you fucking serious? You're scared of a kid?"

A stately vampire, the Old One I'd seen in Faris's memory, the seer of the vampires, stepped forward, dressed in the same thing as before. A long gray silk dress that brushed the floor, her bright-white hair braided back from her face. Hazel eyes sharpened as she moved toward me.

"You mock what you know not."

"I mock everything, Yoda. Get used to it."

Her brows snapped low over her eyes, and I glared back. My guts were clenched into a knot the size of both my fists, sweat trickled down my back and chest, though it was cool in these lower levels. My heart was leaping about inside my chest. Terrified? Yeah, I fucking well was, because for the first time I couldn't see a way out of a situation. Not even with O'Shea and Pamela at my back.

The Old One stared at me, a slow smile ghosting over her lips. "Whoever binds the Tracker to them will be able to seek out the last of the Blood. Those are my words, this is my vision, this is what those who

wish to rule must accomplish. Of course, you would have to be the Tracker who holds the Blood of the Lost."

"Really, did you have to fucking well remind them?" I growled, feeling the room tense around us.

Her grin widened. "Yes, I did. Because I am not sure you can be bound to anyone, Tracker, Immune."

"Good point." I had to fight to keep from stepping away from her. Every instinct I had screamed at me to fight, run, do something. "Anything else you'd like to add?"

"You are afraid."

I arched an eyebrow at her. "Well done, Lady Obvious. You want a fucking medal?"

She banged her cane on the floor, reminding me of Jack. "You, you will either destroy us or save us. Not this Child Empress, the one who has stepped forward, the one they" —she made a sweeping gesture with her cane— "fear."

"You would have Faris lead you?"

She gave the slightest incline of her head. "He is not of the pure blood, but that is better. He is rash, but he is young yet. This Child Empress is barely fanged. An infant unable to control herself or the memories her parents foisted on her."

A murmur rolled around the room and a chime sounded.

"The Child comes." The Old One pointed at the dais that rose up out of the floor, a petite figure on the chair, covered in a gold, gauzy material.

I just couldn't stop myself. "What the fuck, no one told me it was a costume contest."

Again, the gasping murmur went around the room. But I wasn't sure if it was because I was being a foul-mouthed jerk or because additional company had just arrived.

Faris stepped into the room from a doorway across from me. Dressed in black from head to toe, his blond hair was slicked back and his blue eyes were icy with a rage that even I could see this far away from him. Damn, I had to give him props for his timing. His entrance was perfect and his outfit was the complete opposite of the Child Empress's. His eyes flicked over me and he gave me the barest of nods.

Shit, maybe I would be getting out of this fucking mess. Maybe.

The Child Empress stood up, lifting her hands so the gold gauze floated around her. Faris strode forward and no one stopped him, which surprised the hell out of me.

"I have bound the Tracker to me. I will find the Blood; your time on the throne is coming to an end."

The Child Empress didn't answer, except to flick her hand at Faris. A rush of power I could feel, even though it didn't affect me, coursed over the room, crashing into the vampires, throwing even Faris to his knees. So this was why they were afraid. I was the only one left standing, the magic dividing around me like a stone in a river.

Sweet.

I smiled at the Child Empress. "You killed my sister, you little bitch. Know what that means?"

The power rush continued, pinning the vampires hard to the floor. I glanced at Faris who was staring at me, his words echoing to me. "Do not forget your oath."

The bite mark where he'd drawn my blood lit up, the nerves around it dancing a tango. He'd invoked the bite, giving me the speed I'd need to battle this vampire who'd killed Berget, the vampire who would destroy the supernatural world for her own whims. Faris, for all his faults—and fuck he had a lot of them—was right about this.

We couldn't let the Child Empress win.

I ran toward the dais. Three strides and I was there, glaring up at the gold-cloaked vampire, knowing that I had to do it quick. I jerked the short sword from the sheath, the blade catching the light. The Child Empress screamed, high-pitched and full of fear. Her power flowed over me, around me, but it couldn't save her.

"Do not remove her covering!" Faris shouted, his voice pitched with pain. Shit, this little fucker was really doing a number on her own people.

But what did her covering have to do with anything? Would it be like Medusa and her snakes, one look and I'd freeze into stone?

The Child Empress scooted away from me, but I followed easily, booting her in the gut and sending her sprawling over the dais and away from me. Tangled in her stupid gauzy material, she had to rip at it to get away from me. Still, her power strangled her own people, which made no sense. They would help her, wouldn't they?

I turned to look over my shoulder, saw the vampires waiting. But they weren't being held down anymore.

They waited for me to kill the Child Empress.

I was a fucking tool to them. Jaw clenching, I booted the Child again, flipped her over, the gauzy gold material finally tearing free and giving me my first glimpse at her.

Golden blonde hair, brilliant blue eyes, and a face that *couldn't be* stared up at me. Tears streaked her cheeks, and she held a hand out to me in supplication.

"Rylee, please don't kill me." Her voice was older, no longer child-like, but it was hers. The same face I'd seen as I'd walked between death and life. Berget was a vampire; that was what I'd felt when she'd died. Not a true death, but one where she was called back as a blood sucker.

That was what she meant when she'd told me death wasn't the end . . . .

My heart, mind, and soul screamed that this couldn't be, it wasn't happening. I stumbled backward, tripped over the dais, and ended up sprawled on the floor in front of Faris.

He'd known all along. He'd told me not to remove the gauze. He'd bitten me so I would have the speed to kill her. He'd been the one to steal her in the first place.

Rage stole my incredulity. I lunged upward with Jack's sword, the tip catching him along the side of his head, slicing through the skin on his skull.

"You do not understand, Rylee." He held his hands out to me, as if I would give shit about his excuses.

"You mother-fucking bastard!" I didn't think, just swung, using the speed he'd given me with his bite against him. For the first time, Faris wasn't faster than me, and I pummeled him with my fists, my sword slicing into him again and again, though he tried to avoid me. On an equal footing, I was the better fighter, better trained. He was going to die.

I drove the sword into his belly and his hands circled mine. His fingers gripped my wrists, twisting them backward, the crunch of my bones resonating all the way up my arms to my shoulders. I screamed and an answering roar scattered the vampires.

O'Shea loped into the room, Pamela beside him, her eyes as fierce as his.

I had no choice but to let go of the sword, my hands no longer able to grip anything. I snapped a boot up, catching Faris in the jaw and sending him over backward with the blow.

"You do not belong here." Berget's voice drew me back from the rage, but confusion replaced it. I wasn't so sure that was preferable.

I turned to see Berget facing O'Shea and Pamela, but it was Pamela she seemed to be focused on.

Pamela glared back at Berget, so similar in coloring that they looked more like sisters than Berget and I did.

"I'm not leaving until Rylee does," Pamela said, lifting her hands, prepping a spell.

The Child Empress had sent Doran to kill Pamela. Berget was the Child Empress. Clusterfuck didn't even come close to what was happening.

Cradling my arms, gritting my teeth with the jarring every step caused, I ran toward them. Berget lifted her hands, mimicking Pamela, and I knew the power that would flow would kill Pamela, felt it in my gut.

I had to get between them. I had to stop this now. Because if Berget killed Pamela . . . I wasn't sure I could forgive her for that.

"Pamela, don't!" I shouted as I ran, sliding to a stop between them.

Berget's power hit me, dispersed, and I turned to face her.

Her eyes were narrowed with a hatred I couldn't understand. "What the hell are you doing? She can't replace me. I'm your sister. Not her." Berget threw another roll of power at us and again it displaced around me.

"Berget," I shook my head.

"Move, Rylee. It is my right to kill intruders. I rule this place."

O'Shea growled, his lips sliding back over his fangs. I couldn't even lower my hands to touch him, it hurt too badly.

"Is this how it's going to be?" I stared at her, my brain and heart not able to put this together. Berget was a vampire, the Child Empress. Was there anything left of my little sister inside of her? Was what I'd seen as I'd hovered between death and life the real Berget? Was that why she'd said I'd save her?

Her eyes widened, filling with tears, her lips trembling. "You would choose her over me?"

"No. But I can't let you kill her. I can't let you kill either of them."

Berget turned her back. "You need to leave. Take the ones you love more than me and leave."

That was a trip that, for once, I wasn't willing to take. "Fuck off, you spoiled little shit. You're my sis-

ter, and I've searched for you for the last ten years. But I'm fucking well betting you *knew* I was looking for you. Didn't you?"

Her back was still to me, but she nodded. "I did."

"Then don't you give me that bullshit about me loving them more than you. I would have come for you, if I'd known you were here, alive."

Her shoulders slumped. Gods, I wanted to hug her, hold her tight and be grateful she was alive . . . but already I could see that wasn't going to be possible.

And it fucking killed me.

Faris slowly rose to his feet, Jack's sword on the ground beside him. Pamela touched my elbow. Everything around us seemed on pause, waiting on Berget, waiting on her word.

"Let's go."

The Old One stopped us. "You cannot leave. We are not done with you yet."

I glanced at Pamela and she flipped a hand at the Old One, pinning her against the wall.

"Piss off."

"Faris," Berget barked. "You are hereby exiled. I will not die at your hands, not by yours or those of any of your . . . pets."

I didn't turn around, just kept walking. Fuck, fuckity, fuck, fuck. The pain in my wrists had nothing on what streaked through my battered heart. This couldn't be happening.

Focus on one thing at a time. *Get Jack and get your crew the fuck out of here.*

O'Shea let out a growl as we reached the doorway, and I turned to see Faris behind us.

"I'm coming with you," he said, and I felt his power whip through me, my bones that he'd broken snapping back into place with a speed that left the pain just a memory. I flexed my hands.

"You, you're the reason this is happening." I glared at him.

"You won't get out of here alive without me. You think she's really going to just let you go?" His hair was no longer perfectly slicked back, but disheveled from our fight.

I turned to look behind us. Berget's back was to us as she lifted a hand, her fingers flashing in a signal I didn't understand. But by the reaction of the vampires, Faris was right.

Fuck it all to hell and back, the vampire was right.

22

Faris led the way and we raced after him. I still carried the speed his bite had given me, so I picked Pamela up and carried her on my back.

"Jack, we have to get Jack!"

"There is no time," Faris shouted back.

I didn't argue with him, just turned when I hit the intersection and ran to Jack's door. I threw the bolt open. "Pamela, lift him up."

She tried to gather him up, her voice frantic. "I can't. It's like something's blocking me!"

Faris slid to a stop beside us and took Pamela from my back; she let out a squeak until he placed her on his back. "Try now."

Jack rose from the bed, lifted easily now that my Immunity wasn't messing around with Pamela's spell. The old Tracker never twitched, never even opened his eyes. I couldn't decide if this was good or not.

We bolted back to the intersection as the other hallways spit out vampire after vampire. There was no way we could fight them all.

"Run!"

O'Shea and I ran side by side, following Faris as he wove his way through the maze of hallways and intersections. Pamela clung to his back, but her eyes never left me. I didn't blame her for being worried.

We burst through a doorway that led into the Palace proper. How could I tell? The night sky beckoned to us through the barred windows. We were in the armory.

"We have to make a stand here. If we kill enough of them, they will pull back," Faris said, letting Pamela slide from his back.

"Why are you doing this?" Pamela asked him the very question that had been floating around in the back of my head.

"I was bound to my lieges, as all vampires are. They made me do things I'm not proud of. I fought where I could, but I was still forced to do much that they wanted."

I rocked back on my heels. "And then you bit me."

He shook his head. "No, I bit another Tracker." His eyes lingered on me for a moment before sliding back to the door we'd come from. "They're coming. If you are going to grab a weapon, do it now."

Cases of old-school weapons beckoned to me—swords, spears, shields, and lances. All just tucked behind a thin sheet of glass.

The closest case held long-handled lances with wicked curved blades on the end. I smashed my elbow into the glass, the sound of an alarm went off as I reached in and grabbed the lance I had my eye on.

"Pamela, take Jack over there and lay him on the floor. You stand back, hit them where you can," I said, pointing to the far side of the room. She ran to do as

I said, putting her back to the wall, placing Jack in the corner furthest away from what was about to happen. I didn't know what to expect. Would the entire nest of vampires come after us? The door would work as a bottleneck, helping us and hurting them, surely they wouldn't be so stupid as to send everyone after us.

Would they?

I faced the doorway; the sound of my own blood pumping through my veins echoed in my ears, dulled the thump of the running footsteps.

The vampires and their pets erupted out of the doorway in a flash of skin and fangs. Faris grabbed the first one, slamming him into the floor, the vampire's head bursting like a melon. The next vampire or pet, I wasn't sure which, came for me. I spun in a circle, swinging upward with the lance, burying it deep into the creature's throat, removing his head from his shoulders with the single blow. Much as I hated to admit it, even to myself, the bite Faris invoked on me was a freaking godsend, giving me both speed and an increase in strength.

O'Shea was already on his second vampire, the sound of his teeth snapping through bone accompanied only by the scream of the vamp at his mercy. A woman leapt at me, but froze in mid-air, her face a comical twist of consternation. Then she burst into flames, the fire swallowing her in a single flash of heat and leaving behind nothing but a faint dusting of ash floating down.

"Good catch, witch." I didn't dare give Pamela a smile, settling for a thumbs up over my shoulder. The three vamps left facing us slowly withdrew.

O'Shea shook the one he held in his mouth, a rag doll of bones and skin, then threw it at the retreating vamps.

I opened my mouth, the desire to taunt them, to finish them off, something I couldn't stop. Faris moved to my side and slapped his hand over my mouth. "Time to go, Tracker."

I pushed his hand off me and dropped the lance. The weapon wasn't mine, and if I continued to carry it, I would likely use it on Faris. And while he was a real piece of shit, I wasn't sure everything that had happened really was *all* his fault.

Even if I wanted to blame him.

Bypassing the security guards—who were no doubt coming to check on the alarm I'd set off—the four of us, Jack floating along beside us, worked our way up to the roof where, true to his word, Blaz waited. When he saw Faris, his head snaked forward, and he pinned the vampire to the roof top with a single foot.

Why is this vampire here? More than that, why is there a connection between the two of you?

"He invoked a bite so I could kill the Child Empress."

And did you?

"No. I didn't. Let him up, Blaz. For now, he's with us." Fuck, Jack was going to kill me when he woke up. If he woke up. I glanced over at him, took in his skin tone, the uneven rise and fall of his chest. Everything was spinning out of control. This place, it had torn up my life more than I ever could have thought.

I was going to lose Jack too. Tears stung the backs of my eyes.

The old Tracker is sleeping deep, but he isn't dying. Not yet, anyway.

I helped Pamela up onto Blaz's back; she lifted and secured Jack into place and O'Shea leapt up, wedging himself once more between the spurs of Blaz's back. I climbed up, exhaustion sweeping over me. Faris didn't mount up; instead, he did one of his shifts, cutting through the Veil. I had no doubt that he would beat us back to London.

"Let's go." I tapped Blaz's back, rapping my knuckles against his scales.

The dragon leapt from the roof of the palace and swept out across the sea. I looked over my shoulder, at the city lit up in the darkness. Berget . . . gods be damned, how could this be happening?

For once, Blaz didn't respond to my unspoken questions. He left me alone, which was what I wanted.

We flew to where Eve and Alex waited. The Harpy rose in the air when we drew close. She was trying to speak to me, but I ignored her. Alex barked and yipped, waving frantically at us.

I couldn't deal with anyone else's issues right then. Fuck, I couldn't deal with my own, what the hell made me think I would be able to help anyone else?

I was numb, my heart and mind tangled up, confused and shocked at everything that had happened. Had it happened? Maybe it was like some sort of waking dream, a nightmare sent to steal my sanity and break what was left of my heart. I clung to Blaz's back and closed my eyes, but didn't sleep.

Blaz kept silent through the flight, Pamela fell asleep at some point, and as the sun rose behind us, London came into sight.

I will drop you at Jack's home. I see it in your head as the place you wish to go.

"Thanks," I whispered, my voice carried away by the wind rushing around us.

Blaz circled low, landing out by the pond where the Beast had nearly taken me. So much had happened between then and now, it seemed a preference to have the Beast on my ass than the truths I tried to deal with now. Or not deal with, as the case was.

Everyone dismounted. I sent Pamela into the house with Jack. Eve landed and Alex bounded over to me, grabbing me around the legs.

"Rylee, Rylee, Rylee. Safe now?"

I scrubbed my hands over his head, scratching behind his ears. "Yeah, we're safe now."

"Yippity!" He yelped, flipping over backward and racing toward the house after Pamela. The distant sound of Pamela rebuking him for running into her drifted back to us.

"Thanks, Blaz. You know how to find me when you want to cash in your favor," I said, feeling strangely formal. But maybe it was just easier than breaking down in front of him, because at that moment it was all I wanted to do.

I couldn't keep doing this by myself. Who did I have to help me, to turn to when I couldn't keep it together anymore? O'Shea bumped his head into my hand and I closed my eyes. The truth hurt more than anything else. O'Shea like this was better than not at all, but it wasn't enough. My thoughts drifted to Will. No, I couldn't do that, didn't have it in me to be disloyal to O'Shea with him here beside me. Even if he was trapped as a wolf.

I needed someone who could stand with me, I needed a partner. Not the lost children who were drawn to me, but an actual partner.

Do not be afraid to cry, Rylee. You must let this out. It will eat you up from the inside, hollowing you until there is nothing left. Until you are good for no one.

"Shut the fuck up, Blaz!" I spun on my heel, let the anger fuel me. That emotion was far more familiar, far easier to deal with than the emotional overload that seemed determined to grab me in its clutches.

Blaz snorted, then launched into the air, winging back toward his lair.

Goodbye, Tracker.

"Goodbye, Blaz."

Eve hopped over to me. "Rylee, are we staying here?"

"I don't know." I brushed past her, heading toward the house. "Go rest, Eve. Please."

"Rylee, what's wrong?"

"Eve, not now." Gods, it was taking everything I had not to snap at her as I had at Blaz.

But unlike Blaz, Eve listened. Walking alongside me, she was a silent support. We reached the main doors and she hopped into the air to go and roost on the roof.

I paused, feeling like an ass. O'Shea was right there beside me. I put a hand on his head. Maybe things wouldn't be so bad. I pushed the door open and we headed toward the library, where I thought I could be alone for a minute or two. I just needed to deal with what had happened. Deal with it, and then I could move on.

Right.

Of course, I'd forgotten a few minor details.

Like the fact that Doran was here. O'Shea and I stepped into the library to see the Shaman standing with his back to the open window, the red curtains swirling out and around him. Which, in and of itself, wouldn't have been too bad except that Faris choose that moment to show up, cutting through the Veil as we walked in.

He saw Doran and, without a word, lunged toward him.

Pamela and Alex ran in, no doubt hearing all the excitement, and Alex promptly threw up on the rug. She lifted her hands to prep a spell and the two blood-suckers careened around the room, sending books and furniture flying.

Yeah, all in the space of about three minutes.

I couldn't do this anymore. I turned my back on them, left the room. If they wanted to kill each other, so be it.

Doran screamed for me. "Rylee, he's going to kill me!"

I stood outside the door just feeling . . . done. Then I looked down at O'Shea, who was still at my side. Doran was the one person who might be able to help me bring O'Shea, the man, back. I steeled myself one last time, then turned and headed back into the library to see Faris holding Doran against the wall.

"Faris. I need Doran."

"He is a pet of *hers.*"

"He's not, he took blood from me. Before I left." Gods, could nothing be simple anymore. "Play nice boys or I'll kill you both."

The Daywalker and the vampire stared at me, like they weren't sure I was being serious. Alex was cringing in the corner, making sure not to look at the puddle of vomit he'd left on the floor. Pamela stood there, her eyes on me. Waiting for a signal.

"Doran, come take a look at O'Shea. And you better fucking well tell me you can bring him back or maybe I'll let Faris do what he wants with you."

Faris let Doran down and the Daywalker made his way over to me, his green eyes shadowed. "You don't seem yourself."

"Just look at O'Shea." I pointed at the wolf at my side, in case he hadn't noticed the massive black wolf with the silvery gold eyes.

Doran ran a hand over the area above O'Shea's head, but never touched him. "He's becoming a Guardian." His eyes flicked up to mine. "But you knew that, didn't you?"

"Yes."

A few minutes of this air touching and I was about ready to shake the Daywalker until his fangs fell out.

"I'm not sure. I think maybe, but I can't tell. He has to want to come back, I think," Doran said, still staring at O'Shea.

"What do you mean he has to *want* to?"

"There are two parts of him, and the man in him is buried deep. If he doesn't want to come back badly enough, the wolf will be all that's left."

Every muscle in my chest tightened with a fear that I'd been holding at bay all this time. "How long?"

Doran shrugged. "A week at most. Maybe less."

I closed my eyes, feeling the loss for what it was. I'd had O'Shea with me for days now. Why hadn't he wanted to come back when he was right with me?

Maybe he didn't want to come back to me. Maybe he was happier as a wolf.

Faris snorted. "He can't be brought back. He's been too long in wolf form. When the collar came off it was a matter of seconds before he glazed over. The backlash is too much for him."

I went very still. "You were there, when the collar was taken off?"

O'Shea growled and inched toward Faris.

"Wait." I held up my hand. "Are you telling me *you* took off the collar, knowing what would happen?"

Faris smiled at me, and for a second, I thought maybe I'd been wrong. That had been Milly's doing, that she had taken the collar off.

"Yes, I took it off him. You are not for the wolf, Rylee. You will belong to me. I must bind you to me if I am to take the throne from Berget. There is no other way and I won't have a wolf—"

"Don't you fucking well use her name in front of me!"

Gods help me; Faris, how could I have ever trusted him? Even for a second? He'd lied to me time and time again. He wasn't in this for anyone but himself. That much was apparent.

"Get the fuck out of here, vampire. The next time I see you, I will kill you."

Faris was on me in a flash, our bodies slamming into the far wall with a thud that knocked books from the shelves. I tipped my head sideways, an invitation for him that he couldn't resist. It would blind him to what I was going to do to him.

His fangs drove into my neck, his desire for my blood making him stupid. I held out my hand. Doran tossed me a silver letter opener from the side table. I caught it and drove it deep into Faris's neck.

He yanked back from me, his teeth tearing a ragged wound across my neck. I jerked the silver letter opener out and jammed it in again. Faris stumbled back from me and O'Shea placed himself between us.

"Do we understand each other?" I asked, my voice even and calm.

He snarled at me, coughed on a mouthful of blood. "You don't understand, and I'm bloody well done trying to explain. I won't be there to pull your ass out of the fire again, Tracker."

"Fuck you too." I tossed the letter opener back to Doran, who wiped it off on his pants and set if back on the side table.

Faris turned, stepped sideways and jumped the Veil. I watched him closely, could almost see how he did it this time. If only I could pull that trick . . . not that it would get us all home.

Doran approached me, lifting his hand to my neck. "You need to get this stitched. It's going to be quite a scar when it heals, even with my stitches."

Jack stepped into the room, surprising me. He tottered toward us and I wondered if how he'd been looking in the dungeons had been an act. He'd certainly perked back up quickly.

"I'll get the thread and needle, you stay here." The old Tracker said as he left the room before he'd ever really come in.

Doran cleared his throat. "Why did you let him bite you? You know it only deepens the chance he *will* be able to bind you to him."

"Because he is no different than anyone else. Everyone wants something from me, and with Faris, it's my blood. It makes him weak." I lifted my eyes to Doran's, let him see a side of me I didn't share easily. I was so done. The shattering truths that had been exposed to me had knocked the stuffing out of me more than any knock-down, drag-out fight could have.

Jack was right, I'd not really given much credence to what he'd said before I'd left to find O'Shea. Everyone wanted something from me, and I was fucking tired of it.

So fucking tired.

Jack came back with the needle and thread, and Doran stitched me up. But again the emptiness swallowed me up and their voices seemed far away, distant and out of focus.

I interacted with them on the surface. I could see they were worried, that they all knew something was wrong with me. But I couldn't explain it and didn't want to try.

Days passed and the darkness that lay heavy on me dug in deeper and deeper. I existed, I ate, and I didn't sleep. I spoke with the others, but something was deeply wrong, like when the Hoarfrost demon's poison had stolen my ability to function. This was the same, only worse, because I knew there was nothing I could do to fix it. The darkness and hurt, grief and pain were a part of me.

Pamela tried to get me to help work with her, Alex tried to get me to play tag, and Eve offered to fly me along the coast.

Only O'Shea didn't ask anything of me. His eyes seemed to have stopped shifting and were a pale gold, so pale that in certain lights they did look silver.

Deanna came over, tried to help O'Shea, but like Doran, there was nothing she could do.

Four days had passed, four days of waiting and not knowing what to do next. Waiting for Doran to say all of O'Shea was gone.

I lay on my bed, staring up at the ceiling. Alex lay on the floor beside me, his head resting on the edge of the bed. His eyes were sad and every once in a while, he'd let out a whimper, reach out, and touch me with the tip of his claw.

O'Shea lay beside me on the bed, his nose buried in the crook of my neck. I wanted things I couldn't have, comfort that apparently I wasn't allowed.

I threw my arm over my eyes, hating the way my eyes burned with unshed tears. Hated the weakness in me.

Someone knocked on the door, and then slowly opened it.

"Rylee, I know I told you to let her go. But maybe I was wrong. You need someone who knows you better than you know yourself right now . . . and I don't fucking well know you that well. Track her, maybe she can help you where none of us can." The door clicked shut, and Jack left me alone with my boys.

My heart clenched and the tears I'd been holding back threatened to break the damn. I blew out a sharp breath, sniffed back the tears, and Tracked Giselle. I couldn't feel her body—there, way far to the west at home in North Dakota—but I knew it was there.

But that wasn't what I wanted. I needed the woman who I would always think of not only as my mentor, but as the mother I'd needed, the woman who trained me, and taught me to stand for myself. She knew me, knew my heart, knew my strengths and my weaknesses. I wasn't sure there was anyone who knew me better. I reached for her, Tracking her spirit, or at least trying to. Maybe she was gone, truly gone, and I couldn't reach her. Or maybe like O'Shea, she just didn't want to be with me.

That was it. I couldn't hold it back anymore. The tears that I'd held at bay for so long, I couldn't stop them. Curling onto my side, away from O'Shea, I sobbed into my pillow. One person could only be asked to take so much pain and I was done.

I was just fucking well done.

His mate needed him. Her body shook with grief and sadness that welled out of her like a spring. Like it would never stop. The half creature stood and nosed her. She pushed him away, gently, but away.

The half creature frowned, a tear slipping from his eye. He was hurting for her too. The wolf hopped off the bed and nosed the half creature, directing him to the door. Sniffling, tears streaking down his furred face, he reluctantly opened the door and then closed it behind him.

The wolf went back to her, his mate, and jammed his nose into her face, licking her tears away. She tried to push him away too, but he persisted, forcing her to acknowledge him.

Her arms finally slipped around his neck.

"Liam, I need you, please . . . please don't leave me here alone." Her words were broken with her pain, broken with her fears.

A sharp stab ripped up through his guts and a memory of what he had been floated to the surface. A man. He'd been a man. That was what she needed. The wolf whined and backed away.

She needed him to be both. The wolf to protect her body. The man to protect her heart and her soul.

He shook his head, whined again. But that would mean going back, that would mean giving up his freedom. It would mean trusting the man in him to be strong enough . . . .

His eyes never left her, the shake of her body; the soft sobs escaping her lips. Swallowing hard, the wolf knew that this was the moment.

He was either her mate in truth or he had to leave her, and let her find another who could be all she needed.

I couldn't stop the tears. Maybe that was a good thing; maybe I needed to let it out, like Blaz had said.

O'Shea had licked my face, tried to get me to stop, but he couldn't understand that this was why I hadn't wanted to let loose, to let the grief overtake me. That I was afraid of the pain, and would rather have my body broken and bleeding than my heart.

Distantly, I knew that perhaps this was more than just the grief and the pain, this was a type of shock, the things I'd seen I couldn't un-see . . . gods, why did it have to be Berget? I'd sworn an oath to Faris that I would kill the Child Empress. An oath that I couldn't break, I'd sworn it on the blood of the lost, and I suspected that if I didn't fulfill the oath, something very bad would happen.

O'Shea let out a low, pain-filled groan. I rolled over, expecting to see him, the wolf him, flat out on the floor.

Not the man him. The O'Shea I'd first known, crouched, his knees bent, his dark hair hanging long, brushing his broad shoulders. He tipped his head up, his pale, silvery-golden eyes the same as the wolf's, no longer the deep, dark eyes he'd been born with. He didn't quite have a beard, but it was close.

We stared at each other, shock rippling through me.

Liam. I didn't realize I'd said his name until his arms were around me, pinning me to his chest.

"I'm here. I'm here."

I sobbed into his shoulder, clung to him and didn't care how needy I might seem. For once, I couldn't be the strong one. For once, I had someone to hold me.

"How? I don't understand . . . ."

He pulled back a little, his one hand stroking the side of my face, tucking my hair behind my ears. "I don't know. You needed me. I think that was enough."

"I needed you long before now."

"But you never said it. I think . . . I needed to know that I wasn't just another one of your wards, someone who needed you—I needed to know that you needed me too. My wolf needed you to want him as an equal, not a dependent."

I leaned my forehead against his, let my hands trace his body, up over his shoulders, his neck, and the sides of his face. I could hardly believe this was real, that this moment wasn't a dream, that I would wake from and be left staring at a wolf, and not a man sleeping beside me.

With my eyes closed, I was more than a little afraid to open them again, to see that my fears had been brought to life.

"Liam, don't do that again, don't disappear," I whispered, reveling in the way his hands stroked my back, slid down to my waist and then worked their way up to my shoulders. Gods, I had missed him.

"Only if you don't call me O'Shea anymore. Just Liam from now on." He gave me a soft grin, and I hiccupped back another sob, fighting of the building emotions in my chest.

His lips found mine, and at first it was a soft kiss, a sweet, gently soothing kiss. His lips pressed against mine, moved to my cheek, kissed away the last vestiges of my tears. But that wasn't what I wanted or needed. I needed him to be with me, really with me, to claim me for what I was to him.

My tongue darted out, dipped into his mouth, and I pressed myself against him. A low rumble rolled out of him and he kissed me back, wild and fiercer than I remembered. But right. This was right.

A moment of understanding hit me. We'd been waiting for each other all along, waiting for this moment of rightness. That was why he'd not been able to let Berget's case go. Why I couldn't just kill him even when there had been moments I could have, why I'd tried to help him when his eyes had been opened to the supernatural. Why even the mere thought of losing him completely had made me more than a little bit crazy. Why I'd chosen him over Berget. And would choose him over Berget again if I had to. With Liam, there was no choice, he would always come first.

He tore at my clothes, ripping them off me, t-shirt tearing like tissue paper. I helped him, shimmying out of my jeans, feeling my panties rip as he jerked them off my hips. His lips made a trail of fire from my mouth to my neck, lower to my aching breasts, lower yet to the juncture of my thighs. I arched into him, reaching up to grab the bed frame as he mouthed me. Not just pleasure, that was too mild a word. Between us, there was a connection, a bond of understanding that had nothing to do with forcing a bond on each other as Faris would do. Or even what had happened with Blaz.

Liam was with me because he wanted to be, and I was with him because there was no one else who understood me and loved me the way he did.

Another rumble slipped out of him, the vibration snaking through my core and tipping me over the edge of pleasure.

I couldn't stop the noises I made; didn't care who heard them.

Until the door opened.

"Rylee, are you all right?" Pamela's voice ended in a squeak, and then Liam was flung off me and slammed into the wall.

"Shit, Pamela. Stop!" I yelped, grabbing the sheets and wrapping them around me.

"He was hurting you . . . I heard you scream. Where's O'Shea, he's supposed to be protecting you?" She had her hands up, ready to thump Liam again.

I glanced over my shoulder, expecting to see a very pissed off werewolf. Nope. He was laughing. Bent over at the waist, laughing so hard his shoulders shook.

"Please tell me you don't want kids." He managed to spit out.

Apparently I made a face, because Pamela shot a glare at me. "Who is this?" And then her eyes widened and she took a good look at him, his dark hair and pale gold eyes.

"Is this O'Shea?" She stumbled back, her face going bright red right up to her hair line.

"Liam, meet Pamela; Pamela, meet Liam. Now get out." I shoved her out the door, locking it behind her.

There was a distant pattering of feet, no doubt to run off and tell everyone what she'd seen. Good grief, how much had she seen?

Liam's arms came up around from behind me, his body fitting against mine. "Well, I suppose it could have been worse."

"Yeah, how so?"

"Could have been Milly walking in on us. She would have asked to stay and join in."

He nipped my shoulder and I spun to stare at him, shocked he would make light of what had happened with Milly. Laughing, he scooped me up and then tossed—yes tossed—me onto the bed. "I do believe we were interrupted, and just as I was getting to the good part."

I lay there on the bed, staring up at him, gratitude and love flowing over me. I had him back, and this time there would be no letting go of him. This time, there would be no separating us, not for anything. Or anyone.

He slid on top of me, his hands and lips, tongue and teeth re-learning my every curve. I groaned, unable to stop touching him. I grabbed his ass and pulled him into me, gasping at the thickness of him as we rocked together.

"Rylee, this isn't a race," he murmured into my ear.

"I don't feel you slowing down."

He chuckled, and then kissed me, as I slid my legs around his hips, locking my ankles together, riding the sweet rhythm that pulsed between us. More than the physical connection, there was something more, something I hadn't ever had. An understanding, a completion of my heart and where it belonged. With him, with Liam.

"Rylee," he whispered my name, nothing else, just my name and the tears started up again. I couldn't stop them, no more than I could earlier, but this time, it wasn't the pain of loss, but the bittersweet knowledge that the rest of my life would be like this. Stolen moments of love, laughter, and life fitting in the tight spots between the death, pain, and loss. This was my future, not prophecies, not fate. Liam, this moment and all that it represented was everything I never knew I even wanted, and yet now I had.

Within all the darkness of my life, I had found the brilliant spot of light that pushed away the shadows. Even if just for a moment of two.

He kissed my tears away. "Let it out, you've got to let it out. That much I've learned. Holding it in will only make you crazy."

So I cried and we made love, spending the night in each other's arms. Not speaking much, except to speak words of love, just living. Breathing.

Healing.

I woke up in the early hours, well before dawn, before any light crept in through the big window. A nightmare, intense and lingering, stealing any rest I had managed. Berget, Berget haunted my mind, an abscess of pain that at some point would need to be purged. Anxiety hummed along my synapses, and a sheen of sweat coated my lower back. I rolled to my side, sheets sliding down over my bare hip, baring my overheated skin to the cool air.

Liam slept flat on his belly, face turned to the side, dark hair unruly and curling over his cheek. I brushed it back, and he mumbled in his sleep, words that made no sense, and yet my heart thumped harder in recognition. Without waking, he reached for me as he rolled to his side, and pulled me into his arms, facing him. I pressed my cheek against his chest, listened to his heartbeat steady and strong. His arms tightened around me, so that there was no space between us; our bodies flush against one another. Peace, pure and soothing, flowed from him into me, calming the anxiety and pushing back the nightmare that had followed me into the waking world.

"Go back to sleep, Rylee." He mumbled into my hair, his breath shifting the strands around my ear.

I curled in tighter to him, sliding an arm across his hip, feeling the scar where the Guardian had clawed him, where Alex had infected him. Safe in his arms, I closed my eyes, and let my fears go. In that moment, with him I knew that we were both where we finally belonged.

With a sigh, I lifted my face to his without opening my eyes and kissed him softly.

"You are the best thing in my life."

He kissed me back, murmuring against my lips.

"Love, go to sleep. Because I have no doubt that tomorrow, something will crawl up and into your life that you or I will have to kill."

I chuckled against his skin. "You know me too well."

"That I do. That I do."

23

Liam watched her sleep, traced the scars on her body with his fingers in the early morning light. She'd brought him back from the wildness that the wolf had kept him tied with.

He let out a sigh, a smile tipping up the edges of his lips. Everything seemed simple now, an illusion for sure, if he knew Rylee's life at all. They were together, as it should have been for a hell of a lot longer than it was, and between the two of them, they would take care of things. Of their pack. Again, his lips quirked upward.

Their pack. Laughing softly to himself, he stood and searched around the room. There were no clothes that would fit him, so he settled for a towel, wrapping it around his waist. His nudity wasn't really an issue, though he suspected that the others in the house might not appreciate him strutting through in the buff.

His memories as a wolf were strange, disjointed. More about scents than anything else. Liam stepped out of the room, stepped over Alex sleeping by the door.

Much as he knew it was the werewolf's fault he now carried the virus, he couldn't really be angry at him. Alex was important to Rylee, and even Liam could admit that he liked the werewolf's antics, saw the joy he brought into their lives like nothing else could. He crouched down, scrubbed the back of Alex's ears.

"Hey, want to go for a run later?"

Alex blinked sleepily up at him. "Yuppy doody, Boss."

Liam stood and strode down the hallway, freezing when he caught the scent of a witch. His head knew it was probably little Pamela, but the wolf in him wasn't so sure. Moving very slowly, he worked toward the scent, tried to calm himself as he went. He would have to be careful around the young witch, making sure he didn't lash out, that the wolf didn't try to take control again. With his back against the wall, he slid down the hallway, the scent of witch intensifying.

There was more than one.

He wanted to shift, slide back into the wolf form. Fear grabbed at him. If he did, would he be able to shift back? He thought about Rylee, lying in bed, needing him. Not because of what he could do for her, but just needing him, for whom he was.

He dropped the towel and shifted into the wolf, the change taking him quickly and with ease. This time was different, though; he, Liam, was still in charge. The wolf was his now, not the other way around.

Creeping forward, his nose far more sensitive in this form, he picked up scent he would know anywhere.

Milly.

He fought the urge to go running toward the witch, tackle her to the ground and tear her throat out. If she was here, then she needed something, she was here to take something from them.

Trotting, he made his way the library door and peered in. Milly had her back to the doorway and she was reaching up, her hands lingering on the different books on the shelves.

How the hell was he going to stop her? A soft snuffle of a child's tears brought his head around. Pamela was tied up in a spell, her arms and legs splayed out against the wall.

He couldn't do this on his own. Spinning, he ran back to Rylee.

I was dreaming that Liam was back, that he had held me all night while I cried out the tears I'd been saving up. That his touch and heart had healed the worst of the wounds I had. I stretched in the bed, reaching out to find an empty spot, still warm where he'd lain.

Sitting up, I scrubbed my hands through my hair. The door creaked open and Alex crab-stepped into the room.

"Rylee better?" His eyes were full of uncertainty and maybe even a little bit of fear. I smiled at him.

"Yes, I'm better."

"Boss good too?" He lifted his eyebrows.

I knew he didn't mean . . . "Yes, the Boss is good too." Very, very good.

The door pushed open and Liam, wolf Liam, stepped in the room, shifting with a spooky ease back to human.

"Milly is here. She has Pamela spelled in the library."

"Fucking hell." One full day, just one freaking day was all I wanted.

I didn't have any weapons, and I hadn't bothered to pick through Jack's extensive collection. I jerked on a shirt and my pants.

"Alex, go get Doran. Quickly!"

Alex saluted and ran out of the room. Liam shifted back to wolf form. At least I knew he could shift back and forth now.

I ran out of the bedroom, down the hallway, and skidded to a stop just inside the door.

Milly was bent over several of the tomes that Jack had hidden from me. In particular, the black demon book, and the violet-skinned blood of the lost.

"What the fuck do you think you're doing?"

Her head jerked up. "I needed the information in these. I need to borrow them."

I couldn't stop my mouth from dropping open. "Are you bat-shit crazy? This isn't a fucking library and we aren't friends anymore." I moved sideways, touched Pamela, and the spell on her disintegrated, dropping her to the floor.

"I'm sorry," the kid said. "I thought I could take her on my own."

Milly snorted. "Training will always win out."

I walked over to her, ignoring the look of fear on her face. Yeah, I would kill her one day, but even I wasn't cold enough to kill a woman who was with child. Shit, it would have been easier if I were that cold.

"You can't have those books. End of story." I yanked the Black one out of her hands and shoved the

Violet one, pushing it off the table. If she wanted it bad enough, she'd have to turn her back on me.

She tipped her chin up and tried to look down her nose at me. "I chained your wolf once, I could do it again."

Liam let out a snarl that filled the room with a menace even Milly couldn't miss.

"You think reminding him of that is a good idea?" I stared at her, wondering how she'd gotten in here without anyone noticing. "You've been watching Faris jump the Veil, haven't you?"

She didn't answer me, just spun, flicked her hand, and the violet-covered book shot to her hand. I lunged toward her. "Milly!"

She ignored me, and jumped through a slice of the Veil to the gods only knew where. It didn't matter, not really. Her time would come soon enough.

Doran and Alex showed up about thirty seconds too late.

"She's ducked out already?" Doran walked across the room and picked up the black bound book. "Was this what she was after?"

I nodded, dread filling me. "She got the violet-covered one."

Liam shifted, moving to stand behind me, naked but seemingly unashamed.

Doran grinned at us, eyes sparkling. "Well, well, well. What have we here? Rylee, I can see why you were so loyal."

Liam leaned down and kissed my neck, right where the stitches were ready to come out, but his eyes stayed on Doran.

The Daywalker laughed and lifted his hands. "No need to mark your territory, Guardian. I know who she belongs with. It's Faris you're going to have to watch, not me."

A growl slipped out of Liam. "Faris is not going to survive our next encounter."

Doran snorted and waved at him. "Listen, you go and shave that crazy beard and get a shower in while I chat with Rylee."

I shook my head. "No, wait here; I'll get you some clothes, Liam. Try not to kill each other."

I left the men there, trotted down the hallway, and worked my way through the mansion to the other side where Jack's quarters were. I knocked softly on his door.

"Go the fuck away."

"Jack, I need some clothes."

There was a muffled thump and then the door swung open. Jack glared at me. "Clothes? What the fuck do you need my clothes for?"

"Liam."

His tri-colored blue eyes widened, and for the first time, I saw him shocked. He grabbed a set of sweat pants and an over sized t-shirt. I took them and ran back to the library, leaving a cursing Jack behind.

Doran and Liam sat across from each other. Liam had the brown book of prophecies in front of him, and Doran had the red. I handed Liam the clothes and he slipped them on. We spent the next three hours reading through the books, making an attempt to find what Milly had wanted. I took the black book, and read through the demon prophecies.

"Shit, I'm going to have nightmares tonight." I pushed the book at Jack. Pamela was sticking close, as was Alex, who seemed to have decided that Liam was the freaking cat's pajamas. Alex had his head on Liam's knee, eyes flicking up every once in a while to see if Liam was paying him any attention.

It took me a while, but I finally figured it out. Liam was the first werewolf that had accepted Alex for what he was. Alex finally had a pack member just like him. Fuck, it made me love Liam even more at how easily he'd forgiven Alex for turning him. Then again, it hadn't been just Alex's saliva that had caused the problems.

"If you don't quit making googly eyes at him, I'm going to puke," Doran said, but he was smiling, his eyes laughing.

"You shut up over there or I'll ship you back to Berget." The room went very still and I let took a deep breath, letting it out slowly. "Let it go, I can freaking well crack a joke about my psycho sister if I want to."

Doran just shook his head. "Don't joke about that. I am eternally in your debt, which is a long time for someone like me. She carries not only her own memories, but the abilities and powers of both her adoptive parents. Which is part of the problem. She cannot handle all those memories and all that power. She is not to be trifled with."

Jack leaned back, contemplative. "What about pied? We could fucking pie her, instead of trifle."

Doran's jaw dropped, and I laughed at his expression. "That's an awful pun, Jack. I like it."

That night, after making sure Pamela and Alex were settled, I made my way up to the rooftop to spend some time with Eve. I'd not been kind to her and I needed to make amends.

She eyed me warily and I waved her over. "I'm better. I'm sorry for the way I treated you, for pushing you so hard when you were hurt."

"You didn't push me, Rylee. I want to help. I just don't know my own limits yet. When I have a chance, I'd like to train with Eagle again. I think I could still learn much from him."

"Of course. I think that would be great." I reached up and touched her wings. "Thank you, Eve. You are the best Harpy I've ever known."

"What happened to you?" She ducked her head so she could look me right in the eye. "Something changed."

Liam stepped out of the doorway and Eve saw him before I could answer. With a screech, she ran a hopping, wing flapping run over to him, dancing around him. "You're back! I knew you were strong enough. I just knew it! Anyone who can fall off a Harpy and survive is tough enough to survive anything."

He made his way over to my side as Eve launched into the air, circling around several times before soaring higher, using the thermals to lift her out of sight and behind the clouds, screeching her excitement into the wind.

"I didn't think I'd made that much of an impression on your crew," he said, moving up to stand beside me.

"You're a part of our family. They've missed you. Or maybe just missed the fact that you can get away with yelling at me when they can't."

He laughed softly. "Not a family. It's more than that. A pack." He slipped an arm around my waist.

ABOUT THE AUTHOR

Shannon Mayer is the *USA Today* bestselling author of the Rylee Adamson novels, the Elemental series, and numerous paranormal romance, urban fantasy, mystery, and suspense novels. She lives in the southwestern tip of Canada with her husband, son, and numerous other animals.

COMING MARCH 2017 FROM TALOS PRESS

BLIND SALVAGE

A Rylee Adamson Novel
Book 5

"My name is Rylee and I am a Tracker."

When children go missing, and the Humans have no leads, I'm the one they call. I am their last hope in bringing home the lost ones. I salvage what they cannot.

Crossing into Ogre country is dangerous when you're a polite, respectful gal. Which means I already know I'm in for a wild ride, despite the backup I've brought along.

Even when things start to go sideways, and enemies close on us from every side, I still believe we have the upper hand.

How very blind can one person be when it comes to a salvage?

$7.99 mass market paperback
978-1-940456-99-7

AN EXCERPT FROM *BLIND SALVAGE*

Liam screamed my name as the giant's hand closed around us. Ignoring Liam was hard, but I had to. I had to focus. Before the log-sized fingers curled tight on me, I yanked my swords free and slashed upward with them, cutting through the giant's fingers. Two fell off; two others were left hanging by tendons and ligaments, blood spurting out around us.

Squealing like a two-story stuck pig, the giant dropped us. Falling, I realized—belatedly—that we were a hell of a lot higher up than I'd thought. I hit the ground with a solid thud, and the crack of my ribs filled my ears as I slammed into a barely protruding rock. *That* was going to leave a mark. Alex rolled across the ground beside me, snarling up at the giant.

"Stinky nasty bugger. No touching Ryleeeeeeeee!"

Hands jerked me to my feet. "Rylee?" Liam was trying to help; I know he was. But I couldn't breathe, and pain shot through my middle, a band of red-hot knives jabbing into me with each tiny bit of movement. I forced myself to shove him away, to stand on my own. If he knew how badly I was hurt, he'd try to carry me too.

"Go. We have to go," I managed to gasp out.

Far too slowly for my taste, Liam led now, Alex limped along beside me, and somewhere in the next ten steps I found the ability to breathe again. Broken ribs were a bitch at any time, but when trying to outrun a massively hungry and fingerless peeved giant—well, let's just say I could have done without.

The slam of the giant's foot into the ground scooted us forward faster yet, and my ribs protested yet again, stealing my ability to breathe. We were just twenty feet from the open arch of the castle entrance way. Pamela pushed herself off Liam's back and turned to face the giant. The look on her face was one I was beginning to know all too well.

Eyes narrowed, chin tipped up, she lifted her hands and flung them toward the giant. Two fireballs erupted from her fingertips, hitting the giant in the chest.

Damn, I wish I'd thought about that . . . nope, never mind. The giant patted the fire out, almost calmly, and then snarled at us. His jagged teeth had hunks of flesh and armor clinging to them, and from between them protruded a thick, long tongue that he used to clean his own face with in single lick.

"Fuck, that is nasty," I spit out, along with a gob of blood. "Move it, Pam. Your fireballs are just pissing him off. Just get inside. I don't think he can follow."

"What? Why not?"

"Giants aren't real smart and as soon as we're out of sight, we're out of mind."

Gods, I hoped that my memory was right. Grabbing her by the arm, I ran as fast as my labored breathing would allow into what I hoped would be the safety of the castle.

Right, I'd forgotten for a moment about the creatures we'd not been able to identify, a part of me hoping Pamela had taken them all out.

The creatures that had been firing on us were not trolls or ogres.

They were gods-be-damned big-ass red caps. I did a fast count. There were at least twenty red caps. Two arms, two legs, built like a man, but their faces looked as if they had been smashed with a shovel, flat with just slits for noses, and no lips to cover their blocky square teeth. Each of them was close to seven feet tall, carried a wicked iron pike, had heavy iron boots, and then there was their namesake. On each of their heads was a cap made of some sort of viscera, blood from the organ poured down the sides of their heads, and stained their skin a rusty brown.

"We can't outrun them," I said, as I slowed to a stop.

Liam grabbed my arm. "Yes, we can—"

"No, we can't," I snapped. "They can't be outrun, not on their own turf, at least."

The red caps started pounding the butt of their pikes into the ground at their feet, each thump bringing them a step closer. They had ringed us. From what I knew of them, which wasn't a lot, we were in for a fight. Trained warriors who bathed themselves in the blood of their victims. Yeah, not really how I wanted to start my week. Freaking stupid Mondays.

"Pamela, to my back." Thank the gods I'd been training her. She responded without question, pressing her back into mine. Alex tucked his butt in next to mine.

Liam didn't question, just slid his back against ours.

"Head shots, people," I said, my words calmer than I felt. Twenty red caps was no small feat to take on at the best of times.

As if in response, as I steadied my stance, something shifted inside of me, and one of my ribs pressed against my right lung. Shit, this was about to get tough.

Their pikes still thumping into the ground, the red caps were twenty feet away in all their blood and viscera glory. This close they looked like Dox on steroids, all muscle and small beady black eyes, bloodstained skin, with armor stretched taut over their bodies. My guts churned; injured, I was going to be more of a liability than a help in this particular situation. As if to drive the point home, pain rippled sharp and intense through my chest.

Four red caps engaged us, and I spun my swords out, crisscrossing them to catch the downward blow of a pike. The red cap forced me to my knees, the stone biting through my jeans. Alex leapt forward, snagging the red cap's belt and yanking him off balance.

The red cap spun toward Alex, giving me his back. Thinking I was the weaker of the two of us. Perfect. He snapped his pike back in order to drive it into Alex's side, but I beat him to the punch.

I drove my sword through the base of his neck, then yanked the blade to the left, beheading the big fucker before he could complete his swing.

"Good job, Alex."

Alex blew a raspberry at the red cap. "Bloody stupid messy bugger."

Yeah, he'd definitely picked up the local lingo.

"Hmm. A pack." I wasn't going to argue with him, not over something like this. I was pretty sure there was going to be a lot to argue about in the future. Sure, things were good now, but we were both too pig-headedly stubborn to back down, even from each other.

"What now?" Liam moved so that he was behind me, his lips against my ear. "What's the next step?"

Gods, if only I knew the answer to that, I'd be a Reader like Jack or Giselle.

Milly was pregnant, had stolen the violet book—a book Jack hadn't wanted even me to read.

Faris was as twisted and untrustworthy as any vampire I'd ever known, and he was back on the shit list where he belonged. Where I should have left him from the first moment I'd met him.

Berget . . . that was where things got confusing. She was still my sister, but I realized now that she was gone outside of my grasp for good. The Child Empress had tried to kill Pamela, had set that fucking Dr. Daniels and her Beast on me, whether or not she meant to. How did I reconcile that with the child I had known? I didn't. Couldn't.

There was no way for me to save her. Once and for all, my sister was gone.

"There's nothing left for us here," I said softly, knowing in every fiber of my being that it was true.

"Are you saying what I think you're saying?"

I smiled up at him and kissed him, my heart heavy with sorrow for all that had been lost, and yet light for all that had been found. "Yes, it's time to go home."

real damage that I could see. The giant's skin was thick, and the red caps weapons weren't spelled to cut deep like my swords.

Unfortunately for them, the giant caught on faster than I had thought he could, and in a matter of minutes, he'd eaten four more of them, armor and all.

"Rylee, we have a problem," Liam said calmly, like he was telling me about the upcoming weather.

I turned away from the giant and his snacks. Ahead of us another legion of red caps trotted into the castle courtyard. Three rows of ten—maybe that wasn't a legion, I didn't really know for sure. But another thirty red caps? Shit.

A body went flying by us and I ducked, rather belatedly. I turned to the giant, who had demolished the last of the red caps and was now eyeing us up. I saluted him with my sword, another idea forming.

"You remember this?" I called up to him.

Apparently he did, as he flexed his hand with his newly regrown fingers. He roared and I did the only thing I could think of. I ran toward him.

A roar came from outside. The giant was still stomping around, and pissed as all get out. He gave me an idea. A bad idea maybe, but it might be the only chance we had.

"Pamela, knock out that arch."

She spun, clapped her hands together and then flung them apart. The arch over the entryway blasted apart with the force of her spell, and as the dust settled, a loud, booming laugh floated down to us.

Garbling his language, whatever it was, the giant stomped into the courtyard, scooping up the closest red cap, and jammed him, pike and all, into his mouth.

I blinked several times. That had been the hand that I'd cut off his fingers. And while they were maybe a bit on the short side, they'd grown back. Son of a bitch, I didn't know giants had *that* ability.

The red caps were torn, half of them engaging the giant, the other half standing in our way. Better odds than we had before. Liam fired the crossbow, the bolt taking the closest red cap in his right eye. With a scream, the red cap went down to his knees, and then fell forward onto his face. Liam was already reloading the crossbow before the red cap hit the ground.

"Pamela, out front," I said. "I'll keep an eye on the big bastard."

Trusting my crew, I let them take the lead. Which meant I had to let them guard my back while I watched the giant take out the red caps one by one. Their fighting style was guerrilla, striking hard and then darting out of the giant's way, inflicting blows, but not any

21

What his mate was thinking, he had no idea. But now he had to find a way to get her, the witch child, and himself out of this nest of blood and death. His nose was filled with it, the scent of rotting death, new death, blood, and pain. The smells made his nose twitch and his skin crawl. The witch child clung to him, fear rolling off her in waves. He didn't like the fact that she had a hand on him, but he allowed it. She was a part of their pack, after all.

"Shouldn't we go back for Rylee?" The child whispered, her voice right in his ear. He couldn't answer her, so he just shook his head. His mate would find a way out; they just had to meet her wherever it was she ended up. They wandered for hours, avoiding those that looked for them, hiding where they had to, never fighting.

He took a deep breath and caught the smell of food, fresh cooking meat. Moving in that direction, he took deep breaths, drawing in the scents all around him, searching for anymore of the blood drinkers. His lips curled back as he walked, just thinking about them. The one that had bitten his mate was bad, but these ones, they were worse. They were mad, a sickness infecting their minds . . . and they weren't even true blood drinkers, they were like shadows that darted around trying to be something they weren't.

"Do you smell that?"

He just trotted along, towing her with him toward the food. They rounded a corner and a large cooking area opened up. She ran forward and grabbed a pot off the stove, shoveling food into her mouth, then grabbing another pot and putting it on the floor for him. They ate in silence, but at the sounds of footsteps in the hallway, he nudged her away. They hid behind a large table, working their way around until they could peer around it without being seen.

The footsteps drew closer and the blood drinker's shadows came in line with the doorway. There was a glimpse of auburn hair, but more than that, the scent of his mate. The scent of where he belonged.

Creeping forward, he moved to the door, watching them take her away from him again.

With a low growl, he flicked his head from the witch child to his mate.

"We'll get her back, O'Shea," she said, her eyes fierce with a fire that surprised him after he'd felt her fear for so long. "I'll kill them all if I have to."

He gave a soft woof. Perhaps the witch child was a better fit than he'd first thought.

Stepping into the hallway, they turned and once more followed where his mate led.

My handlers walked me to the intersection and took a left, trotted me down a set of stairs, and then took